THE DEVIL HOUND

In Search of Family

FRANKLIN E. LAMCA

THE

DEVIL

HOUND

IN SEARCH OF FAMILY

FRANKLIN E. LAMCA

Woodhall Press
Norwalk, CT

woodhall press

Woodhall Press, 81 Old Saugatuck Road, Norwalk, CT 06855
WoodhallPress.com
Copyright © 2022 Franklin E. Lamca

Cover design: Asha Hossain
Layout artist: Amie McCracken

Library of Congress Cataloging-in-Publication Data available

ISBN 978-1-954907-30-0 (paper: alk paper)
ISBN 978-1-954907-31-7 (electronic)

First Edition
Distributed by Independent Publishers Group
(800) 888-4741

Printed in the United States of America

PRELUDE

Father Thomas, a man of despicable scruples, never wanted to become a priest. He was forced into the priesthood by his parents. Father Thomas is not a man of faith; he is an agnostic at best and he hates all things religious. He uses his position in the Church to prey upon young women. Expelled from his position at the Vatican, the Church transferred him to the remote Swiss village of Erlach. There, he raped a young woman, and when caught in the act by his superior, Father Benedict, he beat his elder and left him for dead. Father Thomas blamed the attacks on two itinerant Gypsies. The court's sentence for the Gypsies was hanging.

Father Thomas assumed the local parish leadership, at St. Maria's Church, with Father Benedict in a coma and discretely rendezvoused with his lover, a French spy named Emily De Fontaine, at the church rectory.

The two Romanian Gypsies, Bojko and Raiko Celje, adopted by an Italian circus owner, Bernardo Scalisi, are heirs to Bernardo's fortune. Bojko was trained as a circus trapeze artist, while Raiko studied to become the business manager. The Gypsies, who had met Father Thomas while the priest was living in Rome, face continual persecution by the Church and law simply because of their ethnic background and Father Thomas's hatred toward them.

Father Thomas has pursued the two Gypsy brothers across Europe for nearly two years. Catching them, only to have them escape his grasp. During one such apprehension, the priest permanently injured his leg and now walks with a profound limp. Consumed with hatred, Thomas lives for the day when he can see the two Gypsies hung.

CHAPTER ONE
THE INTERLUDE

St. Maria's Church Rectory, Erlach, Switzerland
June 1752

Father Thomas closed his dark eyes and inhaled deeply to recapture the fragrance of Emilie's lilac perfume. His French lover's scent would linger in his room for hours after she was gone, but for now, she was still there with him, pleading to spend the night.

"There's nothing I'd rather do, Emilie," he told her as he pulled her close, brushed her blonde hair aside, and looked into her bright blue eyes. "But remember, it's only been eight weeks since those heathen Gypsies raped the Welti girl and left Father Benedict for dead. Well-wishers keep coming in droves to place flowers at the base of the Madonna and Child statue, where the attack took place."

Emilie drew her athletic body back a short distance from his embrace and looked pleadingly into his eyes. "But, with Father Benedict in the hospital, we have the rectory all to ourselves."

Father Thomas snickered as he looked around the room. The limestone building's ancient walls were adorned with medieval portraits of nameless saints, all wearing halos and painted in dark colors on wooden backings. A large brass crucifix with an emaciated Christ hung prominently over the high ornate headboard of Father Benedict's bed.

"This was the old priest's room. You should feel honored. You're probably the first woman to be entertained in this bed chamber in its two-hundred-year history. I wouldn't be surprised if God causes the walls of this rectory to cave in on us at any moment."

Emilie shook her head in a gesture of confusion as she glared at her muscular lover. "Don't you go getting superstitious on me now," she said. "It's too late for you to catch a strong infection of religion. Wouldn't it be better if you give up your holy charade and cast off your priestly garment? Frankly, you sound like a total hypocrite. We both know you hate being a priest. You're not even a *real* priest—you're a priest without faith!"

Thomas pushed his lover back from him with anger and sat upon the edge of the bed. The priest retrieved his glass of wine from the nightstand next to the bed. Without offering a drink to Emilie, he lifted the glass to his lips and emptied its contents into his mouth. He swallowed hard and set the empty wine glass back on the nightstand.

"Be patient, my love," he said as he tried to shake off his brief attack of conscience. "Our time is coming. Once I have done what I must do, we'll have more latitude to live the way we want."

An encounter with his conscience was a rare event for the priest. Possessed by a demonic spirit, he had told so many lies during his evil life that lying became easier than truthfulness. Tonight, only forty-eight hours from the scheduled execution of the Gypsies he felt he had brought to justice, the weight of his actions bore down on him, if only momentarily.

"What could be so important that you'd allow it to delay our being together?" Emilie asked.

The priest felt trapped in his circumstances. The air he breathed became heavy and oppressive. He began to sweat. His bedclothes wrapped around him like a spider's web that trapped him like an insect. The priest's self-spun web of deceit held him fast while his deadly spider of self-destruction kept him entrapped—a spider whose presence he could sense but an enemy he could not identify. What was his spider, his adversary or his demon? Was it the woman who lay beside him, always controlling and demanding? Was it the Gypsies, persistently elusive and professionally embarrassing? Was it the Church he served, morally demanding and sexually repressive? Or was it merely his insatiable appetite for evil? Father

Thomas could not identify his spider, but he knew it possessed him and that the demon had the potential to destroy him.

In a desperate effort at freedom, Thomas tore loose from the tangled blankets, threw his feet over the edge of the bed, and stood up. He struggled toward the window above his nightstand like a drowning man fighting his way to the surface and pulled back the brown tapestry curtain. His strong hands hurriedly unlatched the double panes and thrust the hinged windows open. The fresh evening air rushed in and hit his face like a splash of water. The priest inhaled deeply and leaned his head out of the window with elbows resting on the marble window seal.

Father Thomas struggled to suppress his conscience and to regain his composure. He took another deep breath of fresh air and withdrew from the window to face Emilie. He held up the index finger of his right hand and thrust it out toward her. "I just need to do one thing," Father Thomas said in the most authoritative voice he could muster, "and then my vengeance will be satisfied."

Just then, thunder boomed in the distance, and Emilie could see his imposing figure outlined against the flashes of light. The priest trembled as though in a seizure and began to speak with a determined voice; deliberate, yet somewhat raspy. His words betrayed the deep emotion that welled up inside of him.

"The first thing I must do," he said as he held up one of his fingers," is to attend the execution."

Destroy them. Yes, Destroy the Gypsies! The voice known as Damian, and heard only by the priest, called out in his head.

"The hanging will be the day after tomorrow, and I wouldn't miss that execution for anything in the world. Raiko and Bojko Caumlo have eluded me for over two years, but I finally caught them."

We caught them; yes, we finally caught them, and now they must pay, Damian cried out.

"I want payback for my hard work. The Gypsies disgraced me in Rome and ruined my promotion to Bishop. It's their fault I'm here in this despicable excuse for a town. I won't be happy until they're dangling at the end of a rope with their feet kicking and their necks stretched."

Yes. Those Gypsies ruined our chance to work within the heart of the Papacy. You could have been a Bishop, a Cardinal, or even the Pope! Oh, what great things we could have done for our satanic master.

A bright flash of lightning illuminated the night sky as Emilie looked across the bedroom at Father Thomas' tear-streaked face. She watched him as he turned sideways and stared up at the clouds like a werewolf drawn toward the light of a full moon. Several flashes in rapid succession rattled the wavy leaded glass in the narrow window. She watched in terror as the lightning glare reflected a heinous yellow-green glow in the priest's eyes. Emilie, a woman of strong constitution and not prone toward the supernatural, felt a cringe of fear possess her.

"It's no wonder the Gypsies called you a 'devil hound' at their trial. You have so much hatred inside you that you are blind to all else. You've tracked them relentlessly, sacrificing all that's holy upon your altar of revenge. You frighten me with your propensity for evil. Sometimes I think you'd prefer to hound those twins than be with me."

Father Thomas turned away from the window and moved slowly toward her. He did not smile; he did not speak. He stopped in front of the bed and looked down at her with determination. Emilie sat on the edge of the bed and trembled.

Emilie tried to stand up, but the priest placed his hands on her shoulders and held her down. She looked up at him and trembled—afraid and shaken. Emilie did not trust Father Thomas, but at the same time, she became excited about what the priest might do to her. He looked powerful as he towered over her. She was both frightened and stimulated by him. Strong and determined men attracted her to them like a moth is attracted to a glowing lamppost. Men of determination and power had always been a part of her life.

In a micro-second, her mind flashed to the men in her life:

Her father had been a powerful banker but a non-attentive parent.

When yet a teenager, her handsome fencing instructor, Jacques LeBlanc, had stolen her teenage heart but used her for his gain. Jacques had paid with his life, but not before teaching her the power of the sword. He instilled a sense of confidence, determination, and mastery of fencing. Later, Emily went to Versailles to train in the court of Louis XV, who used his status as King to charm and take advantage of her.

Emilie liked to believe her exposure to these strong personalities had not weakened her; they had made her stronger and a woman of resolve. Despite her self-assurance, Emilie felt herself trembling at this man's touch. She looked up at the renegade priest, struggling to see him in the darkness and uncertain of what it was he believed.

"I never know," she said, "what it is that motivates you. Everyone believes in something, and when I understand a person's beliefs, I know what motivates them. I know Father Benedict, for instance: he believes in God and the Church's traditions. For him, his life has order and purpose. He considers the parish members his flock and must shepherd them and do good works.

"I even understand the Gypsies: that Italian, Bernardo Scalisi taught them, and they believe the Bible to be the inerrant Word of God   even though you call them heathens.

"I understand my point of view: I believe in loyalty to King Louis XV and France. I tolerate the Church only when I could use it to further the king's objectives.

"But where do you place your trust? You say you don't believe in God or any other superstition, yet you usurp every privilege the priesthood can afford you. On the one hand, you mock God, yet you embrace evil. Just now, when I saw your face glow in the flashes of lightning, I almost believed in the old wives' tale about devil hounds that roam the night in thunderstorms, seeking the souls of humanity. Thomas, I would like to think that I'm afraid of nothing, but you frighten me."

Emilie realized Father Thomas's dark side and unwavering determination excited her and captured her emotions. She could sense the conflict that raged within him, a conflict between the servant of God he was supposed to be and the instrument of evil he had become. Emilie and Father Thomas were co-dependent upon each other's dark side and ambitions, but Emilie realized this relationship could not last forever.

Perhaps she had become like her fencing instructor—a user and manipulator. When the priest had served his purpose, he was dispensable. For the moment, however, she needed him for king and country and to fill a deep void within her heart.

Emilie continued to look up into Father Thomas's eyes. He stared down at her, his face moist with sweat, his breath tainted with the smell of wine. He remained silent and expressionless as he slowly reached forward and brushed her long blonde hair over her shoulders with his hands. Then, the priest gently slid his hands down and placed them around her throat. Lightning flashed, his eyes glowed, and he pulled her face to his as he reveled in the fragrance of her perfume.

Emily loved him in her way because he was a man determined to live life as he saw fit, but she hated him at the same time for the way he used women. Her life had been a life of manipulation by self-serving men, and she realized he was using her now, but Emilie needed to manipulate Thomas to complete her mission. Father Thomas was expendable, but she would allow him to believe he was exercising his male dominance for now. *When I finish my purpose, Thomas will have his day of reckoning.*

Several hours later, as the sun began to cast its morning rays through the open window, like a spotlight of an opera house, Father Thomas, exhausted and spent, fell asleep without insisting Emilie leave the rectory. That was a victory for Emilie. The French woman didn't need to understand this man who had vowed to serve France, but she did need to control him. Any pleasure she could gain from the relationship was a bonus for her, so long as she could coerce him to do what she wanted.

Later this morning, Emilie thought, *we will take the carriage to Freiburg and spend the night. Then, the following day, the hanging. Maybe then Thomas can put all his hatred behind him. I certainly hope so.*

Emilie drifted off to sleep in the knowledge she had manipulated the priest into allowing her to have her way.

CHAPTER TWO
EXECUTION DAY

June 15, 1752, 5:40 am

Father Thomas and Emilie De Fontaine prepared to leave the *Kleine Bär Inn* (Little Bear Inn) in Freiburg, Switzerland, while the severe weather pattern that hung over most of the country continued its deluge.

"Please hurry, Emilie, we must get to the prison before sunrise, or I'll miss the most important day of my life," the priest pleaded. He took her hand and hurriedly ushered her into the taxi carriage, not bothering to protect himself beneath the woman's parasol. He collapsed the parasol and shook off the excess water. He heard a thunderclap and looked up at the lightning, still flashing in the thick clouds.

"Do you suppose they will postpone the execution because of the storm?" Emilie asked as the priest entered the carriage and closed the door.

"Don't be silly. This event isn't a church picnic—it's an execution. Legal matters like this one are punctual. If we don't hurry, we'll miss it." Using Emilie's parasol to thump on the ceiling of the taxi, he yelled, "Driver! To the prison, straightaway!"

Freiburg Prison
5:55 am

Tension grew in the eight-by-ten-foot cell as the Gypsy prisoners heard the large brass bell in St. Jo Anne's Church begin its first strike in a series of six baritone gongs. The bell intended to signal the beginning of a new day, became for the two Gypsies, a signal to end their lives.

Raiko lay prostrate on the cell floor with his cheek pressed hard against the cold stones. He strained to look down the hallway from beneath the door for any sign of movement from the guards. The young Gypsy could hear the unintelligible voices in the prison kitchen as they awaited the time of execution. Suddenly, Raiko listened to the guards stand up from the table and push their chairs back into place.

"They're coming," Raiko whispered, barely audible, as he turned to warn his brother.

Then came the sound of weapons rattling as the guards armed themselves for the task at hand. It was a scene they had played countless times before as they prepared to force the condemned from their cells and onto the gallows.

Raiko saw the shadows of four guards moving across the walls. Footsteps were moving in his direction. Raiko jumped to his feet and held up four fingers to signal the approach of four men.

"Get ready. The guards are coming for us," he said in a panicked whisper. "They'll be here any second."

"Just calm down and shut up," Bojko responded. "We don't want them to hear us talking."

The Gypsies had no weapons, except for those they had fashioned from their cell's sparse furnishings. Raiko had torn narrow strips from their thin blankets and braided them into a makeshift rope. Bojko, standing on Raiko's shoulders, had secured the makeshift rope to the gothic ceiling of the cell through cast iron eyehooks built into the stone for the purpose of torture. They tied their modified wooden bench to the rope.

Raiko got up from his sentry position on the floor and squatted in front of the cell door while Bojko stood on Raiko's shoulders.

Raiko took a deep breath and reached for the stone wall as he strained his muscled legs to lift his brother toward the arched ceiling above the doorway.

Bojko edged his fingertips and toes into the indented mortar seams and repositioned his body to reach a rusted iron chain that hung from the ceiling. He grabbed the chain and held on as he spread his legs against the arched ceiling directly above the cell door. His arms quivered, and his legs cramped under strain, but he held his position with resolve.

Raiko moved to the wall opposite the doorway and stood there with his feet firmly planted on the floor.

The brothers were realists. They understood their inevitable fate. Sooner or later, they must face death just because they were Romani. The date of their execution did not matter. Little difference whether it was today or a year from now—they were doomed. They had nowhere to run and nowhere to hide their ethnic origin. They had weighed the consequences carefully and decided to stand their ground.

The sound of cobbled boot heels scraping against the hard floor tiles came closer.

Then, the sound of metal against metal as one of the guards inserted a key into the door lock. The heavy wooden cell door swung open.

Four guards started through the cell door.

Raiko pressed his back hard against the wall and shoved the battering ram with all his might. Tied to the blankets hanging from the ceiling, it swung like a deadly pendulum across the room and slammed, with its exposed nail heads, into the body of the first guard to enter the cell, blocking all forward movement.

The hangman pushed hard against the guards from behind, and Bojko dropped down from the ceiling onto the guards. The weight of Bojko's dropping body slammed the guards to the stone floor of the cell. One of them hit the ground hard. His head split open like a dropped melon on impact.

The hangman entered the cell with sword drawn. He was about to run the blade of his sword through Bojko's spine when Raiko rushed forward with a club. Raiko brought the club down on the henchman's head with full impact. A sickening thud echoed in the room. The henchman fell with blood issuing freely from his wound.

The one remaining guard looked pleadingly up from the floor. In a pathetic gesture, the guard folded his hands, as if in prayer, and begged, "*Grâce!*"[1]

The young brothers looked at one another questioningly.

"What should we do?" Raiko asked, already sickened by the blood that had spilled so freely upon the cell floor. "I just can't do it!"

Bojko looked at the terrified man and then back at Raiko. "We will chain them to the wall."

Bojko examined the guard who had split his head against the stone floor. He was gone. Then he looked closely at the hangman Raiko had clubbed with the bench leg. "I don't think we'll have to bother anymore with these two," he said. "They're already gone."

Those words sickened young Raiko to his stomach. "Gone? What do you mean 'gone?' I didn't try to kill him." He began to weep. "Oh, my God!" Raiko dropped to the floor against the wall and relieved his stomach of its meager contents.

"Stop whining, Raiko," Bojko shouted. "You did what you had to do. Search the guards for the keys. I'll get these other two chained to the wall and gagged."

Sobbing, and with his heart pounding, Raiko managed to stand up from the floor. Wet tears of remorse flowed freely down his dirty face, cleaning shiny streaks of skin across his trembling chin and onto the cell floor. He reluctantly approached his victim's body and pulled the keys from a hook on the dead guard's leather belt. Raiko gave the sign of the cross and whispered, "I'm so sorry."

The Romani stepped outside their cell for the first time in days. Raiko locked the cell door behind them with trembling fingers, and the two blood-stained brothers ran down the narrow hallway, through the prison kitchen, and out the back door into the courtyard.

"I hear someone coming," Raiko yelled. "Quick! Duck behind the gate!"

The escapees slipped into the shadows when they saw a black carriage race through the prison gates as if late for an appointment with destiny.

---

1 Please

The carriage came to an abrupt halt in front of the kitchen door. It was still rebounding on its suspension when the carriage door flung open. A dark-clad priest sprang from the carriage, leaving his female companion to fend for herself. The priest limped as fast as his injured leg would allow, followed closely behind by the woman into the prison.

"Oh, no!" Bojko cried out, "It's the Devil Hound!"

Bojko rushed toward the coachman, still mounted on the carriage without saying another word. He bounded up the back of the coach like an agile leopard and knocked the coachman from his perch.

Bojko slapped the reins and pulled them hard to his left. The horses swung the carriage around, and immediately the escaping prisoners sped toward the rising sun. The same sun that was supposed to greet them with death now offered them hope for a new day.

CHAPTER THREE
RETURN TO ERLACH

Two Points of View

June 17, 1752

Anton Smith

It was only mid-morning, and already, the day was brimming with excitement. I was a twenty-one-year-old young man—but I acted more like a small child. My heart raced as I hung my head out of the coach window to catch an advance glimpse of my hometown. Suddenly, a firm hand grabbed the back of my shirt and pulled me firmly away from the window and back into my seat.

"Monsieur. Forgive me," a woman's voice said with an authoritative French accent, "but the city gate is narrow, and you could hurt your head as we pass through."

I turned with surprise to see a set of concerned blue eyes glaring at me from beneath the wide brim of a blue felt hat. It was the first I had seen her eyes or heard her voice since we left Freiburg in the darkness of the early morning. She had already been seated when I entered the coach, its only other passenger, with her eyes closed, either totally exhausted or feigning sleep, I'm sure, to avoid conversation.

"Are you from Erlach?" I asked her while trying desperately to put a name to her face. I had been away for four years, but I would never have forgotten her pretty face.

"No..." she replied, as if with caution, "...but I've visited a friend here from time to time." Her hesitation caused me to feel she was not willing to tell me any more than necessary.

I guessed the young woman to be a few years older than me, but not so much older as to prevent me from being attracted to her. Her perfect pronunciation of words, self-assuredness, flawless complexion, straight white teeth, and soft hair left little doubt she was a woman of breeding. Any remaining doubt that I may have had about her high social status disappeared when I saw the beautiful clothes she wore. She wore a pale blue light-weight wool cape, trimmed in fox, to warm her against the chill of the Alpine air; a long matching skirt that hung down across the tops her black laced boots, made of soft Italian leather; and a heavy white silk blouse with pearl buttons. Unfortunately, I understood fine clothes much better than the beautiful women who wore them. I completed a four-year apprenticeship with the tailor's guild in Zurich.

"Thank you for your concern, Mademoiselle," I managed to force out through my embarrassment and suppressed indignation, "but Erlach is my hometown, and I am familiar with the narrow gate."

A forced smile concealed my genuine emotions. It's difficult to impress a sophisticated woman when she's just pulled you away from the carriage window like a mother protecting her child. Trying to salvage whatever dignity remained, I struggled to change the subject. I held a hand to my left ear and leaned toward the window.

"Oh. Listen. Do you hear that?"

The lady sat up on the edge of her seat and leaned across me to get closer to my window. Without regard to our lack of familiarity, the spontaneity of her movement caught me totally off guard. I sat back in my seat with my hands at my side, afraid to make any "improper" move. The scent of her lilac fragrance and the closeness of her person to mine had its effect.

"Oh, yes," she said, as she pulled her face away from the window and looked directly into my eyes. "I hear the chimes of the town clock. How beautiful."

She smiled devilishly at me and continued to press against me much longer than necessary, almost sitting on my lap. I could feel the warmth of her breath against my cheek and the softness of her body against my arm. Her face remained only inches from mine. She continued to smile at me and cupped her ear with her hand as if to capture the sound of the clock's melodic chimes. It seemed strange that this sophisticated woman, who had ignored me for the past several hours, set her airs aside with reckless abandon because of the chiming of an old clock. I couldn't help but wonder if the clock somehow took her back to pleasant memories of her childhood. I did not know, but whatever the cause for her excitement, it vindicated me from my own earlier act of immaturity when I leaned out of the coach window. She, too, must have reconsidered her spontaneous reaction to the village chimes because reality seemed to return to her face. Her smile ceased suddenly, and she resumed her veil of sophistication as abruptly as she had removed it. The lady pushed away from me and resumed her position in her seat. We spoke not another word.

My brown hair blew freely in the wind, and my eyes felt dry as I edged, once again, toward the open window to see ahead of the coach. My excitement peaked. The coach slowed and threaded through the narrow city gate like a camel through the "eye of a needle²". Erlach was my destination, and I longed to see it once again.

Once inside the village gate, my eyes strained in the morning sun to look up at the Roman numerals on the face of the great clock. The Glockenspiel's metal hammer pounded the last of its ten baritone gongs on either side's two heavy brass bells. Simultaneous with the final bell's gonging, a small door beneath the clock opened, and wooden marionette-like figures, dressed in painted regional costumes, danced with exaggerated mechanical precision. Across the *Strasse* from the clock, a mob had gathered oblivious to the Glockenspiel movements. The crowd was listening to the rantings of a priest. The priest spoke with animated vigor.

The coachman pulled back on the reins and called out, "Whoa!" as the rhythmic pounding of the horses' iron shoes broke their predictable

---

2 A small pedestrian gate in the ancient wall of Jerusalem referenced by Jesus in Matthew

beat against the cobblestone *Strasse.* Next, we heard the handbrake as it screeched its rubber brake pads against the carriage wheels' rims, and the coach stopped abruptly in front of the *Rathaus.*[3]

The village of Erlach was busier than usual that morning. Several carriages parked along the main Strasse; their horse tied to the hitching posts lined both sides of the cobblestone street. Pedestrian traffic was heavy. The people were moving in the same direction as the crowd gathered around the priest.

The lady in blue waited for the driver to open her door. She turned to me and smiled and then moved as far away from me as possible. Her body language told me she didn't want anyone to see us and perceive that we were together. Without so much as a mention of her name, she turned her back on me and faced the carriage door. The driver arrived at the door and set a step beside the exit. When the driver opened the door, she extended her hand to the coachman. The lady didn't look back at me as she left. She stepped down from the carriage and walked out of my life. It was as though we had never talked. Without a fond farewell, without so much as an over-the-shoulder glance, she turned her back on me and departed. So much for impressing the ladies.

By the time I had opened my coach door and climbed down from the carriage, the lady had crossed the town square and approached the crowd. A young priest, rather muscular looking and tall, stood before an angry mob. He spoke with words selected more to incite hatred than as a message of Godly love. I gathered my baggage and crossed the square to move closer to the crowd for a better vantage point.

"The night before last," the priest said in a raspy voice that betrayed his state of near exhaustion, "those two Gypsies who raped that innocent Welti girl, and placed the Good Father Benedict at death's door, escaped from the prison at Freiburg!"

The priest paused to allow an uproar from the crowd to run its intended course. He continued, "They escaped on the morn of their scheduled

---

3 City Hall

execution, mind you, but not before killing two guards and critically injuring two others."

Once more, the crowd responded, and Father Thomas quietly swelled with pride at his ability to arouse a mob.

"Everyone knows that I, too, was a victim of their violence. On the day of their attack on Maria Welti and Father Benedict, I set my safety aside and attempted to apprehend them. There were too many of them. They turned on me and injured me.

"Yesterday morning, when they escaped from the prison in Freiburg, I, once again, set my safety aside to do the Lord's work. Despite what they had done to me, I rode, by carriage, to the prison in the futile hope I could find some redeeming quality in their miserable souls."

The priest paused while the citizens of his parish nodded in wonder at his amazing grace for the wicked. They mumbled words of praise for him.

"Unfortunately, I arrived at the prison while the breakout was still in progress. The Gypsies assaulted my coach driver while I was inside the prison and drove off in the stolen carriage."

Sounds of outrage erupted from the crowd while the priest held up his hands to quiet the outburst.

"After helping the local authorities in Freiburg, all I could, I rode all night to return home to Erlach. I'm exhausted and must now return to the rectory to rest. But once I rest, I vow to go after the two heathens and track them down. If necessary, I will hound them to the ends of the earth. This man will not rest until he facilitates justice!"

A roar went up from the crowd as the citizens of Erlach apparently approved with pride the decisive leadership their interim priest had demonstrated. Thomas seemed satisfied he had accomplished the desired effect. The priest waved to the crowd and looked in the direction of the young French woman. He nodded over his left shoulder toward the village's back gate to indicate he would meet her outside. Then he turned and walked away from the disbanding assembly toward the city gate.

I moved back across the square and ducked into the doorway of the *Rathaus*. My objective was to observe what would happen next without appearing to be a busybody. The apparent alliance between these two very different people didn't sit right with me. My curiosity demanded answers.

The lady-in-blue—as I had begun to think of her—went back to the coach and tipped the driver. He had patiently waited with her luggage. She grabbed the handles of her bags, looked around as if to make sure nobody was watching her, and slipped out the back gate of the village. I gave her a few minutes' head start and then took my one small bag and walked in the same direction.

Before proceeding, it seemed prudent to stop at the gate and peer around the corner. That turned out to be the right decision. I stood at the city gate and looked to my right. I saw a black carriage parked next to the wall, and a couple stood in front of it. The carriage concealed the couple's identities, but their legs were partially visible beneath. I dropped to my knees and looked under the carriage frame for a better view.

What I saw shocked me: A pair of soft Italian leather boots, with a long blue wool skirt hanging down across the tops, stood toe-to-toe with a pair of dusty brown shoes protruding out from beneath a long black robe. The proximities of their bodies to one another left no doubt in my mind that they were embracing. The embrace was not the Padre/Parishioner-everything-will-be-fine kind of a hug I would have expected to see, but rather, the honey-I-missed-you kind of a hug I would have preferred receiving myself. They disconnected after a too-long embrace, climbed into the priest's carriage, and drove off together. My gut feeling told me there was something very wrong with that picture, and I knew they'd come back into my life.

Emilie De Fontaine

After spending two horrific nights in an uncomfortable inn that afforded me little rest, I boarded the carriage in Freiburg. I spent the first night at the *Klein Bär Inn* with a friend, but when things didn't go well for him (two escaped convicts stole his carriage), he left me there, rented a horse, and rushed back to Erlach. I had to stay there one more day for reasons I chose not to discuss.

The early morning journey from Freiburg had been arduous, and it took its toll on my disposition, making me a poor candidate for conversation with the hayseed of a young man sitting next to me. I decided to feign sleep to avoid conversation in the hope I could eventually fall asleep despite the continual bumping of the road and being jerked from side to side by every rut that our idiotic driver seemed to find purposely.

The late morning sun felt warm against the right side of my face as I sat in the carriage with my eyes closed. Suddenly, the carriage hit a rut, and the jerking motion threw me to my left and against the young man sitting next to me. A cool breeze blew in my face from an open window caused me to open my eyes. As I looked at the young man, he seemed unaware of my proximity to him and continued to lean out the window of the carriage door transfixed on whatever lay ahead.

I hadn't noticed much about him during our ride through the night and had kept my eyes closed, feigning sleep most of the morning. But now, his agility and solid body began to intrigue me. Much to my surprise, I found myself uncontrollably scratching my left arm when it didn't even itch, a sure sign, based on my previous experience with me, that I was attracted to this young man. He reminded me of my late fencing instructor, a man who stole the flower of my innocence—he used me because of my inexperience. Later, I made sure he got what he deserved. Pierre La Blanc taught me a valuable lesson; much more than fencing; No man will ever take advantage of me again. I, Emilie De Fontaine, will control my destiny.

My fellow passenger withdrew from the window, looked over at me before I could resume my feigned sleep, and looked into my eyes. He smiled. It was apparent he found me to be attractive too.

"Can you hear the distant chiming of the village clock?" he asked. Before I could even answer him, he once again leaned out the window.

Then, I did something uncharacteristic of me. I moved over closer to the young man and leaned across his body to join him in the excitement of looking out his window. It felt good to be close to him. Perhaps, in the pleasure of the moment, my brush against him was a little too close for respectability and, maybe, a little too long in duration. Indeed, my ego got the better of me, and the enjoyment of knowing that my feminine charm was having its effect on this babe-in-the-woods made me feel more like a woman. Whatever my motives, it is evident that this young man—a few years my junior—was not a man familiar with the wiles of a real woman. Pleased with the apparent fact that my charm could have such an effect and noticing that the narrow gate of the village was approaching rapidly, I withdrew from the window and moved away from the young man.

When it was apparent that we were within a few feet of the narrow gate and he was still hanging out of the window, I impulsively grabbed him by his coat sleeve and yanked him away from the door window with all my might. Startled, he turned and stared at me through raised eyebrows.

"What's wrong?" he said.

I shrugged my shoulders and looked back at him with a half-smile while I shook my head in disbelief. "You could have hit your head on the gate and been killed!" I said as the realization that my action caused embarrassment to well up inside of me. I don't know who had the reddest face, him or me.

By this time, we were inside the village gate. I needed to regain my composure and act in a manner that reflected my station in life. Besides, Thomas would be waiting for me, and it was imperative he didn't think I had cozied up to this young man. I pulled myself against the far side of the bench seat and terminated the conversation as though it had never happened. Staring out the window prevented me from looking at the person beside me. The uncomfortable feeling that his eyes were burning a hole in me persisted until the coachman opened the door and helped me out of the carriage. The young man must have thought it odd that I neither said goodbye nor looked back at him. Thomas was nowhere in sight, but he mustn't see me talking with the other passenger.

CHAPTER FOUR
FATHER BENEDICT'S RECOVERY

June 20, 1752

Ross Welti perspired profusely and hung onto his horse as it raced down *Rue des Chanoines* in Freiburg. St. Nicolas Cathedral had been visible for more than an hour on his approach to the city: The church situated on a hilltop, fifty meters above the River Sarine; its tower another seventy-six meters above the *Rue*. The immensity of the nearly five-hundred-year-old cathedral overwhelmed his senses as he rode ever closer to the high doors at the front of the building. Exhausted, his heart raced as he halted his steed, dismounted, and ran inside the cathedral. Inside, a group of priests stood assembled like a choir before a robed priest wearing a high hat and holding a gold staff in his right hand. Ross approached the rotund Bishop and stood before him, panting, and waiting to be recognized. Irritated by what he perceived to be a rude interruption of the services, the bishop sensed the intruder's urgency and held up his hands in a gesture to quiet the assembly.

"Is something wrong?" Bishop Roten inquired.

Ross tried desperately to communicate through his parched mouth, but his dry tongue refused to form the words he fought to speak.

"Calm down, my son," the bishop said as he removed a white napkin from atop the silver communion cup he held in front of him. Raising the chalice to Ross' mouth, he commanded him to drink its contents.

Ross shook his head "no," at first, nervous about drinking wine blessed for a communion service.

"Please, you need this much more than I. I'm sure the Lord will understand."

Ross Welti reached out and took the cup. He raised it to his lips and drank the wine until the cup was empty. He wiped his mouth on his right sleeve and then handed the chalice back to Bishop Roten. Ross nodded in appreciation.

"There now," the priest said as he smiled and put his annoyance at the interruption aside. "What is the nature of your urgency?"

The farmer from Erlach, who had so graciously assumed responsibility for the care of Father Benedict, struggled against his humility. The very idea of interrupting a servant of God had gone against every precept of respect for Church authority he had ever known. Ross struggled to speak: "Your Excellency, I am sorry to interrupt, but Father Benedict has regained consciousness."

The bishop's smile left his face, and his countenance became more attentive. "Woke up? Do you mean to tell me that he has regained consciousness?"

"Yes, Your Excellency." the messenger said. "That's the word the doctor used...conscious! Anyway, Father Benedict is concerned that he will not last much longer and has sent me to bring you to him. There is something he feels you must hear from his lips. Please come back to Erlach with me now. We may not have much time."

Bishop Roten turned to his assistant and said, "Take this man directly to my rectory and feed him."

Then, he looked at Ross' weary face and said, "After you have rested, we will ride back to Erlach in my carriage. But for now, you need some rest. We will try to depart immediately—certainly within the next few hours."

11:45 am, June 21, 1752

It was nearly lunchtime of the next day when the bishop's carriage, with Ross' horse in tow, skirted the walls of Erlach to avoid recognition and arrived at the Welti farmhouse. Ross' wife and daughters—Anne and Maria—heard the approaching carriage. They rushed outside to greet the arrivals. The carriage pulled up to the house and stopped next to the rose trellises beside the front porch.

Ross hopped down from the carriage and embraced his anxious wife and daughters. The bishop, a man of heightened senses, remained on the carriage and observed the tranquil beauty of the pink Seven Sisters roses that climbed the trellises against the porch.

Ross Welti took his wife and daughters over to the carriage and stood before the bishop to make the introductions. He waited patiently for His Excellency to look at him, but the bishop's attention was not on the conversation. Bishop Roten looked toward the front door and inhaled deeply to absorb the enticing fragrance of fresh-baked bread wafting from within the Welti farmhouse.

Ross sensed the urgency to introduce his family and take the bishop directly to Father Thomas. He took the initiative and cleared his throat to catch his guest's attention. "Your Excellency," Ross nearly shouted. "May I present to you my wife, Eva, and my daughters, Maria and Anne?" Unfortunately, the introductions fell on deaf ears of the preoccupied bishop who could think of nothing but the smells of bread, bratwurst, and sauerkraut cooking inside the farmhouse.

"Bishop Roten?" Ross asked as he waited to reply to a question he had presented.

The sound of his host's voice snapped the bishop back to reality. Embarrassed, he fought to concentrate on the introductions and the purpose of his visit.

"Aah…yes. I am sorry. What were you asking?"

"I was asking you, Your Excellency," Ross said, "if you would prefer that I take you to see Good Father Benedict straightaway?" He had decided the introductions could wait. The most critical issue was to take the bishop to the priest before Father Benedict relapsed into unconsciousness.

"Yes," the bishop said as he pulled Ross Welti closer to whisper in his ear, "we need to see the Father straightaway, but I think it would be best if we had the ladies wait for us in the kitchen. I don't want our conversation to upset them."

Ross Welti agreed to Bishop Roten's request, aware of a review of the events surrounding Maria's sexual assault, and the attempt on Father Benedict's life could be traumatic for his daughter. Consequently, Ross asked the ladies to wait in the farmhouse kitchen while the men conducted an uncomfortable interview in the recovering priest's bedroom.

The bishop struggled to set the tantalizing aroma permeating the Welti kitchen aside temporarily. The bishop and Ross Welti climbed the narrow stairs of the farmhouse to the second floor. When they reached the hallway at the top of the stairs, illuminated by the light coming from long, narrow windows at either end, the bishop noticed eight doors: four on either side of the hallway. He was led to a wooden door, identical to the other seven, midway down the hall on his left. Ross knocked, waited for the priest's reply, lifted the iron latch, and entered with the bishop.

Ross Welti and Bishop Roten found Father Benedict sitting up in his bed, propped against the tall carved wooden headboard, with two down-filled pillows behind his back for comfort. He wore a white nightgown, his legs covered with a blue sheet, the border of which displayed a two-inch embroidered field of edelweiss.

"*Bon journo,*[4]" Bishop Roten said as he greeted the priest and extended his right hand. "Or would you prefer, *Guten Tag*[5]?"

Father Benedict smiled back as he leaned his pale lips forward to kiss the bishop's ring of authority. "It is of little consequence to me, Your Excellency, in what language you wish me a good morning. Any morning is a good morning that I can, once again, open my eyes to see the light of day."

---

4 Good day
5 Good day

The bishop shook his head in empathy and knelt beside the bed. The bishop brought his eyes level with the priest's eyes. "You have been through so much suffering for the Lord's work. When Ross Welti came to Freiburg and told me of your dire circumstances, I came with all haste to hear your testimony. If what he has told me is accurate, I must act with all haste to correct this most reprehensible wrong. So please, Father, tell me in your own words, the events that occurred on that Saturday, back in May."

Father Benedict made the sign of the cross and looked up at the ceiling as though he were looking into the eyes of God. Then he began his account of the events of that evening: "I was in the church rectory, preparing dinner around 6:00 pm. I expected two friends to join me for dinner as they did every Saturday evening. You see that young priest who you sent me, Father Thomas, normally leaves about that time of day to patronize the local pubs and to visit a certain young French woman."

"Oh, dear," the bishop replied. "Do you know that for a fact?"

"I've never actually followed him, but I have it on good authority from several parish members that he does. I do know, Your Excellency, that whenever he comes home, if he comes home at all, he smells of strong drink. And, he always has that same fragrance on his clothes."

"Strong fragrance, Father?"

"Yes, always the same fragrance—lilac!"

"Hmm, that's interesting. Please continue."

"Well, as I was preparing dinner, I thought I heard screaming coming from either the stable or the garden. At first, I discarded the noise as children played out in the alleyway. As you may already know, Monsignor, my hearing is not as good as it used to be. Anyway, I tried to ignore the screaming, but it seemed to get louder and more frequent. That is when I decided that it must be serious if it was loud enough for even me to hear. So, I rushed out to my prayer garden, and it was there that I found her."

"Found whom?" the bishop asked.

Father Benedict hesitated as he looked across the bed at Ross Welti's tearful face. "It was the Welti girl—Maria Welti. She was half-naked, her dress torn, her face bloody, her eyes swollen shut, her legs all bruised. I thought for sure she was dead."

"So, what did you do?" the bishop inquired. He leaned closer to the priest and hung on his every word.

"It was then that I heard the stable door screech on its hinges and noticed it slowly closing. From what I thought was the dead Welti girl, I got up and rushed to the stable. When I got there, I swung open the door just in time to see Father Thomas adjusting his clothing. He held his bloody hands against his badly scratched face. I knew then, without a doubt, that it was Father Thomas who had attacked that sweet young girl, so I attempted to apprehend him."

"What did you do against such a strong young man?"

"I cried out something like, 'You Devil.' Filled with wild rage, I lunged at him. He began to fight me off, but I held on to him with all my strength. My heart apparently, could not take the excitement. My left arm went numb, and I had incredible pain in the center of my chest. I must have passed out immediately because that is all I can remember until I woke up here at the Welti home a couple of days ago."

"If what you say is true, and I have no reason to doubt that it is, the judicial system has condemned two innocent men for that devil's crime."

Father Benedict's eyes watered, and tears rolled down his pale face as he told the bishop the rest of the story. "Sadly, Monsignor, the innocents will face hanging regardless. You see, they are Gypsies— twice captured. By the saving grace of God, they escaped from prison and are now in hiding. Despite the Church's stand on people of their kind, I know they are Christians. Therefore, I have prayed for them often since coming out of my coma. Is that wrong?"

The bishop pondered the question with his head bowed and staring at the floor for a moment. He searched his conscience for an appropriate answer. "It is never wrong to pray for our fellow Christians, dear priest, but we must also remember they are Gypsies. I can only suggest that you follow your conscience and pray about this matter."

"Thank you, bishop. I appreciate your understanding. I am convinced that Christ died on the cross for all peoples."

Bishop Roten was uncomfortable giving too much consideration to the subject of Gypsies. Roten did not feel comfortable viewing any Gypsy as a victim. He wished to change the subject before he appeared to be siding with the priest on such a delicate issue. He had the pressing issue of Father Thomas and his guilt with which to deal. The bishop could not postpone the matter.

"I am so happy, Father Benedict, that you have shown remarkable improvement in your health. You did the right thing in sending Herr Welti to me. Now I must consider what to do about Father Thomas."

"Why not simply get the magistrate to arrest him?" Father Benedict asked.

Ross Welti had remained silent during the interaction between the priest and the bishop, boiling with anger and resisting the urge to find Father Thomas and strangle him. Only his sincere respect for the Church and its designated representatives kept him in tow. He could remain silent no longer and moved away from the door where he stood and moved closer to the bed to interject his opinion into the conversation: "Yes. He must stand trial for what he's done to my Maria and Father Benedict, of course."

The bishop stood up from beside Father Benedict's bed and empathetically placed his hands on Ross Welti's shoulders. He felt Ross's trembling body and sensed the anger and hatred that welled up inside of him.

How thoughtless of me not to consider what this poor man has gone through. I have never bothered to ask the rape victim's parents what action we should take against Father Thomas.

He moved back against the bedroom wall, where he could see both Father Benedict and Ross Welti at the same time, and asked: "Where do you think we should go to from here, Ross?"

"Where do I think we should go from here?" Ross shot back. "I think we should punish Father Thomas for his crimes. He should be hung, just like any other criminal who might have done this.

"Your Excellency, when the news of my Maria's attack reached us, I was out in the north vineyard pruning the vines. Maria's sister ran into the vineyard, screaming and shouting in hysteria. Her screams frightened me. When Anne calmed down enough to tell me what had happened, I ran back to the farmhouse and discovered my Maria laying in the back of a buckboard, just rocking back and forth, her knees pulled up against her body, and staring up at the heavens. Some men from our Church had brought her home for us to provide care. My wife was there embracing Maria and weeping so hard I couldn't even get her to talk to me. She just kept screaming, 'My baby! My baby!' I finally could pry my wife away from Maria long enough to lift her off the buckboard and carry her into the house. I took Maria directly to her bedroom and laid her on her bed. She looked awful. Her mother stayed in the room with her while I took Anne downstairs to boil some water. I needed to get Anne calmed down enough to help her mother bathe Maria. All the while, I could hear my wife upstairs, repeatedly saying, 'My poor baby.'

"When I took the hot water upstairs to Maria's bedroom, her mother told me to leave. Anne and her mother undressed Maria and bathed her. All the while, Maria said nothing. She just kept rocking and staring up at the ceiling. Maria remained that way for days. Finally, one morning, she just got out of bed and came down to the breakfast table as though nothing had ever happened. Maria never said another word about it. She has no memory of the incident as far as I can tell.

"All I've wanted to do, since that incident, is to pin the blame on the Gypsies—strangle them with my bare hands—or to hang them. I'd have had plenty of help lynching them, too. The entire town was ready to resort to mob rule. But now, I realize the error of my rash judgment. The Gypsies weren't responsible for the attack on my Maria. When Father Benedict regained consciousness and told us what happened, it became apparent we would have lynched two innocent men. Their blood would have been on my hands.

"When I found out it was that evil priest who was responsible, I re-directed my hatred toward Father Thomas. It was overwhelming how quickly I could switch my hatred from the Gypsies to the priest. Only this time, my fury was more intense. To realize that we could have hung two innocents while a man we trusted remained silent was more than I could handle. I wanted to kill him, too, only this time, I wanted him to suffer a long death. Hanging seemed too kind for him. I think that's why my wife sent me to bring you here. It was to keep me acting rashly in administering justice to that evil priest."

The bishop hesitated to consider what he had just heard before answering Maria's Father. He had total empathy for this family, and he, too, wanted a resolution to this dilemma, but he always held the good of the Church as his priority. Bishop Roten weighed his words carefully. "What is it you want? Is it justice you are looking for, or are you seeking revenge?"

The girl's father glared at the bishop and boiled with anger that the man could ask him such a question. It had been his little girl who had been beaten and raped, not the bishop's daughter. What did this celibate priest know about children and the love a father has for his daughter? Ross remained silent, starring tearfully into the bishop's face, while the veins in his neck bulged beneath his skin.

"Now, now Ross, we have other things to consider in this matter," Bishop Roten continued.

"Other things to consider? Things like what?"

"Well, Ross…there is the integrity of the Church to consider. Right now, only a few of us know about what Father Thomas did: you and your family know; the doctor who examined your daughter and cared for Father Benedict, the priest, of course, since he too was attacked, and Maria, who can't remember anything.

"I'm asking you to consider what the consequences of making this general knowledge available to the parishioners would be. It may cause some of your local church members to lose confidence and trust in the Church. For some, it might be a loss of faith in God. Ross, let me be frank with you." The bishop hesitated as he lost eye contact with Maria's Father, and he weighed his following words carefully. He looked back at Ross Welti with a nervous twitch in his right eye and fought to regain his authoritative demeanor. "If the parishioners find out it was one of their priests who committed this dastardly deed, it may cause a severe division within St. Mary's Church. As Bishop, I've seen this sort of thing and the wagging tongues that inevitably follow and completely tear the heart out of a local assembly."

Ross sucked in his lower lip and bit down on it, trying to consider all he had just heard. Was the bishop suggesting Father Thomas go unpunished by the local authorities because he held a priest's office? Was he suggesting his physically and psychologically injured daughter, and the seriously injured Father Benedict, allow an evil man to walk away without consequences, free to find new victims? Anger took hold of him, and a unique feeling of betrayal began to overcome him. First, he felt the betrayal of his family by Father Thomas. The sense of betrayal by the Church he loved and the bishop who represented it now. Ross held back the words he wanted to speak. He knew he would only regret his angry words later. The Welti family belonged to the Church through his family's traditions and faith in the organization. He also had his son's career, serving in Paris, to consider.

Ross Welti looked over at Father Benedict—still propped up against the headboard—in the hope the priest would interject some words of wisdom. The old priest was silently gesturing with his hands, fingers extended, and his palms turned down as if to say, "Calm down."

Bishop Roten perceived the silence as an indication he had regained control of the situation. Satisfied, he felt the need to end the discussion. He placed his hands on Ross Welti's broad shoulders and inhaled the cooking's hunger-invoking aroma in the kitchen. "What do you say we go downstairs and enjoy some of the delicious-smelling food your wife and daughters are cooking?"

The bishop hurriedly knelt and bowed his graying head against his folded hands that rested on Father Benedict's bedside. He uttered a quick succession of Latin words that Ross did not understand and blessed the ailing priest. The heavy-set bishop rose to his feet with some effort. He then ushered his host out of the bedroom and down the stairs to have lunch.

CHAPTER FIVE
DEFROCKED

Saint Mary's Church of Erlach
4:00 p.m. June 20, 1752

The hot afternoon sun bore down unmercifully on the tired chestnut mare that labored to ascend the steep cobblestone alleyway behind St. Mary's Church, pulling Bishop Roten's carriage and its two occupants. Finally, the alleyway leveled off behind the open limestone carriage house. Leather reigns pulled against the brass bit in the mare's mouth to signal a stop. Two men, the judge who had presided over the trial of the Gypsies, and Bishop Roten, leaned forward to peer into the building.

"Looks like his carriage and horse are in the stable, Your Excellency," Judge Rene called out.

"Good. Father Thomas must be here. The sooner we get this over with, the better. I do not look forward to what I must do. But let's get some water and oats for my mare. The old gal brought Ross Welti and me here from Fribourg. She must be exhausted."

The two men who came with the magistrate unhooked the bishop's mare from the carriage and led her into the carriage house, where he put her in a stall and provided oats and water. The horse went straight to the water and drank with vigor.

"We'll leave the horse here in the stall. I'll be spending the night here at the rectory anyway," the bishop pronounced. "You only live a few blocks here. I'm sure you don't mind walking home."

The judge nodded in agreement. "The exercise will do me good."

The two men went out through the carriage house's side door and entered Father Benedict's "Garden of Meditation," as he called it. They paused beside the statue of the Madonna and Child. In front of the sculpture, they looked in amazement at the flowers and candles left there by well-wishers. Judge Rene did the sign of the cross.

"Pathetic, isn't it, Bishop?"

"What's that?" Bishop Roten asked as sweat poured from beneath his black hat.

"It was right here, in front of the Madonna and Child, amid all these beautiful roses Good Father Benedict planted, where Father Thomas forced his passion upon that poor innocent child of God."

Bishop Roten wiped the sweat from his brow and the tears from his eyes and looked toward the rectory. He struggled to hold back his rage. "As I said, let's get this done. The sooner I can send that despicable man on his way, the better."

"Send him on his way? What about bringing criminal charges against him?"

"I'm afraid I must ask you not to allow the prosecutor to bring any charges against him," Bishop Roten pleaded. "Father Benedict has already agreed not to bring charges against him, and the Church can little afford the scandal. I'm afraid letting word get out that a priest did this horrific act would only cause parishioners to lose confidence in the Church's integrity. Please, your honor, allow the Church to handle this internally. I do, however, feel sorry for those poor Gypsies."

The judge got a sheepish look on his face that betrayed a look of guilt. "That won't matter at this point," he said. "The Gypsies have already escaped from the prison, but not without killing two of the guards. When we recapture them, there will be murder charges filed against them."

The judge and the bishop turned and walked up to the flagstone path to the rectory. When they arrived at the door to the rectory, His Excellency was just about to knock when he saw movement through the kitchen window. He saw a tall, slender woman carrying two white wine glasses toward the house's inner part.

The bishop pointed through the window and asked, "Do you recognize that young woman?"

Judge Rene leaned against the glass and held his open palms beside his head to shade against the reflection of the afternoon sun on the window.

"Yes," he replied. "That's the French woman I described to you. That's Emilie de Fontaine."

Bishop Roten did not bother to knock. As acting Bishop, he had the authority to enter any Church property unannounced. Bishop Roten opened the kitchen door and entered the rectory. He proceeded through the kitchen and continued in the direction they had seen Emilie go.

In the rear bedroom of the house, the bishop could hear a man and a woman laughing. Without a second of hesitation, he boldly approached the open bedroom door. There, he found a partially clad priest lying on Father Benedict's bed with a scantily clad woman standing beside him, holding two glasses of white wine.

Even for a devil hound as evil as Thomas, the shock of being discovered was overwhelming. The priest jumped out of bed, clothed only in his underpants and the guilt of his conviction. He quickly wrapped himself in a sheet. His feeling was not unlike Adam's in the Biblical account of Genesis when Adam stood before God and became aware of his nakedness. Emilie exhibited no shame at all.

The bishop was outraged. "How dare you bring that shameless woman onto church property? I want you both to get out of this rectory and out of this town. You can consider yourself defrocked and excommunicated from the Church. You are forbidden, ever again, to wear the cloth of a priest. You have brought shame to the cloth and the Church."

Father Thomas suddenly remembered the trophy handkerchiefs he had collected from the women he had seduced during his career as a priest. He was especially concerned about the lavender embroidered handkerchief that smelled of lilac fragrance he had taken from Maria and sewn into the lining of his robe. That one would tie him to the attack on the girl. He trembled in fear as he tried to contrive a way to get his hands on his robe and to tear out the lining discreetly.

"Yes, Bishop," he said in a shaky voice. "I'll get my things and clear out immediately. Just give a minute to get dressed." He reached for his jacket, but the angry hand of the bishop grabbed Thomas' wrist.

"You will not leave here wearing the clothing of a priest!" Bishop Roten said in a firm voice.

Thomas knew it was futile to push the issue, especially in the presence of Judge Rene. He would have to leave the robe, but it would only be a matter of time before someone discovered his bizarre collection of "trophy" garments. He searched the rectory closet until he found a few civilian garb articles and then departed Erlach with all haste.

You messed up this time! A voice within him spoke. *But we will get even. This revenge on the Gypsies has not ended. We will find those Gypsies and be done with them once and for all.*

"Yes. You are right. We will find them," Thomas uttered audibly.

Emilie looked across the carriage seat at Thomas with her head cocked and mouth open in a questioning manner. "What did you say, Thomas? To whom are you speaking?"

Thomas snapped back to reality and spoke without looking directly at Emilie. "Nothing, Emilie. I was only thinking out loud."

Emilie shrugged her shoulder and shook her head. "You seem to be doing a lot of that lately. Sometimes I worry about you."

"What now, Thomas?" Emilie inquired. "What do you intend to do? Where will you go?"

"I can't stay here with you. The King has ordered me to return to Versailles, and it must be soon."

Thomas pondered his options for a few seconds and then turned toward Emilie. "Paris would be a good place for me. I need to get away from these country peasants and return to civilization for a while. How long will you be in Paris?"

"I don't know," Emilie replied. "The war with England is growing more intense and will probably spread to the colonies. I will most likely have to go to New France or Philadelphia within the year. Why do you ask? Are you thinking about staying with me? If you think you will stay with me—forget it. King Louis will want me at Versailles. I can visit you from time to time in Paris, but you must be on your own."

Thomas did not reply. Instead, he slumped down in his seat and considered Paris.

What a great time you can have, Thomas. So much to do and so many opportunities.

Thomas didn't reply to Emilie. He smiled and nodded his head and silently agreed with Damian.

CHAPTER SIX
ANNE WELTI

One Year Later
June 15, 1753

Anne Welti had few cares that extended beyond her family's farm near Erlach, Switzerland. She would be seventeen the following December, old enough to consider marriage, but young enough to fear the seriousness of such a union. To date, Anne expressed little interest in the steady parade of young men from her Church who wished to become serious suitors to the tall, slender redhead. She was aware of her apparent attractiveness. Having a twin sister was like looking into a mirror, and her sister's beauty was her own. Still, she maintained a modest humility, avoiding the sense of arrogance she observed in her female friends. Some young men found her sense of personal honesty and modesty most attractive.

Anne had definite ideas about potential suitors' qualities: honesty, faith, gentleness, love of children, intelligence, and respect for women. Because of her high standards, she maintained a stubborn indifference to suitors who did not meet her criteria. She resisted her parent's constant prodding amid reminders. Anne's parents constantly reminded her that peers would grab up all the good men.

It was July, Anne Welti's favorite month. She enjoyed the warm days and scents of early summer. The white blossoms of sweet-smelling edelweiss blessed Northwest Switzerland with a fragrance pleasing to the senses. Simultaneously, the beauty of red geraniums, which adorned nearly every window box in the region, pleased the eye. It was the season for refreshing swims in the cold waters of Lake Biel or just lying on the banks of the lake and daydreaming about romance. Anne loved to fanaticize about the man she would someday love, and she hoped to find him soon. She would sit for hours, conjuring up imaginary images of the soon-to-be-but-not-yet-met young man. Romance occupied her every thought—but they were her private thoughts—thoughts she shared with no one else.

This day was one of those lazy daydreaming days. Anne sat in the shade of an apple tree in the family apple orchard near the farm's west boundary, overlooking Lake Biel. Puffy white cumulus clouds drifted slowly across the lake in a pale blue sky, and green stalks of barley waved gently in the breeze, revealing only the slightest hint of their ripening golden hues, six weeks before the harvest.

She sat on a green woolen blanket with her curly bright red hair braided in long pigtails that hung down the back of her head, midway to her waist. Anne leaned forward and shooed a honeybee away from a wild yellow flower. She picked the flower and held it to her nose to enjoy its sweet fragrance. Carefully, she placed it in her hair above her ear and wished she had a mirror. Life felt right on the farm. Anne was at peace there. She hated to think she, someday, might have to leave it behind. Adulthood brought with it so many changes. But those were problems she would have to deal with, when and if they came. For now, she would enjoy her life and take a *Que sera* attitude. Anne leaned her head back against a tree and closed her tired eyes. She was soon sleeping peacefully.

The young woman had not been sleeping long when the sound of approaching foot steps awakened her. Anne could hear the voices of men talking nearby, but they seemed unaware of her presence. They stopped only a few feet away, on the other side of a short wall of stacked fieldstone that served as a boundary between her family's farm and their neighbors'. She rose quietly to her knees and lifted her head to peer over the stones. She could hear the two men talking: one, an older man, the other younger. She recognized them: It was Herr Smith and his youngest son. They were discussing their grapevines.

"I've cut this section back to its base and grafted on new Chasselas vines. I had to travel to Neuchâtel to buy them, but it was worth the trip," Herr Smith told his son. "As you can see, the new growth is taking hold just fine. If the weather holds, we'll have a banner crop this year. If that happens, we'll have cause for celebration at the wine festival in September."

Then, Anne heard the younger Smith speak. She knew his name was Anton, but she had never been allowed to meet him. As a little girl, Anne would wave to him when she would see him working in the fields with his father, but seldom did he acknowledge her greetings. *After all*, Anne reasoned, *I was only a child then, and he probably thought I was just a silly little girl. I thought he was so handsome then—and he still is.*

She listened as she heard his adult voice clearly for the first time.

"I think you were wise in grafting new vines, Papa. I remember how unproductive this section was when I left here four years ago."

His voice sounds so deep and mature now. I cannot believe how tall he is grown. Wow! Has it been four years since he went away?

Anne could not believe how silly she felt. She had known about his existence for most of her life, yet she barely knew him.

If only my family were not so bull-headed about Calvinists. Oh well, summer has only just begun. I will find some way to meet Anton—regardless of my parents' prejudices.

The Weltis were a faithful Catholic family. Never had any member of this family been anything but a good Catholic in anyone's memory. The local parish priest, Father Benedict, could always count on the Welti family whenever the Church was in need. Money or labor made little difference. The Church got the best of whatever the family had to give, and they gave it willingly. Every Sunday would find the family dutifully attending mass, and all the Welti children received instruction in the Catechism. Their devout loyalty to the Church served as an example to all.

Family tradition had it that the Welti family fought hard to maintain the Church's integrity during the Reformation. Many family members rose to arms in fighting the spread of what began with Martin Luther as a reform and grew known as Protestantism. The movement was labeled "heresy" and spread with like-minded thinkers across Europe. Resistance to change by the Pope resulted in an armed confrontation.

When the followers of another reformer, named John Calvin, spread the Presbyterian doctrine, or "Reformed" Church across Switzerland and later Scotland, the Welti's remained steadfast in the Catholic faith. They didn't depart from tradition. Many Welti men served in the Papal army, and many had served in the priesthood over the years. Among Roman Catholics in Switzerland, the Welti name commanded respect.

Anne thought a lot about Anton Smith over the next several days working around the farm. She found herself continually looking in the direction of the Smith place, trying to catch a glimpse of him working outside or finding excuses to walk up to the apple orchard just in case he came back. Twice, she walked down to the lake where she remembered he used to swim with his brothers, but it all to no avail. He could not find him.

One early morning, when Anne was working in the milking barn, she began to think about what it would be like to be married. She knew that the life cycle involved mating from growing up on the farm. Every farm animal and every bird had a mate to reproduce. It seemed natural enough, and of course, she accepted mating as natural. Her curiosity caused her to wonder what it would be like when she married.

Anne wanted to be married and have her own family someday. She could not imagine life any other way, yet the thought of a husband carried with it some anxiety. Anne wasn't sure how she'd react the first time a man touched her, and the idea of being alone with a man frightened her.

What if I panic, cry, or refuse to be with my new husband? What if the act of love is painful or ugly? Why do I think about love so much?

Anne was aware that she thought of love and sex often. She began to wonder if thinking about it so much was normal for a girl her age—or any age.

Could I be like the harlots I have overheard her brothers discussing? Is it possible, I too, am a wanton woman? Am I a woman with no self-respect, condemned to an eternal hell? Surely not! I have never done anything wrong—only fanaticized. Certainly, curiosity is not the same thing as actually doing the act. If only I had someone, I could direct my questions to without fear of ridicule.

Anne did not want sex to be cruel, and certainly not painful. She hoped her husband would be gentle and to want her, and only her, for the rest of his life. She wanted her physical union to be beautiful and fulfilling and between only her and her husband.

Anne's mind remained in a constant turmoil of being torn between wanting life to go on the way it was and wanting to have a family of her own. She had begun to think about marriage a lot more recently. Her thoughts about marriage had intensified the day she saw Anton and his father talking near the apple orchard. *Could Anton Smith be that special someone of her dreams? How she wished she had someone to talk to about marriage and sex, but she did not feel comfortable asking questions.*

Anne saw her mother walking toward the barn alone and decided now was as good as any time to ask questions.

If I cannot talk to my mother about marriage, who else is there?

"Mother," she began nervously when her mother drew near, "Can I talk to you about marriage?"

Her mother was shocked. "Well, yes, of course. What is it you want to talk about, honey?" her mother replied with apprehension.

Anne hesitated for a moment, unsure how to begin, but now that she had taken the initiative, she was determined to follow through with the discussion.

"Mother, when it's time for me to be with a man, how will I know what to do?"

"Anne Welti!" her mother said in a state of shock, "What, in heaven's name, are you asking me? I mean, is there something I need to know? What do you mean by 'when it's time for you to be with a man?' Are you seeing someone?"

Anne was offended by her mother's harsh reaction and her series of seemingly condemning questions. "No, Mother, I'm not seeing anyone special. I mean, I do not have a suitor. I'm not doing anything wrong. What I meant to ask is, how did you know what to do when you were alone for the first time with a man."

Her mother was embarrassed and stumbled over words to find the right thing to say. She looked away and down at the ground, avoiding eye contact with Anne. Finally, with an air of righteous indignation, she snapped, "Your father is the only man I have ever known. What do you mean by implying that I have been with anyone else? I'm a good Catholic woman and wouldn't commit the carnal sin of being with a man who is not my husband. Young lady, watch your mouth!"

"Mother!" Anne responded, sorry she had ever brought up the topic of sex, "All I was trying to say is I'm nervous about finding a husband. When I do find the right man, how will I know what to do to please him?"

Anne's face began to redden, and tears formed in her eyes from the frustration of this hopeless conversation.

Mrs. Welti felt inadequate to handle this conversation. She wished she had prepared a mother-daughter talk in advance. She should have known, at some point, Anne was bound to need advice and guidance, but this happened so unexpectedly. She knew Anne was becoming a woman, but she had told herself there was still plenty of time to prepare. Anne was still such a child in so many ways. When did it happen that this little girl grew up? Suddenly, her little girl was curious about being with a man?

"When you love a man," Mrs. Welti struggled, "and you are, of course, married to him, it will all come naturally to you."

She knew her answer sounded stupid and unprepared, but it was the best she could come up with on such short notice. She searched her mind for a better way to put it. "Since the beginning of time, people have just, naturally, known what to do when the time was right. There's no way to instruct someone on what to do. You do what comes naturally. You will know when the time is right."

The conversation was becoming increasingly difficult for Anne's mother. She could see the perplexed look on Anne's face, and she understood the fear Anne was facing. She went over to Anne, put her arms around her, and hugged her. She wanted to tell Anne what to do, but it was too complicated to put into words that were—for someone who had not experienced lovemaking.

Mrs. Welti felt inadequate. These questions weren't fair! She thought back to when she got engaged to Ross. Her mother didn't know how to give her advice either. Her mother took her to the priest and a nun to explain it. Mrs. Welti didn't want that to happen to Anne. She kissed Anne on the forehead and spoke.

"Darling, the only advice that my mother gave to me was vague and of not much help to me. She said: 'You are obligated to give your husband sex whenever he wants it. Just don't give him sex too often, or he'll want it all the time. Women don't enjoy sex—only men enjoy sex."

Anne drew back, and with tears in her eyes, she said, "Mother. Is that true? Do only men enjoy sex?"

"Darling," her mother chuckled, "if women don't enjoy being with their husband, then I'm in real trouble. I've found that when you love your husband, the relationship is enjoyable for both of you. As far as not giving your husband too much sex is concerned, I find myself being the one who initiates the encounter sometimes. A woman should strive to remain attractive to her husband, so he wants her. Never make your husband beg for your affection. Affection comes from the heart."

Mrs. Welti thought back to that awkward time after becoming engaged to Anne's father. Her mother took her to the parish priest and a nun for counseling.

How ridiculous that was. My parents took me to talk with people who had never experienced marriage to explain marriage and sex. It was like asking a fish how to fly or asking a camel how to swim.

Neither the priest nor the nun had the slightest idea what romantic love, either emotional or physical, would be. She remembered asking the priest how he could know what it could be like being married, and he said, "A doctor can know how to amputate a leg without amputating his leg. I can advise you on marriage without having been married."

The priest was annoyed by her questioning of his priestly advice. Conversely, his short answer did nothing to satisfy her lack of confidence in the priest. Seeing the embarrassment of her dear mother, however, she resigned herself to the counseling procedure.

I do not want that same experience for Anne. I don't want the embarrassing lectures, threats of Hell's damnation, or fears of failure for my daughter. I want Anne to have the confidence of marital love and the wonders of a blessed physical union. Love and marriage should be something extraordinary for Anne.

My marriage has been outstanding because of the man I married. Ross is sensitive enough to understand the needs and anxieties of a new bride. The wedding night was fearful for me. The first night of our marriage had not been a successful consummation of the wedding vows, but my husband never ridiculed me for needing to wait. He had been loving and understanding enough to realize I needed a little more time. When consummation did happen, a few nights later, it was an actual act of love, and I respected him for his patience. Respect is the solid foundation upon which we built our undying love. It is a love that has endured for over thirty years and is still growing.

Anne was about to ask her mother another question when she heard her father's footsteps coming into the barn. Anne wanted to continue the conversation, but she knew it would have to wait for now. She and her mother had never had a serious talk about love and its physical implications before. Today had been a wonderful time of special closeness with her mother, and she would cherish it. Her mother had spoken freely to her for the first time. Anne appreciated the openness more than any talk she could remember having with her mother. She was amazed at how much her mother was willing to share with her. Her mother's willingness to discuss such personal matters caused an immediate mother/daughter bond.

Mrs. Welti leaned over and whispered, "Baby, when you're engaged to a man, we'll talk again, but there's no sense in rushing it. Yes, let's talk about it then, not now."

While the discussion had been uncomfortable for both, it had been a long-overdue conversation. Anne felt much closer to her mother for having talked openly about sex. She needed her mother's guidance, and she needed her mother's recognition of her as a woman, not just as her daughter. Anne was not a little girl anymore, and her mother saw her as a young adult for the first time. Anne looked forward to the day when they would again discuss the subject. She needed to know a lot about sex, and the subject fascinated her, but she did not want to appear too eager. She had to drop the issue for now, but she knew she could approach her mother again when the opportunity availed itself.

That night, in the privacy of their bedroom, Anne's parents lay quietly on their bed, embracing. Marie Welti could no longer keep the secret to herself. She giggled, which aroused the curiosity of her husband lying next to her.

"Woman, what is so funny?" he queried.

"You'll never guess what our daughter asked me today in the barn?"

"What?" he asked.

There was another giggle and then prolonged silence.

"Woman, are you going to tell me, or do you intend to keep me in suspense for the rest of the night?"

Marie searched for the right words to answer her curious husband. She realized what she was about to tell him would certainly shock and concern the girl's father. He had always been so protective of his beautiful Anne. Marie leaned beside his ear and whispered her reply. "She wanted to know about marriage, Ross."

Ross Welti rolled away from Marie and sat straight up in the bed. "She wanted to know about what? Marriage? Is someone courting her? Why don't I know about this? Who is he?"

"Just calm yourself down and lower your voice," Mrs. Welti responded. "Anne said that no one is courting her. She just wanted to know what sex was going to be like."

That was the wrong way to put it to the father of such a young and beautiful girl.

"What do you mean she wanted to know what sex is going to be like? Is there something wrong with that young woman? I'm going to talk to Father Benedict about putting her into a convent. That girl is too young to be thinking about sex."

"Calm down, calm down!"

Mrs. Welti knew her husband couldn't think about their daughter as a young woman. She also had trouble accepting that fact.

"Our little girl is growing up fast, Ross. Soon, we need to introduce her to some good Catholic boys. After all, many girls her age are already married—with children. Maybe Father Benedict and Sister Mary Daniel can help us. They'd know how to go about making some introductions to proper young men."

Ross Welti thought about it for a few minutes trying to absorb the shock of finding out his baby wanted to know about sex and marriage. Eventually, he spoke: "You're right. We need to get that girl counseling about marriage. I'll talk to Father Benedict tomorrow. Don't forget," Ross added, "Father Benedict counseled you when we got engaged, and it seems to me he must have done a good job. You've been a wonderful wife."

"No, Ross, you absolutely will not take her to them for counseling. Introductions are one thing, but marriage counseling—never!"

The powerful sound of her voice surprised even her. Marie was unaccustomed to being defiant to her husband, yet she knew what was best for her daughter as a mother.

Anne's mother tried to soften the impact of her response. "As far as introducing Anne to young Catholic men, that's fine for Father Benedict to do. However, when it comes to counseling our daughter, you will not have an unmarried man who has never experienced either marriage or sex counsel our daughter. Socially and religiously, I acknowledge Father

Benedict's qualifications, and I welcome his guidance. But when it comes to matters of the heart—that's my job. I must have my way on this, Ross. Please don't put her through the same embarrassing humiliation I went through when we got engaged."

Ross Welti peered into the darkness of their bedroom, seeing only the outline of his wife's face. He lay silently in bed and said nothing at first. Finally, he broke the silence by inquiring, "I didn't realize the counseling with Father Benedict had been embarrassing for you, honey."

"No," she replied. "I'm sure neither you nor my father had any idea how embarrassing it was for me. It's a horrible experience for a frightened teenager, who knows nothing about marriage or sex, to be forced into a counseling session with a man of authority, to discuss intimacy."

Ross thought about it for a minute and then replied, "Honey, you knew Father Benedict."

"Yes," Marie said. "But you will recall that at the time of our wedding Father Benedict was a newly appointed priest to our diocese. The priest is a warm and wonderful old priest now, but he seemed cold and stern when he was younger. I'm sure, at that early point in his experience, our session was as embarrassing for him too. We both hated being there."

Marie disliked bringing it up again, but she felt compelled to say, "After what happened with her sister and that evil Father Thomas, talking to a priest about sex would most likely, be uncomfortable for Anne. Please, Ross, don't make our daughter sit through such an awkward experience!"

Even though Ross couldn't see Marie in the darkness, he could read the intensity and the earnestness of her request in the tones of her voice. He knew that intensity all too well, and he knew better than to challenge it.

"Ross," Marie requested, "Let's just sleep on it and discuss it further in the morning."

Her request to discuss the subject later sounded good to him. Ross loved Marie, and he had learned, over the years, to trust her maternal instincts. He was also a firm believer in never letting the marriage bed be the place to settle disputes. It was a formula that had served the Welti marriage well for twenty-nine years, and there was no need to change it now.

He slid back down beneath the blankets, and he held his dear wife close. She felt warm and tender and alive. Twenty-nine years of marriage had not dampened his desire for this wonderful and loving woman. To Ross, she was still the twenty-year-old bride he had married, and every time together was just as intense as their wedding night. This night would be no different.

Outside Anne's curtained bedroom window, the moon shone full and bright. Fireflies flickered in the shadows of the moonlit orchard, and crickets made their high-pitched sounds. A barn owl hooted a love call across the barnyard, and a female responded to his invitation. Heidi, the family dog, lay sleeping in the kitchen.

Alone in her bed, Anne dared to wonder when love would fulfill her with a husband to hold her tenderly. For now, all she could do was a dream.

Paris
June 1753

The carriage from King Louis' personal stable in Versailles turned many heads as it wound its way through Thomas' seedy neighborhood in Paris. The carriage came to a stop in front of a brick apartment building where a young woman, dressed in blue, quickly opened the carriage door, and hopped down before the footman had a chance to assist her.

"Return to Versailles," the woman said to the driver. "I won't be needing the carriage. There is no need to wait for me."

She picked up her bag, applied lilac perfume to her neck and wrists, and reached for the door handle of the apartment building. The door suddenly flung open from within. A young woman, her dress and hair in disarray stepped through the doorway without a greeting as she counted the money in her hand, and then shoved it down the front of her dress.

The lady from the carriage held the door open as the lady of the night came through and hurried down the street. The perfumed lady climbed the stairs to the third floor and flung open the apartment door.

Thomas, aroused by the opening of the door sat up in bed with a start, and rubbed his eyes to focus on the doorway.

"Emilie," Thomas managed to utter through swollen glands, "what a pleasant surprise to see you here."

Emilie tossed her bag across the room at Thomas. "Still in bed at noon?" Emilie said in a voice just shy of shouting. She drew in a deep breath, shook her head in disgust, and said, "Thomas, you are disgusting. This apartment reeks and I can still smell the woman I passed at the front door of the building."

Thomas, still hung over from the night before, rubbed his head and flung his feet over the side of the bed. "I know what you're thinking," he said, "but you are dead wrong. There was no woman in my apartment last night. I have been wrongly accused. I slept alone."

Emilie was not in the mood for an argument. "Whatever! I really don't care to discuss your morality."

Thomas stood up from the bed and held out his hands to receive Emilie into his embrace. She walked across the room and accommodated him.

"You smell like cheap wine, Thomas. Let's get out of here and find something to eat."

Emilie and Thomas went to a sidewalk café a few blocks from Thomas' apartment where they often dined when Emilie was in Paris. Emilie, over-dressed for such a neighborhood attracted attention, which she relished. Seated at a table next to the building, Emilie raised her right hand and snapped her fingers to get the waiter's attention. Recognizing her from her past visits, he rushed to the table with a wet cloth and wiped the table. The waiter apologized, took their orders, and left them alone to talk.

"Emilie," Thomas started. "I have discovered that the woman who was raped in Erlach, is staying at a convent in Zurich. She had her baby there, a son, about three months ago."

"So, what is that to me?" Emilie asked. "Are you admitting to me that you are the father of the child?"

"All I'm saying," Thomas replied while avoiding Emilie's eyes, "is that since I have been accused of the rape, it would be poetic justice for us to take the child away from her. The Welti girl is putting the baby up for adoption, according to a nun that I have been in contact with, and I'd like us to adopt the child."

Emilie didn't answer right away. Instead, she slipped into deep thought: *I wonder if Thomas thinks I am gullible enough to believe him. I know he raped that girl. But he needs me to help him by posing as his wife to pull off the adoption, and I need him to help me with my new assignment to New France for the king.*

"Alright. I'll help you with completing the adoption in Zurich. But you will need to take the baby to New France and wait for me there. Find us a place to live and I will join you there as soon as I am done with my assignment in Philadelphia."

Thomas sat back in his chair wide-eyed and asked, "Philadelphia? What are you going to do in Philadelphia? That is a British colony."

"That, my friend is none of your business," Emilie replied.

CHAPTER SEVEN
ANTON SEES ANNE

One week later.

Good Heaven! This down-filled mattress feels good!

Anton stretched his body fully out and yawned with pleasure that he had enjoyed such a good night's sleep. His comfortable bed on the family farm was much better than the one in his small, rented room in Geneva. It had taken him four years to fulfill his apprenticeship with the tailor's guild—four seemingly endless years! He was only nineteen years old when he began his training. His apprenticeship had taken almost twenty percent of his entire life. It was no wonder he had been homesick for the farm and his family. Now he had completed his apprenticeship, and he intended to enjoy his vacation. He had looked forward to a summer holiday at his parent's farm all winter, and now it was time to relax.

Young Anton Smith used his time in Geneva wisely. He took advantage of every opportunity to utilize his talent. Anton realized he needed to get as much experience and training from the masters as possible. Even at this early stage of his development, the young man had developed a reputation as an excellent tailor and fashion designer. At age seventeen, he was already well on his way to becoming successful in his trade, thanks to the early start he had received at home.

The Smith family had been farming and tailoring for generations. He grasped the tailoring skills his parents taught him early and then moved very quickly beyond needle and thread basics. His parents recognized

Anton's talent and realized his talent was too great to be limited to the mundane types of clothing their local clientele demanded. Through friends in the garment industry, they arranged for an apprenticeship for Anton in Geneva. There, he developed his talents far beyond the level he would have gained in their small shop. He possessed a rare ability to see fashion beyond its present stage and mix fabric and color. He had the daring to try new and innovative designs.

Anton's accelerated apprenticeship was very demanding, but he possessed a determination to grasp all he could learn. He worked hard and combined his artistic flair with craftsmanship. His natural ability challenged even the talents of his more learned masters, and his abilities didn't go long unnoticed. Soon the fashionable elite of Geneva stood in line to buy his fashions. His contacts in Geneva expected a bright future for Anton when he returned to Geneva.

Anton felt no sense of urgency to get out of bed. He took his time to enjoy all the morning sounds of the farm that he had missed so much. Anton remained flat on his back like a man of leisure. He loved to hear the familiar farm sounds of horses whinnying, chickens clucking, and cows mooing. The sound of the voices of two women engaged in conversation beneath his window suddenly disrupted his peaceful morning. One of the voices was his mother's, but he didn't recognize the other. He raised his head from his pillow and listened carefully, trying to discern the identity of the other female. The longer he heard, the more familiar the woman's voice became.

Who in the world could that be? He tried desperately to put a name with the voice—he almost had it—yet he couldn't seem to unlock his memory enough to pull out the word.

He rolled out of bed, still wrapped in his comforter, and pulled back the white curtains to look down onto the yard beneath. Below, he could see his mother on the lawn in the front yard, talking to a plump young woman dressed in her Sunday finest.

A feeling of anxiety overcame him immediately, and the smile so recent upon his lips turned to desperation. *Oh, my word! It's Hildegard!*

Anton Smith had reached the point in his life where the fantasy of having a wife had crossed his mind. He had no suitable candidates in mind. Almost all women seemed beautiful to him, but no woman Anton had met possessed the unique charm he was looking for in a mate; a charm, yet undefined, but one he knew needed to be a part of the "special someone" who would make his life complete. Whoever that "special someone" was going to be, Anton was confident that Hildegard Shultz was not the woman of his dreams.

Anton dropped his quilt to the floor and reached for his pants. He pulled up his pants, grabbed his shirt and shoes, and hurried quietly down the back stairs of the farmhouse. Anton ran through the kitchen, out the back door, ran through his mother's flowerbed, and jumped over the back fence with his clothes still under his arms. Then the young man ran up the hill and through the cover of the apple orchard. Anton ran hard until he felt he was safely out of sight of the obnoxious Hildegard Shultz. Totally out of breath, he dropped to the ground and laughed hysterically at his close call.

Anton pulled on his shoes and socks and then buttoned his shirt and leaned back against the trunk of an apple tree. He looked up at the tree's sagging branches, heavily laden with green apples, not yet ripened by the summer sun. Then he drew in a deep breath of fresh air and looked toward the west, out beyond the farmhouse, to the beautiful Lake Biel he had loved so dearly as a child. It glistened blue and shimmered like a jewel, rich in flawless perfection, treasured and rare, a one-of-a-kind keepsake, meant always to be an heirloom of the heart. Beyond the piled stone fences, a dirt road followed the lake's edge and continued south into the nearby village of Erlach. From his vantage point, the buildings looked small, its houses like miniature fixtures in a toy village.

Beyond the edge of fields of ripening grain and the trees that lined the rocky shores of crystal-clear waters of the lake, Anton could see a small island he and his brothers considered as their own when they were children. He allowed his mind to carry him back to another moment in time when life was much more straightforward. It was the time of his childhood when he and his brothers would swim out to their domain, fifty yards from the shore.

There, they were free to allow their imaginations to run wild on their island. It was a place where they could pretend, they were royalty. The island was their kingdom of fantasy, where they ruled it with absolute authority. On this island domain, no injustice was allowed, and only happiness prevailed under the imaginary role of the Smith siblings. There, they destroyed dragons with their swords and successfully fought against oppression. It was a good time in their lives, and he wanted to revisit that time and place.

Anton sat on the warm ground and leaned against the old apple tree and felt the warmth of the alpine sun on his face. He soon drifted off to a peaceful sleep. When he awoke, he had no idea how long he had slept. Anton looked up into the sky and judged that more than an hour had passed from the sun's position.

Once again gazed toward Lake Biel and thought about his childhood kingdom. He wondered if the island had changed. His curiosity finally won out. He headed for the lake.

Anton descended the hill through the apple orchard, crossed the grain field, and climbed the fence beside the dirt road. He slid down the steep bank on the other side of the split-rail fence and crossed the road into a wooded area. There, he found the narrow path that led to the lake.

The path had become overgrown with vegetation in his absence. He reckoned with all the children in his family grown, no one used the path anymore, at least not as frequently as he and his brothers had used it. He meandered down along the winding path, taking the time to stop often to pick ripened blueberries from the bushes growing wild along the way.

As he drew closer to Lake Biel and noticed familiar landmarks, memories of his childhood raced through his mind. He saw the old oak tree where his two large initials, "A.S.," still scared the rough gray bark. Twenty yards ahead, he could see the enormous flat boulder where he and his brothers would lay sunning on hot summer afternoons when they were supposed to be working in the orchards.

Anton arrived at the lake's edge and stopped atop an enormous boulder he recognized from his childhood. He walked to the edge of the boulder and recalled how they would dive into the water and race to their small island offshore. Anton stood there quietly in the sun, and shaded his eyes with his right hand, and gazed out across Lake Biel's peaceful waters. His mind recalled the laughter of his childhood, and he visualized his two brothers as they splashed each other with the cold water and enjoyed the thrill of their youth. It was a pleasant time for him, and he cherished the memories.

Anton suddenly hesitated as something caught his attention. *Was there someone on the island? Who would be out there this time of day?* He looked again, but his eyes struggled to focus against the bright sun. He strained his eyes to see. There was no further movement. *My eyes must be playing tricks on me.* Perhaps the memories of his childhood had begun to seize control of his imagination.

Why not just swim out to the island now? But then again, I really shouldn't swim so far alone—but then—why not? A devilish grin came across his face as he realized he was going to do it.

The thrill of adventure had won out over logic. Anton stood on a large protruding rock and stripped naked, just as he had done so many times before with his brothers. He carefully folded his clothes and neatly put them on some bushes that grew beside the rock to keep them off the damp ground. Then he walked to the edge of the rock, sat down, and stuck his toes into the water.

Oh, I've forgotten just how cold this lake can be.

He would have to try another approach to getting acclimated to the cold water. He was never good at gradually wading in like his older brother, Johann. For him, there was only one way to get into the water: dive right in and get it done! Anton ran and jumped immediately into the cold water before he had a chance to rethink whether he should do it.

Soon he was beneath the icy water. It took him a long while to grow accustomed to the water, but soon he was refreshed by the coolness of the mountain lake. He surfaced and began to swim for the island of his childhood.

Either the swim to the island was farther than he had remembered, or he was out of shape because he grew exhausted and needed to rest. He rolled over and floated on his back to give his tired arms a rest. Gently, he began to backstroke toward the island. He rolled over and started swimming. Noiselessly Anton glided through the water, this time seemingly without any effort. The swimming skills he had acquired as a boy came back to him. He remembered how to relax while he swam toward his destination.

Anton's arms once again grew weary, and he needed another rest. He rolled onto his back and closed his eyes against the glare of the sun. It felt warm on his face, and he could hear the cold water splashing against his partially submerged ears as he backstroked in a continuous motion. Anton glided, unnoticed, past a mallard duck as he neared his island. He continued until he felt the familiar brushing of the lake grass against his legs as the water grew shallower, indicating he was getting close to the island. Soon he heard water splashing against the shore and felt with his feet for the mud and the rocks on the shallow lake bottom in the shallows.

He had no sooner gained his footing in the water than he noticed someone was sunning upon a sizeable protruding rock ledge on the island. Several feet above the water's surface, the shelf was about twenty feet out in front of him. His quiet backstrokes had gone undetected by the sunbather. He stood there in the three feet of water, doggy paddling to maintain his balance. He wiped his eyes to clear his vision. He looked on, still undetected, at the figure on the ledge. His heart jumped, and he realized he was in a place he shouldn't be.

On the ledge of rock, there was a beautiful young woman in the clear light of day. Her long red hair hung softly down across her bare shoulders, and countless freckles caressed the skin of her beautiful, rounded face. Her freckles gave her a look of youthful innocence. He had never seen a woman this beautiful before. She was gorgeous, and although he knew he should stop starring, he couldn't stop looking at her.

Anton Smith found himself in an embarrassing situation, and he didn't know what to do. He had very few options: He could introduce himself to her and apologize for his intrusion, or he could remain silent and quietly leave without looking back. Anton wanted to do what was right, so Anton quietly left.

Quietly, Anton backstroked away from the shallow water of the island toward the mainland. Anton knew he was in deeper water when he felt the water become colder. The young man took a deep breath and dove beneath the surface — going as deep into the water as he dared. Anton swam beneath the water's surface and headed toward the shore from whence his swim began. He held his breath for as long as possible and then surfaced again for air.

He looked back toward the island and could see the large rock where the young woman had been standing only a few minutes before, but he couldn't see her.

Has she seen me watching her and hidden? Have I frightened her?

Anton felt guilty for participating in an encounter he had no control over or preplanning. *I've done nothing wrong—at least not intentionally. I'm as much a victim of this chance encounter as she is. The only difference is that I saw her, and she did not see me—or did she?*

Anton floated on this back for a while, then rolled over and swam toward the shore. He thought of the beautiful young woman and how he wanted to know more about her all the time. The excitement of his accidental encounter made him smile. Yes, perhaps he had gotten away with something naughty

CHAPTER EIGHT
AN EMBARRASSING MOMENT

Anton's swim back to the large rock where he had left his clothes gave him time to reflect on what had just happened. He had been silently embarrassed by what he had done, and yet he couldn't free himself of his guilt. Yes, Anton hadn't intentionally spied on the girl, yet he had deliberately watched her for much longer than he should.

I am like King David when he watched Bathsheba bathing in the privacy of her pool.

He was embarrassed about the accidental meeting, but the unexpected encounter's suddenness caused him to wrestle with his conscience. It made him feel both guilty and thrilled.

Anton swam silently to the rock from which he initially dove into the water. He kept a low profile to avoid being seen by the girl on the island. The youth tried to remain in the water for as long as he could endure the cold, but soon the cold water chilled his body, and hypothermia began to set in. After about fifteen minutes, he began to have uncontrollable shivers. The setting sun cast long shadows out into the shallow waters where he waited, and evening insects tormented him. Anton dove beneath the waters to escape their torment. He could endure the cold water and insects no longer. Convinced the shadows and bushes would conceal his escape, he painfully crossed through the bushes. They scratched his flesh and pierced at his feet. Anton carefully stepped through the briars and bushes and crept low to the ground to conceal his profile against the shoreline. He followed the shoreline back to the rock where he had initially undressed. Anton crept along the shoreline, thinking of nothing but the warmth of the clothing that awaited him on the bushes. He soon recognized the spot where he had left his clothes and strained his eyes in the dimming light to find them.

Where are they? He couldn't believe his eyes! His clothes were gone. He thought he had remembered where he had put them, but they weren't there. It seemed impossible, but his clothes had disappeared. Was this some joke? Did one of his family members follow him to the lake and then hide his clothes from him? He began to panic at first, but then he realized if it was a joke, the prankster wanted him to panic and look like a fool. He would wait for a couple of hours and then return home when the sun went down.

When I get home, I'll not say a word about this incident. I'll wait until the time is right, and then, even the score on my terms.

The late summer afternoon sun soon passed behind the high mountains, and darkness set in. Anton, completely naked, shivered in the chill of the mountain air. Anton's body itched and stung from the scratches he incurred hiding naked in the bushes. However, he was determined not to play into the hands of the jokester by returning home without his clothes. He was not going to face the embarrassment of being made a fool. He waited for the cover of darkness. It was the only alternative Anton had to ridicule. So, wait, he did.

When darkness arrived, Anton Smith walked cautiously down the road, careful to keep to the right side of the road if he had to duck into the bushes at the encounter of other travelers. Whenever he came to an open area or an intersection, he crouched low and ran as fast as possible until he reached cover once more. The trip home was arduous, but he made progress. Soon was to the open fields of his family farm.

Just a little further, and then I can leave the road.

In the distance, ahead saw the outline of his family's apple orchard outlined along the hill's ridge.

Just when Anton felt he was out of danger, it happened: "Hello, who's there?" a woman's voice called out.

Anton was caught unaware. The sound of the female voice cut through him like a sharp sword. He stood for an instant paralyzed, unable to move. Regaining his wits, he quickly dashed for the bushes beside the road.

"Hello," the voice called again, "Is that you, Anton?"

Anton knew that he had to respond and respond fast. He recognized the voice of the caller as that of Hildegard Shultz. It was apparent she had not seen him well enough to realize that Anton was naked, or it would have been evident in her voice. He was safe for now.

"Yes, Hildegard, it's me," he replied from within the bushes.

"Oh, Anton, you startled me. At first, when I heard you, I was afraid it might be a bear."

"I am bare all right," Anton snickered.

"What did you say?"

"I said...it could have been a bear, all right."

Hildegard couldn't understand why he did not move forward and come out of the bushes. "Where in the world are you? Why don't you come out of the shadows and walk with me?"

Anton stuttered as he cleared his throat to find a reason for his peculiar behavior. "I–I have a touch of a cold, and I'm afraid I'll make you sick. Besides, I'm late for dinner and have to take a shortcut across the field to get home."

Hildegard refused to be put off by the Smith boy. She had always hoped the opportunity would avail itself for the two of them to find themselves in a social situation where Anton would notice her attraction to him. Maybe even a courtship would ensue. She wasn't going to let this opportunity get away from her.

"Wait right where you are. I want to ask you something important. Do *not* leave!" Hildegard exclaimed.

Hildegard hurried in the general direction of where she had last heard his voice. "Talk to me so that I can find you."

By then, the full moon had begun to rise over the hill and vastly improved the illumination of what had been the shadows just a few minutes before. The orchard's outline became clear enough for the trees to cast their shadows in the silvery moonlight. Time was running out for Anton's concealment.

Hearing Hildegard's footsteps drawing closer to where he hid, he crouched in the bushes and looked in her direction. He could begin to make out some of her features in the new light. He knew he had to act quickly to avoid discovery. Springing from the cover of the roadside bushes, he climbed up the steep bank beside the road, crossed over the split rail fence of his property, and sprinted across the open field toward the apple orchard.

From her vantage point, just yards away, Hildegard soon discovered the reason for Anton's peculiar behavior alongside the road that night. To her amazement and delight, she saw the bare backside of Anton Smith streaking across the open field. He ran for all he was worth in the full light of the July moon. Anton sprinted with every ounce of energy and speed he possessed, onward, toward the cover of the apple orchard and the protection it would give him. Through the orchard, he continued slowing because of the sharp tree branches that reached out and scratched his unprotected body like demons in the darkness. Anton slowed to a brisk walk, panting and gasping to relieve the aching demand from his lungs for more oxygen. He was in very familiar territory, and he could have found the rest of his way home blindfolded. His feet, limbs, and torso burned with cuts inflicted upon him during his flight. He perspired freely despite the chilling night air. His salty sweat flowed into his numerous abrasions and burned, but he could see the lights from the Smith household and knew safety was at hand.

Back on the road, a bewildered young lady watched Anton run across the field and disappear into the shadows of the apple orchard. "Well, I'll be!" she said with her mouth agape.

Suddenly, Hildegard realized the amusement of the situation and began to laugh hysterically. She laughed silently at first, then boldly and uncontrollably. Hildegard had seen the area's most handsome bachelor in his totality.

The farm's main building served a dual purpose: a barn and a farmhouse. The large building had been constructed of stone and carefully fitted logs. The corners of the building accurately fit into place and are caulked to withstand the test of time. The farmhouse was over two hundred years old and just as straight and true as the day Anton Smith's ancestor completed it. Stone fireplaces graced the main living quarters and added beauty and functional design to the house. The fireplaces burned warmly on cold winter nights and drew a draft that burned the logs efficiently to white powdery ash. The builders of this farm were as much stonemasons as they were carpenters. The quality of its construction was self-evident throughout. More than just a functional house, the structure's aesthetic quality was pleasing to the eye and balanced and symmetrical. The center of the building measured forty by forty feet square. The family expanded the building on either side via additions. The three additions moved out from the center of the house. Each addition was smaller than the previous one and looked like the extensions on a telescope.

The family housed the farm animals in the lower rear portion of the building, with the Smith family's living quarters directly in front of the barn. The short summers kept the odors to a minimum. Strict, self-imposed sanitation standards made cohabitation possible and easier to care for the animals during the winter months' deep snow. It was a system that had endured effectively for centuries.

Anton crept around the side of the house. He saw that his mother had hung laundry on the clothesline to dry with wooden clothespins. Carefully plucking a semi-dry pair of pants from the rope clothesline, he quickly put his legs into the damp material. His pants were hard to pull up over his shivering legs, already feeling the chill of the cooling evening air. Soon he felt safe from prying eyes. He rethought the day's events and chuckled to himself about the absurdity of his current predicament. Anton found humor in thinking how quickly he had turned from thinking he was in complete control of the situation to feeling inadequate and intimidated. The laugh was for the time being on him, but sooner or later, he would have his revenge, revenge that Shakespeare said, "is best served cold." He would once again have his day!

He climbed the stairs to the family living quarters above the barn, making very little noise in his bare feet. The family of five had already been seated for dinner. Anton's father was praying over the food when Anton entered. He stood silently in the doorway as his father asked the Lord's blessing for the food and the coming harvest. Anton's younger sister, Catherine, looked up at him over her clasped hands. She winked a smile of acknowledgment toward Anton as Papa Smith continued his long prayer. Anton smiled back at her. He knew that she realized it was unusual for him to be dressed only in a pair of pants and without shoes. Catherine looked down at his cut and bruised feet. Her eyebrows raised, and her forehead wrinkled, but she did not say a word. Anton followed the stare of her eyes to her feet. He looked back at her and shrugged his shoulders, and smiled. Catherine returned the smile, and without saying a single word, they both understood that everything was all right. Anton knew, however, that he had some explaining to do to Catherine later.

The prayer ended, and Papa Smith looked up to Anton stood clad only in his pants.

"What in the world happened to you, Son?" inquired the elder Smith. "Where are your clothes? Look at that terrible sunburn and scratches! Son, what in the world were you doing?"

"It's a long story, and I doubt that you would believe me if I told you," replied Anton.

The elder Smith looked questioningly at his son, but it was evident that Anton did not want to discuss it. The elder thought that he was old enough to be entitled to his privacy, so he just shook his head and let the issue rest.

The younger Smith was glad that his papa did not push further for answers. He went over to his Mama first and kissed her tenderly on the cheek. Then Anton nodded gently in the direction of Papa Smith as an acknowledgment of Papa's position within the family. He apologized for being late for dinner and excused himself to his room to get a shirt and shoes.

Anton realized that the eyes of his entire family would be upon him when he returned. He half laughed to himself, thinking again about what had happened. He knew his family would expect an explanation at the dinner table, and quite frankly, he did not know what to say. Anton thought *Papa would say, "Son, what did you do today?"*

When he returned to the country kitchen, he sat in his regular seat at the family table. Seating himself next to his sister Catherine, he fixed himself a dinner plate and began to eat. He tried to ignore everyone hoping that no one would ask him any questions. The family around the table grew silent. The silence was overbearing. He could hear himself chew his food in the silence. Anton looked up from his plate and realized that all eyes were upon him. His family sat silently, staring at him in a silence that demanded an explanation.

The young man cleared his throat and spoke: "Why is everyone staring at me? I just went swimming in the lake. When I got back, I could not find all my clothes. That's all that there was to it." Anton looked around the dinner table. He could see his family was beginning to snicker. "What?"

Unable to conceal their amusement any longer, his family broke into laughter. The joke was on Anton.

"I saw you swimming in the lake alone and couldn't resist the temptation," replied Anton's brother Jesse. "You shouldn't have been swimming alone. It's too dangerous. So, I hung around until I saw you coming back toward the shore, and I knew you were safe. Then I left with your clothes."

Everyone continued laughing at the prank. Jesse swallowed the food he nearly choked on while laughing at Anton and spoke one again. "I could tell someone else was out on the island, but I couldn't distinguish who the other person was. What concerned me was seeing you swimming out to the island alone. You didn't seem to make any contact with the other person. Were you trying to avoid him?"

"I stayed away because it was not a 'him.' It was a young woman, and I didn't want to intrude upon her privacy. I don't know who the young woman was, but she was gorgeous. I wanted to speak to her, but I couldn't."

"You? Bashful?" asked Catherine.

"No. It wasn't that I was bashful at all?"

"What then," she inquired. "Couldn't you get close enough to her to speak?"

Anton was genuinely embarrassed. He thought for a while, how to phrase it. "The young lady was sunbathing, and it would've been improper for me to come forward."

"She was naked?" screamed an astonished Mama Smith! "What were you doing swimming with a naked woman? Dear Lord! I thought that I raised you better than that."

The Smith family were dedicated followers of John Calvin—*Presbyterians,* or *Calvinists*, as some people called them. The Smiths considered themselves devout Christians who shunned all appearances of carnal behavior. Chastity was more than expected; it prevailed.

"No, no, Mama. I was swimming alone and happened upon her merely by chance. 'Predestination,' as the pastor would say. I guess that it had to be."

Catherine and Jesse tried to conceal their humor. Mama and Papa Smith did not see the humor in what they considered as paramount to blasphemy. They felt they had a dangerous situation on their hands regarding the salvation of their eldest son. The parent thought that the circumstances required immediate action.

"Mama, get me the Holy Scriptures!" exclaimed Papa. "We need to take this problem to the Lord in prayer. Anton needs to confess his iniquity immediately."

CHAPTER NINEM
THE SEARCH FOR ANNE

Anton awoke early on Sunday, long before sunrise, the termination of a restless night. The excitement of finding the woman he had seen on his island occupied his every thought. He knew he would never have peace of mind until he found her.

The young tailor had formulated a plan. It was a plan that Anton had reviewed several times in his mind and intended to execute that very day. He wanted every detail of their first meeting to be perfect. Anton might never get another chance to impress her. He needed every detail to be perfect.

Anton Smith got out of bed and went over to the white ceramic wash-bowl he had set out on his dresser the night before. The water was not hot, but it was room temperature. Anton splashed water on his face and used his wooden-handled lather brush to prep his sparsely distributed whiskers for shaving. A shave was all that his young beard required every two or three days, but he felt like a man today. Every detail needed to be covered. He gazed into his mirror and grinned at his reflection.

Today is my day, he thought. *Everything is going to work out for the best.* He couldn't keep from smiling as he thought how perfectly his plan was coming together. It was too perfect not to be God's will. His hope of finding his mystery woman grew stronger within him every waking minute. *My plan must work. I must find her.*

He finished shaving, made easy by his lack of facial hair, and dried his face before he hurried down the stairs.

"Come on, everybody," Anton urged as he entered the farmhouse kitchen filled with the smell of freshly cooked bratwurst. Even in his excitement, the alluring fragrance of breakfast was overwhelming. He walked briskly over to where his mother sat and reached down to steal a tiny morsel of meat and a piece of hard roll. "Hurry up," he urged, "and finish your breakfast so we won't be late for church. It's terrible to walk into the church after the worship service has begun."

"Be still, my heart," his mother teased as she looked up at his clean face. "Is this the same young man who makes us late for church every Sunday morning? My goodness, your time in Zurich has certainly matured you."

Anton realized that his zeal had become apparent. "Maybe I am a little anxious today, Mama, but the day is so beautiful, and I don't want us to have to rush. Let's take the time to enjoy our drive along the lake." He leaned down to his mother and kissed her on her forehead as he snitched another piece of bratwurst off her plate.

The family did as Anton requested. They cleared the breakfast table and hurriedly washed the dishes as they prepared to leave for town. Soon the family carriage was moving briskly along Lake Biel with Anton at the reins.

Ross Welti, who sat next to his son on the driver's seat, looked questioningly across Anton. "Son, whatever happened to your suggestion that we leave early to enjoy the beautiful morning? We will be at the church at the rate you are driving in record time. Slow down, Son, or you are going to bounce your mother out of the carriage and onto the road."

"I'm sorry, Father," Anton answered apologetically. "It's just that I've missed this place so much during the last four years, and I want to take it in all at once. I'll slow down a bit."

Anton pulled back on the reins and slowed the chestnut mare to a cantor. Streaks of wetness formed on the horse's back and bore evidence that it had been working hard.

The Welti family carriage edged ever closer to the village Anton loved. Erlach was a picturesque farming community with a population of less than 2,000. From their vantage point in the approaching carriage, the village looked like a beautiful portrait, painted on an artist's canvas by a true master. The walled village noted for its well-kept white plaster and beamed houses had been occupied for hundreds of years by generations of the same families. Long narrow window boxes filled with bright red geraniums adorned the buildings and gardens; colorful roses of multiple hues delighted the senses. Nothing much ever changed here. It was a town that resisted change, purposely preserved in its past.

The farms surrounding the town were as beautiful and well-kept as the town itself, with vineyards of white grapes that climbed the steep hills in perfectly spaced rows. The Chasselas grapes were coveted treasures that provided fruit for Switzerland's fine white wine, known in German as *Gutedel*.

Terracotta-tiled roofs covered white-washed buildings adorned with red, gold, green, and blue flowers. The medieval architecture lined narrow cobblestone streets, tucked safely behind thirty-foot fortress walls, edging Lake Biel's deep blue waters. The three-hundred-year-old walls embraced its inhabitants like a mother protecting her child.

Apple orchards, laden with fruit, basked patiently in the warm mountain sun, their trunks whitewashed in lime, and their branches trimmed low to the ground for easier harvesting. Brown dairy cows grazed on the lush green summer grass; their udders filled with milk rich in butterfat.

During Anton's four-year absence, the structure of the village had remained virtually unchanged. Erlach showed no signs of new construction. The town's inhabitants cherished the old buildings, and everything remained the same from the time memorial.

Erlach's townspeople continued through the inevitable cycle of life. Some of the elderly had died, new babies had been born, toddlers had become children, children had grown to become adolescents, and adolescents had matured into young adults. It seemed to Anton that this life cycle was the story of Switzerland's villages: the inanimate remained unchanged, while the animate rotated in ever-changing life cycles—out with old and in with the new. Neatly ordered grave markers in the ancient churchyards bore silent testimony to his theory.

Anne Welti was one such adolescent who cycled from childhood to adolescence and young adulthood. She had bloomed like a flower into a beautiful young woman. Nurtured in the security of her family's love, she matured with each passing year. Anne was eighteen years old—a dreamer—about to discover a new kind of love; it would be different from the love she knew from her family.

Every day since his accidental bout with voyeurism, Anton felt consumed with the desire to meet the mystery woman—to know her name—but fate, it seemed, had played a cruel trick on him. Within the village of Erlach, there were two very distinct social circles: one for Roman Catholics; another for Calvinists. They were separate universes, orbiting together in the same galaxy, but always with the potential to collide. They were tolerant of each other only so long as their planets remained within the orbit of their universe.

Inquiries into the identity of the beauty soon made it obvious she was not of his religious persuasion. Still, visions of her bright red hair and fair complexion haunted Anton day and night. He just had to find her, even though he realized involvement with a non-Protestant woman was sure to cause controversy. Regardless of the consequences, the religious difference was a controversy he was willing to endure. He would search for her at the Catholic church.

Anton edged the family carriage through the town gate and drove it toward the village's center to the town square. The square served as a type of line of demarcation. The Catholics had their church on the north end of the town square, while the Calvinists had their church on the south end. He stopped the carriage at the Protestant church and waited until his family climbed down.

"I'll take care of the carriage," he called to his family, "and meet up with you later." With that, he drove off under the pretense of securing a spot for the carriage. Anton waited until his family was inside the church, drove through the town square, and crossed the demarcation line.

The Catholics were practicing what they considered the one true religion, while the Calvinists were in their church on what they perceived as the one correct path to God. The Catholics knew that the Calvinists were going to Hell; the Calvinists knew the same about the Catholics. The world was at peace only because the two faiths had segregated themselves from each other.

He parked his carriage across the street from the Catholic church and waited for the service to end. Music from the colossal pipe organ bellowed from the church and filled the air with majesty. There were many similarities between what he heard from the Catholic church and his own.

Anton wondered what differences could be so significant that it would cause these neighbors to distrust each other so much. What perceived differences made the two faiths want to kill each other during various church history periods and do so in Christ's name. His mind took him back to the Scriptures, and he could hear Jesus say, "Oh ye generation of vipers!"

The sun began to feel very warm on his face as he waited. Comfortable in his seat, the young man began to doze off. He daydreamed of the beautiful young woman he had seen at the lake. Suddenly there was silence, interrupted by organ music and the voices of worshipers singing. The young man realized the change in tempo must be signaling the close of the Catholic Mass.

The music stopped, and the doors of the church opened. People began filing out of the church and shaking hands with the old priest, known as good Father Benedict. The gray-haired priest, still recovering from a heart attack, leaned on his carved wooden cane and greeted the parishioners as they departed the church. Anton sat up and leaned forward to study the women's profiles as they came down the church's front steps. There were so many of them, and they all wore scarves that covered their heads. He needed to get closer or face the possibility of missing the woman he desperately wanted to meet.

He climbed out of the carriage, crossed the cobblestone street, stepped up over the curb, and walked to the bottom of the twenty stone steps that led up to the church. He leaned back against a stone pillar and waited. There, at the base of the steps, he could examine every face that came down.

Scores of people came out of the church, and one by one, Anton searched their faces. Finally, after twenty minutes of desperately searching the ocean of faces, he recognized her long red hair. She was even more beautiful than Anton had remembered. He watched her as she walked. She carried herself like no other woman he had ever seen. She flowed like a well-written poem and possessed the grace of a ballerina on the stage of the opera house.

She wore a red dress, cheerful but subtle enough to suit the occasion. Her red dress made her cheeks glow with a bright illuminating countenance, like a thousand candles upon a church altar.

When she spoke, her voice was just as he had imagined it would be soft and warm. Her voice would be like listening to a hundred violins playing Vivaldi's *Four Seasons*.

She removed her scarf as a gentle breeze lifted her bright red hair and made it flow and wave as though wildflowers grew on the hillside. There was no doubt about it. This beautiful person was the woman he had determined to find. His heart pounded fiercely within his chest.

Anton stood upright from the post against which he had been leaning. He clasped his hands in front of him and shifted restlessly from one foot to the other, pondering what he would say to her when she reached the bottom of the steps. She was smiling and talking with her parents as she descended the steps. Just a few more steps, and he would be face-to-face with her; three steps, two steps, and one! She was there.

The young woman stopped at the bottom of the steps. She stood silently in front of Anton while her family continued walking toward their carriage. It was as if she had expected him to find her. A nervous smile came to her lips as she spoke.

"Good morning, Anton," she said as she held out her hand to him in expectation. "It's been a long time."

Anton's mouth fell agape. "You know my name?" he asked.

"You don't know me, do you?" she chuckled. "I'm Anne Welti. I'm from the farm next to your parents' place."

"Oh, my goodness!" he exclaimed. "The little red-headed Welti kid?"

A voice called from the waiting carriage twenty feet away.

"Anne, darling. Are you coming?" It was her mother.

Anne Welti turned her head toward the carriage and held up her index finger to signal that she would be there in one minute.

"It was nice seeing you again, Anton," she said. "I used to watch you across the fence, working with your father in the fields. It's too bad we never spoke, except for an occasional wave of the hand. Our families were never really friends."

"Anne!" her mother called, "We're waiting for you."

Anne looked toward her mother and then back at Anton. "I do have to go," she said.

Anton was exasperated. He did not want the conversation to end this way.

"Do you think we could talk again sometime?"

"Of course, we can," she replied. "When? Where?"

He was elated at her willingness to meet with him. He searched his mind for an answer. "What about tomorrow—right after lunch—down by the lake—where you go swimming?"

The words had no sooner left his mouth than he realized he had betrayed his secret, but Anne either didn't notice or didn't care because she agreed to his proposal. "Sure, that would be fine," she answered. Then, looking in the direction of her impatient parents, she said, "But for now, I really must go. My family is waiting for me."

Anne turned abruptly and rushed toward her waiting family. She resisted the temptation to turn and wave to him. She knew her family would never approve of her involvement with a Protestant.

He watched as she climbed into the carriage, and it pulled away. He wanted her, and he could only hope she wanted him. His heart pounded with excitement at the possibility it would be so.

The fantasy didn't last long. Reality returned when Anton remembered his own family would be waiting for him. He glanced down the street and across the town square in the direction of the Presbyterian church. Although he couldn't see them, he knew his family was waiting at the curb.

The four Smith family members looked up and down the narrow street, trying to locate their carriage, and the young man who had so mysteriously disappeared before the church service. They could not find Anton. George Smith, Anton's father, stepped off the curb and into the street where he shaded his eyes and looked toward the square at an approaching carriage.

"I think I see him now," he shouted as he waved his hands in the air. "He had better have a good explanation for his bizarre behavior."

Anton eventually pulled the panting horse and family carriage up to where his family was waiting and stopped. With expressions of irritation, four questioning faces told him he had a lot of explaining to do concerning his tardiness and strange disappearance.

CHAPTER TEN
THE PLANNED MEETING

Lunch on the farm was the day's main meal, but Anton was too excited to eat. He rose before sunrise and worked hard to make sure he had done his fair share of work on the family farm, but by lunchtime, he was ready to quit.

Anton dipped the hard-baked crust of his bread into his soup and looked across the table at his father. "Papa, I'd like to take the afternoon off to go swimming, if you don't mind," he said. "I tried to get as much work done as I could this morning to make up for it. Would you have a problem with that?"

Ross Smith looked back at his son with a puzzled look and said, "Son, I think you should do that. While I appreciate your hard work, you're supposed to be relaxing this summer. Take it from an older man; you'll spend the rest of your life working hard to support your family. You're young, and you've just completed your apprenticeship. Go swimming and relax while you can. You have my blessing."

"Thank you, Papa. It's a hot day, and I've been looking forward to a good swim." He put down his bread and stood up to kiss his mother before leaving the table.

"You shouldn't be swimming alone," his mother reminded him.

"Don't worry, Mother. I won't take any chances," he teased. "You have taught me well."

Anton went over to his mother's place at the family table and kissed her gently on the forehead. "Lunch was great, Mother."

"Great?" she questioned. "You hardly touched it."

"Save it for me. I'm just not hungry yet. All I can think about is going swimming." He hugged her and left the kitchen immediately.

When Anton reached the large sunning boulder beside the lake, he found Anne waiting for him; her hair was still wet from a recent swim.

That's a good sign. Anne must have been anxious to see me. I wonder how long she's been here. He approached her smiling and nervously held out his hand, indicating he wanted to shake.

Anne raised her eyebrows and looked questioningly down at his hand. She hadn't expected this formality. She reached out to shake his hand and shook it.

"I didn't have anything to do this morning," she explained, "so I got here early and took a swim. It was a beautiful morning."

She looked down at her hand, still clutched in Anton's grip and dwarfed by comparison. She inclined to pull her hand back, but he continued to hold it firmly in his, as though he had forgotten to release it. Anne waited for him to speak, but Anton didn't say a word. He just stood there in front of her, mesmerized by her beauty and staring into her brown eyes. Anne allowed her hand to remain in his for a moment without trying to withdraw it. She liked the way his hand felt; solid and warm, comforting, and reassuring.

Anne looked into his pale blue unwavering eyes, penetrating and sincere. Anne continued to gaze, spellbound, and she began to feel a peculiar sensation she had never experienced before. It started with a slight fluttering of her heart and an irregularity in her breathing. It wasn't the kind of feeling she got when she was coming down with an ailment, but it was more like the kind of feeling Anne got when she received good news or when someone gave her an unexpected gift. A sudden sense of excitement caused a tingle to run through her body, and while she didn't know what this feeling was, she liked it. Anne wriggled her fingers free. "I'm glad we've finally had a chance to meet," she managed.

Anton snapped back to reality and fought hard for something to say—anything. "Have you eaten any lunch?" he said. "You must be starved."

"Actually," Anne replied, "I brought some lunch with me, and I have enough to share. It's right over here. Will you join me? We can talk while we eat." Without waiting for an answer, she turned and walked over to a shady spot where she had left a brown woven basket beneath an oak tree.

"I'm afraid the blanket is still slightly damp. I used it to dry off from my swim, but it's dry enough to sit on it."

She spread a thin quilt, light blue and white, with multi-colored hearts sewn on its front, across the grass beneath the tree. She motioned an invitation for Anton to be seated. She sat on the ground facing him and leaned back against the tree where he was sitting.

"Strange isn't it," she said.

"Strange in what way?" Anton asked.

"Strange that we have lived on neighboring farms all of our lives, and yet, I've never really known you. I mean, I've seen you working in the fields and the vineyards and apple orchards, but our families have never visited back and forth. Sometimes, I've even waved to you across the fences, and you've looked back, but we never came close enough to talk. Once, maybe four years ago, right before you went away, you came with your father to buy a cow from my papa. I wanted to meet you then, but my mama wouldn't let me come out of the house. Don't you think that's strange?"

"Yes," Anton answered, "I guess it's strange, but I think I'm beginning to fit all the pieces to this puzzle together. You're the cute little girl with pigtails who used to wave at me?"

"I *am* that little girl. Even as a twelve-year-old girl, I thought you were special—you know, in a silly kind of way."

"A silly kind of way? What do you mean by that?"

Anne blushed as red a ripened apple and struggled for an explanation. She hoped she wasn't seeming too aggressive in revealing her secret thoughts, but she had dreamt of meeting Anton for a long time and was not about to let this opportunity escape her.

"What I meant to say is this: little girls tend to get silly crushes on older boys at that age. You were the only boy I saw much, except for the boys at church, and even though we never met, I could tell you were a very nice boy. Just watching you work with your papa spoke volumes of your character."

Anton smiled. "I'm not sure that what you just told me should be considered as a compliment. You just told me I won your approval by default if I heard you correctly. If I was the only available boy because of your isolation out here on the farm, I can't take much pride in that."

"Well, you should," she said with a tone of righteous indignation. "There are plenty of nice boys at church who would love to have my attention."

"Are we talking past or present tense, Anne?"

Anne realized she had made a slip of the tongue. "You're impossible," she answered in exasperation. She handed Anton a ham sandwich wrapped in a red checkered cloth and a gherkin pickle.

He reached out to receive them and smiled, sensing it was time to stop teasing her. After all, he had made the first move by tracking her down and forcing the introduction. He was thrilled she had agreed to meet him and, after all, she had brought along a wonderful picnic lunch. It was time to let well-enough alone.

"Thank you, Anne. I'm quite hungry."

Anton realized Anne had volunteered a great deal of information for a first meeting. They barely knew each other, and yet, it was as though she had been carrying pent-up feelings for him for a long time and needed to tell him so while she had the chance.

Has she been a secret admirer, loving me from afar for a long time?

It seemed unbelievable to him, but evidence pointed to the conclusion that while his attraction to her had been recent, her attraction to him was not. He had nothing to lose by being bold, so he shared with her some of his emotions too: "I've been looking forward to meeting with you ever since...ever since... our encounter at the church." Anton recovered quickly from his near-fatal slip of the tongue. He continued: "To tell the truth, I was afraid you had changed your mind and wouldn't show up.

My stomach has been tied in knots all morning. When my family sat down to dinner this afternoon, I was too upset to eat."

Anne was flattered that Anton shared the excitement about their first rendezvous. His comments confirmed they might have a mutual admiration. She watched as Anton took a bite from his sandwich.

"May I ask you a personal question, Anton?"

"Sure. Go right ahead."

"Why did you come looking for me yesterday morning at the church? It was obvious, to me, that you being there was no coincidence. We had never formally met, and yet, you missed your worship service to find me. Don't get me wrong, I was flattered, but why me? You just admitted you didn't realize I'm your neighbor. Where did you see me?"

It was Anton's turn to blush. He choked on his food as he struggled for an appropriate answer. He prolonged his chewing to give him more time.

Anne smiled and reached down at her side for a cloth bag she had brought with her to the lake. She held out the bag to Anton and said, with a tone of righteous indignation, "Perhaps I can help you with your answer. Do these look familiar?"

He had not gotten away with anything the day he saw her sunbathing.

"Anne," he explained, "when I swam out to the island, I didn't have any idea that I would find a woman there—especially you. But by the time I saw you, it was too late. So, I did the gentlemanly thing by turning around and swimming back to shore. I'm so sorry."

"Well, I have a confession too," she snickered. "While you doggy-paddled around, trying to decide what you were going to do next, I swam back to shore. At first, I was only trying to get out of there before you returned, but when I saw Hildegard Shultz approaching and saw your clothes hanging on the bushes, I recognized the opportunity to get back at you. So, I quickly dressed, and was about to grab your clothes, and quietly slipped away from the rock when I saw your brother coming. I managed to grab only your underpants and then hid nearby. I had to hold my laughter when I saw him grab your clothes, instead, and then run away with them.

I was hiding nearby when you came ashore and ran into Hildegard. I laughed so hard I was afraid I'd reveal my position in the bushes, just a few yards away."

"You trapped me? Anton responded in disbelief. Then after thinking the scenario through, he asked, "Did you see me getting out of the lake too?"

Anne did not respond. She only smiled.

"So," Anne said, to change the subject, "when you showed up at St. Maria's Church, I was surprised to see you, but I knew why you were there.

"I've been trying for days to think of a way to introduce myself. I even considered tearing down a section of the fence that separates our two farms. That way, one of your cows could stray onto our property, and I could return it to your family. Pretty devious—huh?"

The two neighbors were well on their way to becoming friends. Years of living side-by-side without ever meeting had given way to a new realization that it never needed to be that way. The two young people put aside tradition and allowed their hearts to give them a new direction.

CHAPTER ELEVEN
TWO FAMILIES DIVIDED

Anton and Anne's meetings at the big rock beside the lake became increasingly frequent. They would slip away at mid-day, as often as they dared to be together. When the circumstances were right, they would signal the other with a red scarf tied to the apple tree near the stone fence that separated the farms. It was the very place where Anne saw Anton talking with his father. Confirmation was to add a double knot. It was a simple system, but it worked.

Anton approached the apple orchard about half an hour earlier than usual. It was mid-July, and even though it was only 11:30 am, the day promised to be the hottest day of the summer. He hoped to get to the lake ahead of Anne that day and to cool off in the chilling waters of Lake Biel. As he approached the designated tree, his heart raced. There on the tree, beneath the draping branches of ripening apples, he saw the red scarf, double-knotted with the stem of a red rose tucked conspicuously in the loop of the knot. Anton smiled as he reached for the rose and brought it to his nose. He inhaled deeply and took in the sweet fragrance of the bloom.

She does love me; she does.

The giving of the rose could mean nothing else. Geraniums and daisies were for friends, lilies were flowers for funerals, but roses were flowers for romance. He threw up his hands in jubilation and screamed, "Yes, yes, yes!" Today was the best day of his life. Anton and Anne were more than just friends now. The new friendship was the confirmation of what he had hoped and prayed for: She loved him.

Anton held on to the rose as he turned and jumped over the stone fence in one mighty leap. Then he stopped, shaded his eyes, and looked toward the big rock at the edge of the lake.

There she is. She's waiting for me.

He could see her looking up the hill at him. She waved. He waved back. Excitement raced through him like the surge of an ocean's wave. Anton swallowed hard and ran down the hill toward his Anne.

He arrived at the rock, exhausted and out of breath. His urge was to take her into his arms and tell her he loved her.

Anne watched Anton as he raced down the hill toward the lake. She was excited about his enthusiasm to get to her.

He must have understood the meaning of my rose. It can only mean that he loves me too. Come, Anton, come to me. I want to hear you say that you love me too.

Anne watched her love as he ran ever closer. Anton ran down to the bottom of the vineyard. He jumped over the split-rail fence, down the embankment, and across the road. Anton kept coming until he ran through a narrow strip of linden trees that separated the road from the lake. Now, Anton stood in front of her, out of breath and sweating profusely. She didn't care. Anne wanted him to embrace her.

Hug me, she wished desperately. *Throw your arms around me and capture the moment.* But Anne could see that Anton didn't have the confidence for such a move. She perceived he was still too naïve and unsure of presuming her physical acceptance of him.

Anne considered taking the initiative by moving forward to embrace him, but she didn't want to rob him of the opportunity to take the lead. She felt it was his turn to act. After all, she had exposed her vulnerability by offering him the rose. Her bold act seemed to have paid off. There he was, standing in front of her, holding the rose in his hand.

Anne had been aware of her vulnerability from the beginning of their relationship. She knew the first day she watched him from the apple orchard. Anne knew when she heard Anton's voice and secretly peeked at him from behind the stone fence that he was someone she wanted in her life. Anne recognized the girlish crush she had carried for him since childhood was still alive in her heart.

Perhaps, she thought, *I should have denied those feelings and not have encouraged him.*

But it was too late for denial now. It always had been too late for Anne. It was as though fate had sealed their relationship from time immemorial, and there was no way out for her. Her attraction for Anton had grown like a well-nourished rose and blossomed into a love that demanded expression and notice. Her heart told her they were both hopelessly in love, but neither one of them had ever verbalized their feelings. *Why won't he make the first move?* Finally, Anne's prayers received an answer.

Anne stood facing Anton, her heart in her throat, her hands trembling at her side. She could see him moving slowly toward her, his eyes wide, his expression serious. Hands began to reach out toward her. Anton held the rose between his right hand's fingers, his left hand now reaching around her body.

He pulled her toward him. She did not resist his embrace. His breathing was still deep, but not from exhaustion. She pulled him closer and felt the rise and fall of his chest against her warm response. He pulled back his head and looked into her brown eyes. She looked back at him, but lost focus as her lips drew to his. Her attraction to him was as though by some irresistible force. She felt his lips upon her, warm and moist, desirable, and welcoming.

This kiss is exactly what I wanted, and I don't want to stop.

She knew she must stop. Her body said "more," but her mind said, "You must not end up like your sister." Anne resisted the urge to continue and pulled back from Anton's embrace. They smiled at each other, still in a light embrace, when Anton spoke.

"What are we going to do about our relationship, Anne?" he asked. "We can't keep sneaking away to meet like this—as though we're doing something wrong—something evil—something dirty. I want to walk openly with you and tell the whole world I'm proud of you. I want everyone to know I love you."

Anne stepped back and smiled as she looked into his blue eyes. "Would you please repeat what you just said?"

"I said I'm proud of you, and I want everyone to know that..."

"That you *what*?" she asked.

Anton realized that he had never told Anne he loved her at that moment. "I... I love you, Anne Welti." He pulled her close to his lips and kissed her passionately.

Anton had never made love to a woman, but now he wanted to. He found himself possessed with a desire he had never felt before—at least to this level of intensity. He began to take liberties with Anne's person that he had never dared to do.

"No," Anne insisted as she struggled to push away from Anton. "Not now, not yet. I refuse to end up like my sister."

Anton relaxed his embrace, heart racing and mind keeping pace with his heart. The passion of their kiss was still on his lips when he heard approaching hooves on the road leading to the lake.

Anton released Anne and turned just in time to see Anne's father, glaring at him from atop his still-moving horse. Anne's father jumped down before his horse had entirely stopped and ran over to his daughter, trembling with fury. "Young lady, what do you think you're doing?"

"Papa, we've done nothing wrong. We're just friends."

Her father pulled the crying Anne by her right arm and half-drug her to the horse grazing beside the big rock. With one mighty, adrenaline-powered lift, he placed her on the back of his plow horse. Then Ross grabbed the drooping reigns and turned to face Anton, who had followed them over to the horse.

Anton looked at Ross Welti to realize that social decorum had required him to ask the girl's father for permission to court Anne. He had deliberately postponed a technicality because he correctly anticipated what the father's answer would have been. Now it was too late for the protocol.

"Herr Welti," he uttered as he fought to conjure up the right words, "I can explain everything. Our meeting is entirely my fault. I should have come to talk with you about courting Anne, and I didn't, but I assure you, her honor is intact. Please don't be harsh with Anne."

Ross resisted the urge to punch Anton in his face. His anger needed an outlet, but he would save his wrath for a time when his daughter wouldn't have to endure witnessing it. His family had suffered the consequences of aggressive male sexual behavior with Anne's twin sister, and he was not about to stand by and allow any indiscretion to happen again.

"Young man," Ross Welti said as he jabbed his finger into Anton's chest, "If I ever see you on my farm or catch you with my daughter again, I swear, I'll kill you with my bare hands. Just stay away from her!"

"But sir," Anton pleaded, "we were afraid you would send me away because I am a Calvinist. Otherwise, I would have talked with you sooner."

Ross knew the young man was right, but he didn't answer. His daughter was going to marry a good Catholic man, and that was that. He pulled the big gray horse over to the rock and climbed on it behind his weeping daughter. He slapped the horse with the reigns and dug his heels into its side. The horse startled forward, and Anton stood helplessly as his love departed with her father.

Anton crossed the road, climbed up over the embankment, stepped over the split-rail fence, ran directly to their rendezvous point at the apple tree in the orchard, and leaned back against the rough bark of the trunk. Far in the distance, he could see the gray horse cantering toward the Welti farmhouse with two passengers on its back. He watched Anne jump down from the horse and run defiantly toward the back door of the house.

Anton slid his back down to the ground and sat leaning up against the tree with his knees pulled against his body. He rested his elbows on his knees and his chin on his palms. He sat and stared at his island in the lake. His island—their island—was a more peaceful world than the cruel world in which they now existed. He longed to be there with Anne.

The days and weeks passed slowly for Anton without Anne brightening his life. Every day he returned to the orchard to check the red scarf he had tied to the tree, in the hope Anne had tied the double knot requesting a meeting. Every day he checked, but each day his journey to the orchard was unanswered, and in time, the bright red scarf faded into a pale tattered rag. Undeterred, Anton continued to check daily for some sign of hope.

Why has Anne forsaken me? I know she loves me, yet she refuses to meet with me. Is her family holding her hostage?

Anton's heart ached for the woman he loved. Summer was nearly over, and he needed to decide his future. He wanted Anne to be a part of the decision-making process. *Should I go back to Zurich and rent a small shop in the Central Marketplace? Should I move to Paris and try my fortunes there? Should I stay here in Erlach and work with my family in their small shop?*

He needed to talk to Anne, and if she couldn't come to him, he would have to go to her, regardless of her father's threat. He devised a daring plan.

It was early September, and most of the harvest was in the barns. Both families were busy in the orchards picking the remaining apples from the trees and pruning the branches back for the next season. Anton could see the Welti men in their orchard across the fence at work, but the women were not there with them. He looked over at the Welti farmhouse and could see Anne stirring a large black iron kettle that hung over an open fire in their yard.

Anton took a chance. He detoured back to his house, slipped over a fence behind the barn, and crouched low as he followed the grapevines up the hill toward the Welti home. The young man went around the house's side and was within ten yards of where Anne was standing, stirring apple butter as it cooked in the big black kettle. He picked up a pebble and threw it to hit the side of the kettle.

Anne swung around in time to see Anton signal for her to come over to where he was hiding. She immediately ran to him and threw her arms around him. She held him tightly, not wanting to let go.

"I have to see you," he said. "When can you meet me on the island?"

"On the island? Can't we meet at the big rock?"

"No," Anton insisted. "If someone from your family follows you, they could sneak surprise us again. I'll leave a rowboat tied to a stake beside the rock. You can row out to meet me."

"I'll do it, but I can't get away today. Tomorrow's Saturday, and my parents expect me to go to church for confession with Father Benedict. I could be at the boat tomorrow morning at by 10:00 a.m. Would that work for you?"

Anton didn't answer. He pulled her close and kissed her as if there would be no tomorrow. Then she looked into her beautiful brown eyes, smiled, and left, filled with hope rather than linger and risk detection.

Anton arrived at the rock at 9:00 a.m., secured the rowboat to the big rock for Anne, stripped down to only his pants, and swam out to the island. He had been there only fifteen minutes when he looked toward shore and saw Anne arrive at the boat. She tied her horse to a shady tree beside the lake and then went to the boat, untied it from the stake Anton had driven into the ground, got into the boat, and shoved off with an oar. He watched as she rowed the small boat toward the island, her hair blowing softly in the breeze.

Anton waved her into a small cove when Anne arrived at the island. When Anne arrived, he helped her out of the boat. They embraced. The embrace removed all doubt about whether they wanted to be together for a lifetime.

"What's been happening with you since the day your father separated us at the lake?" he asked.

Anne's eyes filled with tears as she prepared to tell Anton her story:

"When we got home, I was angry with my father, and I didn't want to talk to him. I just wanted to go to my room and cool down until my anger subsided. I ran into the house ahead of him and upstairs to my room. I could hear my father telling my mother about him finding us at the lake together, and I could listen to my mother begin to cry uncontrollably at the kitchen table. My father called for me to come down to the kitchen and face my mother. They made me feel as though I had done something evil. I'm not sure if the most challenging part was seeing my mother crying or whether it was realizing that my parents didn't trust my behavior or my judgment.

"They kept reminding me that you're a Calvinist and, therefore, you're not to be trusted. My parents told me you're not a proper friend for me—most definitely, not a proper suitor."

Anton was noticeably hurt. However, Anne's family's reaction to him did not surprise him. He knew they disapproved of his faith. He took a deep breath and listened to Anne's story without interruption.

"I was forced to sit and listen to stories about the strife between Protestants and Catholics that happened during the War of the Reformation. When I reminded them that the fighting was over two hundred years ago, my father didn't appreciate my comments. To him, it was only yesterday. He spent the next half-hour reiterating every horror story that has been handed down from generation to generation by my family.

"Next, Papa reminded me of what happened to my sister, Maria."

"That's your twin sister?" Anton asked.

"Yes. You know what happened to Maria—right?"

"Well, I've heard some rumors. That was about a year ago. It was while I was in Zurich for my apprenticeship. I remember a massive hunt for two Gypsies who attacked your sister and tried to murder Father Benedict. It seems to me there was also a related scandal involving that other priest from your church. What was his name—oh, yes—Father Thomas?"

"Yes," she nodded. "Only it turned out that the Gypsies had nothing to do with what happened to Maria. It was Father Thomas, and he tried to blame it on the Gypsies.

"As a result of the rape, Maria was constantly depressed. She had trouble interacting with other people—especially men. We realized she desperately needed to get away from Erlach."

Anne paused and looked down at the ground as if hesitating to say what came next. "There's something else that I want to tell you, but you must give me your word of honor that you will not tell another soul."

Anton agreed. "My sister became pregnant," Anne said with a trembling voice. "As if the rape wasn't bad enough, she had her rapist's seed within her womb. She went away to a convent and stayed there during her entire pregnancy."

"It must have been horrible for her to spend nine months knowing that she was bearing the child of a rapist," Anton replied with empathy.

"It was difficult for Maria at first. But, as she began to pray and to forgive, she realized that the baby she was carrying was no more responsible for what happened than she was. The baby was, also, like her, a victim. She began to love the unborn child and wanted to keep it."

"Did she keep the baby?" he asked.

"No. The nuns at the convent convinced her that she needed to give the child to a married couple who would love the child as their own. Besides, by the time the baby was born, Maria decided to become a nun and serve Christ. After what happened to her, she didn't think she could ever feel comfortable in a relationship with a man."

Anton pulled his sobbing Anne close to him and embraced her. It was apparent that what had happened to her twin sister hurt her almost as deeply as it did Maria.

"Whatever happened to the baby?" he asked.

Anne backed away from Anton and sat down on a rock beside the lake. "The baby was adopted by a French woman of substantial means named Emilie De Fontaine. Maria got to meet the woman and, after they spent a little time together, Maria felt the woman would be a good mother for her baby and to provide for the baby materially."

"What about the woman's husband? What kind of a father would he make?"

"Well, unfortunately, Maria didn't get to meet him. The couple was about to leave for New France, and her husband was in Rotterdam, making all the arrangements. They had all the necessary papers, and the lady made a significant donation to the orphanage, run by a Catholic order of nuns helping Maria. The French woman also promised Maria she would tell the baby about his biological mother."

"How wonderful that the story had such a good ending, although it must have been heart-wrenching for your sister," Anton added.

"Yes. It was heart-wrenching for the entire family. Knowing that a family member is gone and realizing we will probably never see him again is like having a family member die at birth. Knowing Maria will be happy serving the Lord through the Church is the only consolation my parents have amid all this madness."

"Don't you have a brother who is also serving in the Church as a priest?"

"Yes. That was another blessing for us. Our brother served in Bern, where my sister lived in the convent. He was able to visit her often and comfort her. I think he was influential in her decision to become a nun."

"I can understand," Anton said, "why your parents are so distraught and guarded when it comes to your well-being. However, don't they realize I'm not some stranger who just happened to stumble into Erlach? I'm a man who has lived next door to you all my life. I'm a neighbor who happens to love you very much."

Anne looked at Anton and wondered how his family would feel about her. "What has your family said about our relationship?" she asked.

"What do you think?" he answered sarcastically. "As you said, our families live right next door to each other, but they haven't visited as friends in over two hundred years. Two centuries of hate and mistrust are not likely to change overnight.

"But my concern is for you, Anne. You don't think your parents will send you away as they did to Maria, do you?"

"I don't know what they're capable of when it comes to their religious beliefs, but I doubt they could bear the permanent loss of another family member. They've arranged for me to have counseling sessions with Father Benedict. He's a gentle soul, and I respect the old priest a great deal, but he is without experience when it comes to matters of the heart. He's never loved a woman the same way you love me."

Anton pulled Anne close and struggled with the dilemma that faced them. They could remain in Erlach and continue in a relationship that showed no signs of ever receiving the blessing of either family. They could also move to a larger city to hope for acceptance by more liberal people. Then they might be able to put the entire European social structure behind them and embark on an entirely new concept. Anton struggled for the right words to say to his love.

"Anne, there is one option we have not discussed."

"Another option? What kind of option?"

"What if," he replied, "we consider putting all of this hatred and prejudice behind us and move to a place where we would have more freedom? What if there is a place where religious beliefs are tolerant? What if there is a place where a young man can aspire to whatever level he is capable of without being held back by society?"

Anne's eyes widened as she moved back to consider what Anton had just said. "Is there such a place? Is it near here…" she asked in a trailing voice, as the reality of the unthinkable began to sink into her mind, "…or are you asking me to leave my family?"

Anton cast his vision toward the ground and loosened his embrace on Anne. He realized the gravity of his suggestion, albeit vague, had struck a sour chord with her traditional thinking. Perhaps he should have found a more diplomatic way to tell her what he saw as their best alternative for a successful relationship, but it was too late to take back the words he had spoken.

Anne released his hand, stooped toward his face, and cocked her head to get into Anton's field of vision. She waited for him to speak, but his silence told her what she feared most.

"Speak to me, Anton. You are avoiding my question. I need to know what you expect of me."

Anton pawed his right foot into the ground and shuffled the loose dirt around like a dog trying to cover his function.

"What is it you are keeping from me?" she asked. "What is it that you want me to read between the lines? Do you believe our families will never reconcile with us because of our differences in how we worship God? Are you saying that you believe our families will always be unfriendly to us because of our relationship, and if we marry, we will never have any contact with them?"

Anton took a deep breath and looked into her reddened eyes. He didn't want this conversation to ruin their precious time together, but he knew it was a conversation they needed to have.

"Anne, I would give anything for our relationship to receive the blessings of our families, but the probability of that happening is unlikely. Your family would feel you are going to Hell to marry a Protestant, and my family will think I am going to Hell to marry a Roman Catholic. What chance would we have for happiness?"

Anne began to sob uncontrollably and rushed into Anton's arms. They stood that way for several minutes, sharing each other's fears while sharing each other's comfort. Finally, Anton pulled back and looked into Anne's brown eyes.

"We don't need to make any decisions today," Anton said. "I just wanted to start the thinking process and to have us both begin to consider what our options are. The one thing we do know is we can't go on indefinitely the way we are. Sooner or later, your father will interject himself into our relationship. If he does interfere again, the situation is going to get quite nasty."

"I don't like any of the alternatives. I was so happy when I saw you in our garden. I knew you had come for me because you love me, and all I could think about was being with you again. But this conversation has drained the joy from our rendezvous. It had robbed me of the hope I felt when you held me in your arms. Must we talk about it anymore today? Can't we live in the here and now, treasuring every moment together, without worrying about the future?"

Anton pulled her close to him without saying another word, but he was a realist. He understood the harsh reality of the divisiveness the two opposing faiths could bring. Anton knew that it was time to abandon this conversation and save it for later.

Nothing got resolved that Saturday afternoon. The couple followed Anne's suggestion and spent time treasuring their first meeting together in over a month. After two hours of being together, Anton helped Anne back into the rowboat and watched as she rowed toward shore.

CHAPTER TWELVE
THE COUNSELING SESSION

The cold, damp early morning air felt like a wet slap on Anne's chaffed cheeks. She pulled her gray wool shawl tightly around her shoulders and crossed her arms against her body beneath her wrap. Anne sat beside her father in the family carriage moved ever closer to her dreaded appointment in Erlach.

The weathered farm carriage passed through the city gates beneath the large village clock. Neither Anne nor her father, Ross Welti, took notice of the clock's extraordinary mechanical activity. The clock struck six gongs on its basal chimes, and six painted marionette-like figures came out of the *glockenspiel.*[6] The clock's wooden residents began to dance their hourly ritual. Still, Anne and her father were too focused on their pending appointment with Father Benedict at St. Maria's Catholic Church to notice.

The four steel rims of the wagon wheels clanged hard against the gray cobblestones and echoed a loud metallic sound across the town square. They maneuvered skillfully among the multitudes of early vendors who had come to town to set up their booths for the Saturday market. Ross continued down the main Strasse, filled with fragrances of fresh-cut flowers, grilling bratwurst, freshly baked *brochten*, whole carp cooking on wooden sticks over hot coals, and kettles of sundry food items. Onward

---

6 Large German-style clock with figurine movements

they traveled, past the timber and plaster buildings set upon large stone foundations: the *Rathause*[7], the music hall, the courthouse.

The *glockenspiel* above the city gate had barely finished with its incredible mechanical movements before the loud sound of the dueling brass bells of Erlach's two churches began their thrice per day competition for dominance. The ritual bell ringing occurred daily at precisely 6:00 a.m., 12:00 p.m., and 5:00 p.m.. The more massive bell at St. Maria's was the louder of the two, but from within the city walls, it was merely a matter of which church one was closest to that seemed to dominate. Anne and Ross passed the Calvinist church, where Anton and his family worshiped.

Anne looked longingly to her left at the church and wished Anton were there now to give her a smile of encouragement, or better yet, she hoped he was attending the counseling session with her. She dreaded the meeting her parents were forcing her to participate with their priest, even though Father Benedict was a man she respected as her spiritual advisor. Anne feared the priest would side with her father and ask her to terminate her relationship with Anton. Her relationship was a matter of the heart, not a spiritual issue to Anne. She felt her love for Anton would not affect the way she worshiped. *Why can't they leave us alone?*

Ross parked the carriage along a curb and pulled back on the long wooden brake lever. He climbed down from the carriage on the curbside, tied the horse's reins to a post. Then Ross went around to the street side of the carriage to help his daughter down.

"*Gutten Morgan*," a voice called out from a bench high on the landing of the stone stairs that led up to the church. Ross looked in the direction of the greeting and saw Father Benedict waving from the bench on which he was seated with a cup of coffee in hand. The jolly priest smiled as he set his coffee cup on the ground beside the bench. Then he stood in anticipation of receiving his parishioners. The old priest just seemed happy to be

---

7 City Hall

alive after his brush with death at his understudy, Father Thomas' hands. He continued to smile and waited for the Rosses to climb the stairs. When they arrived, he greeted them both with a warm embrace.

"Isn't this the grandest morning you have ever seen?" Father Benedict asked. "The sun feels so warm on my face, and from here, and I can look down at Erlach as it comes to life. Morning is my favorite time of the day. I get up early and spend time with the Lord. We sit here on this bench, and I meditate as I drink my morning coffee. In the evenings, I prefer the rose garden, near the Madonna and Child statue, in the back of the church. But we don't need to talk about that."

When he saw the painful looks on Anne and her parent's faces, he realized his unwise judgment in speaking about the place where Anne's sister's rape happened. Father Benedict struggled desperately to change the subject and regain the momentum of his cheerfulness.

The priest sat back down on the wooden bench and patted the space beside him as he looked up expectantly at Anne and smiled.

"...So, Anne, please sit down beside me and tell me about the young man you've been seeing. Is he a good Christian?"

Anne was thrown off guard by the old priest's warm and casual approach. She had expected to be ushered into a cold, dark office and sternly reprimanded. Instead, she found herself sitting on a bench in the morning sun, talking to a smiling priest who was talking to her like an old friend.

"Yes," she replied as she looked down the steps at the carriage, unable to force herself to make eye contact with Father Benedict. "Anton Smith is a wonderful Christian man. He has lived on the farm next to our farm all his life. Furthermore, I might add, he attends worship service every Sunday."

The wise old priest raised his right hand to his chin and scratched it as if trying to remember something. "Let's see now...Smith. I've been the parish priest here for over forty years now, and I don't seem to remember Anton Smith in our parish. Where did you say he attends Sunday worship?"

Anne nervously squirmed on the bench as she muttered an inaudible response to Father Benedict's question.

"I'm sorry, Anne. I couldn't hear you. Would you please say that again? My old ears aren't what they used to be," the priest cunningly replied.

Several seconds passed without Anne's response as she pawed her foot against the flagstones beneath her seat.

"He's a stinking Calvinist!" her father exclaimed. "He attends church over there." Ross pointed in the direction of Erlach's "other" church. "He's going to Hell with all of the other rebellious Protestants, and I won't have my daughter and my future grandchildren going to Hell with them."

Anne stood up from the bench, sobbing into her hands. Father Benedict rose from where he was sitting beside her and put his arms around her.

"Now, now, child," he said to calm her. "I'm sure your father is only expressing concern about your mortal soul. He meant no harm."

Ross Welti looked at his daughter and Father Benedict in disbelief. "What do you mean, I 'meant no harm?' I'll tell you about what harm is. If that Smith boy doesn't let my Anne alone, I swear I'll kill him! I better never find him on my property again—or with Anne—on or off my property."

Ross stood up and moved to where his daughter and the priest were standing. He jerked Anne away from Father Benedict's comforting embrace and pulled her toward the steps that led back down to the family carriage. He stopped at the top of the landing and turned to look back at the priest.

"As for you, Father Benedict, I'm disappointed. You're obligated to be a defender of the faith, yet you've failed to speak out against Anne's relationship with that heretic, Smith.

"My family sacrificed life and limb during the war of the Reformation for the Church, and I'll not have my ancestor's sacrifices be all for naught.

"I'm taking my daughter home, and she's not leaving my property until I'm confident she won't sneak out to see that young man again.

"Father Benedict, I expect you to act like a priest and have a serious talk with Anton Smith. You tell him that my daughter is strictly off-limits, and if I find out he's trying to contact Anne, I'll kill him, so help me, God."

Ross Welti didn't wait for a reply. He grabbed Anne's arm and forcibly led her down the carriage steps, still parked along the street. He lifted his crying daughter into the carriage, untied the reins, released the hand brake, and slapped the leather straps across the horse's back. The carriage lunged forward as the early morning shoppers and merchants scrambled to get out of the way of the reckless driver who carelessly hurried through their midst.

Father Benedict leaned against the stair railing and watched sadly as the Welti family departed. Perhaps Ross Welti was right about his expectation of the priest taking a stronger stand in defending "the faith." Maybe he had mellowed with age, but he didn't feel the same way about interfaith marriages as he did as a young priest. He now saw as minor differences what he had perceived as vast chasms in his youth. If Anne and her young man both worshiped the same God, what difference could it possibly make? *Why can't everyone get along?* he wondered.

CHAPTER THIRTEEN
THE DECISION

It was nearly midnight, and Anton laid restlessly on his bed, fully clothed, trying to imagine what had become of his Anne. It had been four weeks since the lake's unfortunate incident when Anne's father accosted and threatened him. He had diligently checked the fence near the apple orchard for a knotted scarf, but there was no indication Anne was trying to contact him. As a result, Anton began to imagine all types of scenarios regarding what happened to Anne. Maybe, her father sent her to the convent with her sister. Perhaps, he locked her in her room. Even worse, perhaps she is being guarded by her family and forced to work at hard labor around the farm. Nothing made any sense to him. Anton was going mad, trying to find a reasonable explanation for Anne's lack of contact.

Unable to sleep, Anton wiped the sweat from his brow and got up from his bed. He moved over to his bedroom window and pulled back his curtains in the hope of catching a cool night breeze. He knelt on the floor and leaned his elbows on the windowsill, and leaned his face out into the darkness. Thousands of fireflies flickered in the night like moving constellations of stars winking at the Earth. The sweet fragrance of ripening apples from the orchard and plump white grapes from the vineyard filled his nostrils with the smells he had all but forgotten during his apprenticeship in Zurich. It had been a wonderful summer at home, but all the joy of his return got lost in Ross Welti's intervention in his relationship with Anne.

The night stillness was suddenly interrupted by the sound of something rather large moving through the rows of corn about thirty feet from beneath Anton's window. Thinking the disturbance was caused by a deer, the young man leaned his head further out of the window. Anton strained his eyes against the darkness. Closer and closer, the sound of movement and the rustling of swaying cornstalks proceeded to the edge of the field like a ghost moving through a haunted forest. The movement stopped, followed by a long pause. Anton leaned out of the window as far as his balance would permit and peered into the blackness to gain perspective.

"Anton. Is that you?" a woman's voice inquired in a whispered shout. "It's me...Anne."

Anton Smith was ecstatic. He could barely believe his ears or his eyes. Anne stepped out of the cornfield and moved toward the house, looking up at him. He grinned widely and jerked back into the window so suddenly that he struck his head on the wooden frame of the opened window.

"Stay there. Don't move, I'll be right down," Anton called to Anne as he held his hand to the lump on the back of his sore head.

Within seconds, Anton was downstairs and out the back door where Anne stood waiting for him with open arms. They rushed wildly into each other's embrace, and Anton lifted her off her feet and twirled her around and around in a dizzying dancelike swirl.

"I can't believe you came to me," Anton said in a joyful proclamation. "I was so afraid that you wouldn't dare."

"How could I not come to you? I love you more than you could ever know. I want to spend the rest of my life with you, regardless of what my parents say."

"I love you too, Anne," Anton replied with surprising ease. "I love you too." Somehow just saying what he knew to be true felt therapeutic and reassuring. He wanted to shout his love for this woman from the highest hill, but he knew they needed time to talk.

"How long do you have before your family realizes you are gone, Anne?"

"How long? What do you mean by that? I'm prepared to stay with you forever if that is what you want. I don't care if I ever go back home."

Anton was surprised by Anne's bold statement. Sure, he loved her, but he wasn't expecting such an immediate and unprepared move.

"We need to make plans, Anne. I was hoping that we could receive the blessing from both families to continue toward a more permanent arrangement before..."

"Before what, Anton?"

"...Before we announce our engagement."

Anne pushed away from Anton's embrace to see his eyes in the darkness of Smith's backyard. "Anton Smith, are you asking me to marry you?"

These new plans are all happening too fast. Without really meaning to do it, I've intimated a proposal of marriage. But how could that be? Both families are diabolically opposed to such a union.

"Anne, there's nothing in this world that I'd rather do than to marry you. But how would we support ourselves if we're outcasts from our families? I have no job, no property, and no money. It would be my responsibility to take care of you, and, right now, I can't do that." Anton felt the exasperating feeling of hopelessness.

Anne moved toward the man she loved and took him by both hands. "I know of a way that might sound a little far-fetched to you, but please hear me out before you say no." She looked pleadingly into his eyes.

"Right now, I'd consider anything to resolve our dilemma," he replied.

"Good. Just hear me through. As you know, my sister and my brother have both gone to New France—Quebec, to be exact. They tell of the unlimited opportunities that await any young person with the courage and grit to exercise their entrepreneurial spirit in every letter they write. I've been thinking that..."

Anton interrupted her train of thought. "Are you suggesting that we run away to the colonies?"

"No, not necessarily 'run away.' More like 'move' to the colonies."

"You would defy your parents?"

"Anton, you're unreasonable. I'm old enough to make my own decisions now. When I was a little girl, I had an obligation to honor my parents and to obey their wishes. I always did that with the utmost respect. I'm not a little girl anymore, and I must be allowed to make my own choices.

"I believe that, although my parents would hate my decision, so long as I was willing to live with my decision, they would honor it. My mother's favorite saying is: 'You've made your bed, now lay in it!' I'm prepared to do precisely that. I love my family and would prefer to remain here in Erlach, but if they can't deal with us as a couple, I'll do whatever I need to do to be with you."

"I don't know, Anne. It's all so sudden, and the colonies seem so far away. You must realize the absolute finality of such a decision, don't you? I mean, once we leave Switzerland, chances are we will never see our families again."

"Yes. I realize that possibility, and it is not what I would prefer. Still, I realize the impossibility of our families ever reconciling to the fact we love each other. I believe even Father Benedict has more empathy for our relationship than my father does. He will never give us his blessing. Besides, I will have my brother and my sister in Quebec."

"But Anne, even if I were to consider your bold plan to go to the colonies, New France isn't where I'd want to go."

Anne let go of Anton's hands and stepped back. "Really? Where would you rather go than New France?"

"I don't know...maybe Baltimore...or Philadelphia. But I would need more of a cosmopolitan area than a frontier town like Quebec. I don't want to sound arrogant, but I've developed my tailoring skills to more sophisticated levels than sewing buckskin and beaver. It's the gentlemen and the ladies of wealth who spend their money on fine clothes, not Indians and trappers. Do you understand what I mean, Anne?"

Anne tried not to sound disappointed, but she was. "How far are Baltimore and Philadelphia from Quebec, Anton?"

"Oh, I don't know, but they both are reachable by ship. No matter how far Philadelphia is from Quebec, it's a lot closer to Quebec than Erlach."

"Would you agree to my visiting my brother and sister from time to time?" she pleaded.

"Once we get settled," Anton agreed, "I will do everything within my power to arrange a visit. But please realize it might take a couple of years before we could afford it."

Anne moved forward into Anton's arms. She felt comfort in the fact that while they didn't have much of a plan at this point, at least they had hope for the future. That was more than they had before their discussion in the backyard of the Smith farm.

"Now, Anne, I want you to go home and get some rest. Think about what we've discussed to be sure you can live with this plan. It would require me to go to the colonies ahead of you to get established. I'll send for you when I know we can make it financially."

Anton's going to Philadelphia without her was something she had not considered. "How long would it be before you send for me?"

"I don't know the answer to that question. I guess it could be as much as a year. Longer, if the economy is not favorable."

Anton felt Anne's disappointment as she relaxed her embrace.

"Look. I don't like waiting for you to be with me any more than you like it, but either we have the resolve to see this plan through, or we don't. Let's give it some thought and meet again next week. Let's meet at the rock next Saturday at 1:00 p.m. to review whatever we can find out about the opportunity in the colonies."

Anne smiled bravely up at him. At least she had enough hope to hang her dreams onto. That was a good start.

"I'll do whatever it takes," she said. "I'll do whatever it takes."

Saturday, September 1, 1753
The Big Rock, Lake Biel

"I took the family carriage and drove to Neuchatel last Monday," Anton informed Anne as they sat perched on the big rock beside the lake.

"Why did you go to Neuchatel?" Anne asked.

"I heard of an agent in that city who contracts people for services in the colonies in exchange for free passage on a ship."

"Free passage? What must you agree to do in exchange for the passage?"

Anton tried to look directly at Anne when he answered, but his eyes automatically looked down at the water beneath where they were sitting. He paused for a few seconds and then began.

"I would need to sign a contract stating that I would be indentured for seven years to whoever sponsored my fare. After seven years, I would receive papers establishing a 'Freeman.'"

Anne's jaw dropped, and her eyes widened in disbelief. "Are you telling me you would be an indentured slave for seven years? You have got to be kidding!"

"No, no, no. Not a slave, I would be an indentured servant."

Anne shook her head, unable to comprehend. "Call it what you wish, but it sure sounds like a slave to me. How would you be able to send for me if you were indentured? Surely you don't expect me to sign a contract like that too. Do you?" Her eyes watered, and she began to sob uncontrollably.

Anton reached over and put his arm around her to comfort her. But his move did not have its desired effect.

"Please, Anne, don't be angry with me. I was researching the possibilities like we agreed to do. I'd never ask you to wait seven years for me, and I certainly never ask you to be an indentured servant. Did you find any information that would help us?"

"Well, I talked with Father Benedict again today when I went to town for confession. I told him I have a friend who was thinking of going to the colonies but couldn't afford the passage."

"You didn't tell him who your 'friend' is, did you?"

"No. Of course, I didn't, but my priest is an intelligent man. He probably could guess it was you. At any rate, he didn't ask, and I didn't volunteer the information.

"What he did tell me is, he knows of men who have gone to Bremerhaven or Hamburg and signed on as deckhands in exchange for their passage. He said the work is hard and long hours, but it sure sounds better than seven years as an indentured servant.

"Oh, Anton, sometimes our being together seems so impossible. I had hoped that our parents would have been able to see that we belonged to each other by now. I don't want you ever to leave me for such a long and dangerous trip, but on the other hand, I know the longer we delay your departure, the longer it will be until I can be in Philadelphia with you. I know that as good a tailor as you are, you will be successful in no time at all. In some ways, I wish you were there already."

"Me too, Anne, but the truth of the matter is, it may take a while to save enough money for me to go. I've used most of my savings to buy the equipment I'll need to take to Philadelphia with me to get started. Perhaps I could sell my equipment here and try to earn enough money in Philadelphia to get re-established?"

"No!" Anne said emphatically. That would only make matters worse. Whatever plans we make together, they must include a plan that will shorten our separation, not lengthen it.

"Now, Anton, I know how proud you are, but I have an idea that I want you to consider before you say no. Will you listen to it objectively?"

"Sure," he said. "Now is not the time to let pride stand in the way of being together. Right now, I'd listen to any idea."

Anne reached behind her neck and unclasped a long gold chain. The chain held a bright red gem, set in a fourteen-karat gold oval, bordered with small diamonds around its perimeter. She held it in the palm of her right hand while Anton looked on in amazement.

"My great-grandmother gave this to me for my first communion. It has been in the family for generations. Family tradition has it that it was left behind by Hannibal when he crossed the Alps to sack Rome. It must have some value, and I want you to have it to finance our new beginning."

Anton was speechless at first as tears welled up in his eyes at the thought that his precious Anne was so committed to their love.

"Anne, how could I ever take this from you? I'm touched, but this is your inheritance."

"Anton, it is only a piece of jewelry. It is something that is supposed to bring women happiness. Tell me how I could ever be happy if we were not together. Without happiness, this is only a trinket. Please take it and use it to bring me happiness," she pleaded.

Anne reached out for his left hand and turned it palm up. She tenderly placed the jewel in his palm and gently closed his fingers around it. Then she leaned forward and kissed Anton on his trembling lips to seal the commitment.

They often met to make plans with little concern about being discovered in the days that followed. It mattered not what their parents thought of their relationship at this point. They needed to make radical changes in their futures, and they were determined to do whatever it took to be together.

They had a plan: Anton would go to Rotterdam as soon as possible, now that they would have enough money to sustain him in Philadelphia until he got established. He would try to sign on as a deckhand to pay for his passage and conserve cash in Rotterdam. Time was of the essence. Anton would not wait until Spring.

Two Romani brothers, Raiko and Bojko, sat hiding in a hayloft near Rotterdam. Bojko, pulled off his shirt and pressed his muscled torso against the gaps in the vertical boards of the barn to catch the cool breeze that blew in from the river.

"Ah. That feels so good. I'm growing weary from the running and hiding; the prejudice and hatred; and the continual stalking by that devil hound of a priest. Here we are, carrying our inheritance that makes us wealthier than most, but living like paupers because we can't settle down long enough to enjoy it. Surely there must be a place in this world for two Romai?

Raiko sat up from the hay and cleared his voice. "Look into the horizon, Bojko. Look toward the river at all those sails on the tall ships."

"Yes," Bojko said as he looked out between the gaps in the wall. "I see them, but what is that to us?"

"Those sails are from ships that sail to ports all over the world. Maybe we should find one of the ships that are going to another a hemisphere," Raiko said. "Maybe we can find a place where people don't hate Romani."

Raiko turned and looked at his brother and said, "Someplace like where?"

"Well, we know that our parents were sold to a Dutch trader and taken to the New World. Why don't we go search for our family? It can't be any worse than here."

The brothers agreed. They would find passage on the first ship headed to the New World. They would find their parents.

CHAPTER FOURTEEN
PASSAGE TO AMERICA

September 15, 1753

The sultry morning breeze began to stir with the sun's rising and clanked the fitted sail ropes against the masts of the ships anchored in Rotterdam's harbor. The triple masts of the French clipper ship, *La Patience,* listed impatiently in the Dutch harbor, like a horse at the starting gate, anxious to begin its voyage to the New World. This voyage would be its third crossing of the Atlantic. Captain Beloux had sailed his ship twice before to Maryland via Baltimore Harbor, but this trip would be different. This time his destination was Annapolis.

Many of the passengers, who awaited the boarding call, still three days away, had already converged on the harbor area and were lodged in one of the several inns that lined the docks. Most booked passengers had sold all their possessions to pay for their third-class passage. One hopeful passenger, a young Swiss tailor, was trying desperately to find an alternative means by which to pay his fare.

The ship would be tight in the third class. Most passengers would travel with only a space of about 6 X 6 feet, usually allotted for each third-class passenger. Overcrowding into the three poorly ventilated levels with low ceilings and few windows would result in sickness and death.

Death was also unavoidable. Captain Beloux accepted that between three and five passengers would die somewhere between Rotterdam and Annapolis if there were no unusual cholera, typhoid, or influenza outbreaks. Infant mortality and death among the elderly was all too common a factor, yet they kept coming, wanting a chance at a new life in the so-called "New World."

Anton Smith rose early, awakened by the cramping discomfort of hunger pangs that gripped his stomach. The young tailor had gone to bed without dinner. He needed to conserve as much of his meager funds as possible. He quietly pulled back the thread-bare soiled blanket that reeked of body odor from countless previous guests and swung his feet over the side of his cot. He stood, still clothed from the night before, stretched, and then picked up his leather boots before tip-toeing quietly from the room he shared with three other men.

Anton descended the stairs as quietly as possible and then passed the inn's owner, a heavy-set man who sat snoring in his chair. The innkeeper never noticed Anton slipping past him and out the front door.

The tailor sat on the inn's front steps and pulled on his brown boots. Today he would try to secure a job as a crew member of the *La Patience* to pay for his passage.

Not everyone scheduled to sail on this voyage was financially in need. However, appearances can be deceiving. At least four persons in the lower-class levels held considerable wealth, in the form of letters of credit from banks they had carefully sewn into the linings of their clothing:

Two such persons were brothers with olive skin and in their early twenties. They were noticeably muscular and sporting new beard growth on their faces.

The brothers, recently endowed with a substantial inheritance from their adopted father, gave the appearance of being desperate emigrants. The latter had assembled to await the ship's departure.

Their goal was simple: to escape Europe with their lives and newfound wealth. They had made it this far, barely escaping the clutches of death, but they needed to remain inconspicuous and out of sight until the sailing. Raiko and Bojko hoped to secure jobs as crew members. If that failed, they would purchase passage and make good their escape in the *La Patience's* third-class section. The New World would offer them a chance for a new life without concern for their ethnic origin.

A tall, Free-African woman and her shorter French husband also concealed their wealth. They were also recipients of an inheritance; hers was from a wealthy employer; he was the bastard son of the same man. The couple hoped for a new beginning as traders on the American frontier where their race and social status would not matter. They, too, would be quartered with third-class passengers.

Later, another wealthy passenger would be more concerned about concealing her identity than hiding her conspicuous wealth. Her name would not appear on any official passenger list. She was a beautiful and strong-willed young woman from a wealthy banking family in Strasbourg, France. She would travel, incognito, covertly serving in the employ of King Louis XIV of France. The mystery woman planned to remain concealed in the captain's cabin for the entire voyage.

Ironically, circumstances brought these six persons (the Swiss tailor, the two Gypsies, the African woman, and her French husband, and the young woman concealed in the captain's quarters) together on the same ship. At this juncture, they were all without knowledge of the other's presence, and in the case of the Gypsies and the tailor, they were completely unaware their paths had ever crossed. A common thread of evil had begun to weave itself through the lives of these six passengers. It wove itself into a fabric of bizarre design known as Father Thomas.

The captain sat alone in his cabin, smoking his long, nicotine-stained clay pipe, pondering his need for additional crew. It was only four days until the scheduled sailing, and he was still three sailors short of the sixteen crew members he needed to navigate his ship. The ship was two hundred tons and ninety-foot-long, equipped with eight guns. Two-hundred-sixty passengers bought passage on the *La Patience.* He knew that it would be a grave mistake to set sail without an entire crew. He would need all the help he could get, especially with the constant threat of Ottoman pirates raiding the shipping lanes.

Captain Beloux leaned on his elbows and peered over the top of his narrow wire-framed glasses, perched precariously near the end of his prominent nose, at the ship manifest. Suddenly, he heard a loud knock on his cabin door. He immediately recognized the annoying five-knock wrap of his nephew/first mate, Pierre, to whom he had assigned the recruitment task.

"Enter," the captain shouted, "and I hope that you have some good news for me about deckhands."

The tarnished brass latch on the cabin door turned, and the first mate stuck his head inside the smoke-filled cabin and proudly reported, "I have found a perfect match for the three openings, Uncle…I mean, Monsieur Captain."

Captain Beloux looked scornfully at his nephew. He told Pierre a hundred times not to address him on the ship as "Uncle." "Well, just don't stand there, you idiot. Bring them in, and let me see what you found."

"Aye, Aye, Captain. I think you're going to like these three men." Pierre opened the door fully and ushered the three men into the cabin for the captain to inspect. The recruits stood silently before the captain, three abreast.

Captain Beloux looked over the three men carefully: one tall blonde-haired and fair-complexioned man and two shorter dark-skinned men—one thin, the other, powerfully built. "You two," the captain inquired, pointing at Raiko and Bojko, "What's your nationality?"

Raiko stepped forward. "We are Jews of Italian residence." The apparent lie was an attempt to conceal their ethnic origin.

Looking again over the top of his wire-framed glasses, Captain Beloux leaned forward on his table to get a closer look at them. He removed the clay pipe from his round, bearded face and spoke with skepticism. "You don't look like any Jews I ever saw. And another thing, that accent doesn't sound like any Italian accent I ever heard either."

"Well, Captain," Raiko replied, "We were born in Romania, but we moved to Italy very young. We are both well-educated and speak several languages. I think you'll find us very helpful to you."

"You look more like Africans or Arabs to me. I couldn't care less what nationality you are, but I don't want any trouble with the other crew members aboard my ship. Besides, how do I know you're not Turkish Ottoman spies planted on my ship to lead us into an ambush?"

"I assure you, Captain, we don't hate Christians. We love Christians."

"What's your experience sailing, young man?" the captain inquired of Raiko.

"Well, sir, neither of us have any experience with sailing, but we have other talents that we can bring to the ship."

The captain snickered with sarcasm through his yellowed teeth. "What talents could you possibly bring to the ship if you've never sailed?"

"Well, Captain," Raiko replied, "my brother and I worked in a circus that toured all over Europe."

"A circus? What in the world is a circus?"

"It is difficult to explain, but it's a relatively new concept. It is like a huge traveling show, which travels from city to city to entertain large crowds with demonstrations of unusual feats."

"Feats? Like what?" the captain inquired.

"Like my brother swinging on the high wires and walking across a tight rope in his bare feet."

"Do you mean like a monkey?"

"Well, yes, sir. But I would like to think of it more like a sail rigger. My brother has incredible high-wire talent."

Captain Beloux smiled and looked across his table at Raiko. "And what about you, young man? Are you also good on the high wires?"

"Oh no, Sir; I am terrified of height. I leave that feat to Bojko. What I'm good at, Sir, is financial management and accounting. The First Mate told me you need a ship's purser. I assure you, Sir, you will never find a better, more honest purser than I."

The captain was impressed with the possibilities these two dark-skinned men could bring to his ship. "What do you expect in pay?"

"We only require passage and meals to the New World, Captain. You do not need to pay us anything. In return, we will work like galley slaves for you. We will work harder than any man on your crew."

That proposition intrigued Beloux. He could always find men in Annapolis who were disenchanted with the New World and looking for passage back to Europe. If these men were all they claimed, it was good for him. "I must warn you, boys, that at the first sign of Ottoman pirates, I will slit your throats and throw you both overboard to the sharks. Do you understand me?"

Both young Gypsies nodded reluctantly in agreement that the threat they both feared was severe.

The captain focused his attention now upon a tall blonde-haired man who stood silently awaiting his turn to speak. Captain Beloux looked him over carefully. *Something is not right here. They are solidly built and fit, yet immaculately dressed in well-fitting attire?* The captain cautiously and silently pondered this unusual man's motives.

"So, what's your story, monsieur?" the captain asked. "You look fit enough, but there's something I find strange about your appearance. Your clothes are too perfect for a sailor or a common laborer. Why would you want to serve on my ship? I want to tell you right up front that we have no room for lazy sluggards here. All hands must pull their weight, or they will find themselves put off my ship—and not necessarily onto dry land!"

Anton stepped toward the captain's table, respectfully nudging Raiko aside. He held out his calloused hands, palms up, and displayed them to the skeptical captain. "Captain, with all due respect, I have worked hard all my life. I grew up on a dairy farm near Erlach, Switzerland, and I am not unfamiliar with hard labor."

Beaux examined Anton's hands and then pushed his chair back from the table. He slumped in his chair and drew on his pipe while he pondered this unusual man who stood before him. "So then, monsieur farmer," he asked, "what do you propose to bring to this voyage that would make me want to hire you?" Smiling, he added, "We don't have any dairy cows on board."

"While I am, indeed, a farmer, Captain, I'm also a skilled tailor. I've served my apprenticeship in Bern and Paris and am a Suisse Tailor's Guild member. You can see examples of my work, even now, as I stand before you. I make all my clothes."

Anton looked across the table at the captain's old uniform and tried to conceal the smirk he felt creeping across his face. "Not to offend you,

Captain, but it appears to me that you could use some help with your uniform as well."

Cpt. Beloux looked down across his time-worn uniform and smiled in agreement.

"Most importantly," Anton continued, "I can serve as your ship's tailor, and I can mend your canvases. All I ask in return, like these other two gentlemen, is passage and meals to the New World."

The ship's captain nodded in agreement at his nephew's latest find. Beloux now had the three crew members he needed, albeit inexperienced, and it would not cost him a cent of pay. He looked over at Pierre and said, "First Mate, sign them on and show them to their quarters...and start training them immediately. They need to be operational before we set sail three days hence.

"Aye, Aye Uncle...I mean, Monsieur Captain." Pierre saluted his perturbed uncle and then turned to lead the three newest crew members out of the cabin.

The training of the recruits was intense for the three remaining days before the scheduled sailing. When word spread among "old salts," the three new men had no previous sailing experience, the recruits received no mercy. Anton, Raiko, and Bojko worked sixteen to twenty hours a day doing the most disagreeable jobs imaginable. The primary antagonist among the crew was a sturdy, but aging sailor named Henri. Henri functioned as Bojko's boss, trainer, and mentor, but he became a jealous menace. Henri was a loud-mouthed braggart, territorial and guarded about his role on the Le Patience. The man did nothing to conceal his contempt for Bojko, even though the Gypsy demonstrated extraordinary ability on the riggings. Bojko realized it would be a very long voyage if he had to remain under Henri's supervision, but he was determined to do it. Perhaps it would have been better to pay for the passage, but he and Raiko were determined not to let anyone know of their wealth. Their gold and letter of credit from the bank remained sewn into the linings of their clothing.

On October 1, 1753, *La Patience* was ready to set sail for America with 260 passengers and an entire crew of sixteen men.

CHAPTER FIFTEEN
THE MYSTERY PASSENGER

5:30 a.m. October 1, 1753

The *La Patience*, a ship of English registry, prepared to depart Rotterdam on the morning tide. While of the English registry, the ship was owned by French ex-patriots and commanded by Captain Beloux, a one-tenth owner and man of dubious character.

A strong wind blew in from the North Sea and brought the high tide and a canopy of dense cloud coverage. Superstitious sailors murmured among themselves about the weather. They felt it was a bad omen to leave in such ugly weather, but none dared allow the captain to hear their murmuring.

A team of twenty-four men, twelve each in two longboats, would labor on long oars to tow the ship's two-hundred-ton bulk into the Maas River's current. As dockhands pushed the *La Patience* away from the dock with their long wooden poles, a cavalcade of flowers descended from the deck. The top deck's railings were lined with teary-eyed passengers waving to friends and family who crowded onto the dock for their final farewells. Several passengers shouted promises of reunions, which any rational person would have known, could never be kept. Still, it was better to be unrealistic than to deal with reality in their aching hearts. Going to the New World was a serious commitment, and few of the *La Patience's* 260 passengers would see Europe, or their loved ones, again.

"Get those passengers off the top deck," Captain Beloux shouted from his position beside the ship's pilot, who stood with his hands on the wheel. "I can't see the towboats, and they can't hear me!"

"Everybody below deck immediately!" the First Mate shouted, "You can come back after we've cleared the harbor."

Despite the crew's urging, the passengers were reluctant to move away from the railings, hoping for one last glance at loved ones waving from the dock. Captain Beloux mobilized available hands to herd the passengers below, a necessary exercise repeated by the crew on every departure.

Two hours of labored efforts by the longboat rowers eventually pulled the massive clipper ship into the Maas' current. The forward motion of the wind allowed the slackened tug ropes to be disconnected. Soon the morning breeze filled the sails on the ship's three masts. Since the ship's departure, Captain Beloux had the complete steering control of his boat for the first time. He sailed with the ebbing tide of the river in a westerly direction — toward the North Sea.

Late in the afternoon, the *La Patience* neared the inlet's mouth to the North Sea, just as the orange August sun's bottom edge began to touch the top of the western horizon. The passengers started to notice an increased bouncing of the ship and could hear the water slapping against the ship's hull. The nearer to the mouth of the inlet they moved, the more they could feel the North Sea, empowered by the evening breeze, forcing its way into the River Maas.

"Clear all of the passengers from the top deck," the captain shouted as he initiated his customary safety precaution at this point of every voyage, "I don't want anybody falling overboard when we hit the choppy waters of the inlet."

But then he issued a most unusual order, which none of his crew was expecting: "I want the entire crew, save the First Mate, to get below."

The crew looked questioningly back at Captain Beloux, but the captain stood firm in his order "Get below now! And don't come topside until I tell you."

With puzzled expressions amid an undercurrent of questioning murmurs, the crew reluctantly obeyed the captain's orders and retreated below deck. The captain's nephew, Pierre, kicked the hatch shut and stood on it as the ship sat bobbing in the increasingly rough water. Pierre looked with searching eyes toward the north shore as the silhouette of a longboat appeared on the horizon, rowing its way toward the ship.

"Put a pin in the hatch and lower a rope ladder over the starboard side," he commanded his nephew as the longboat drew nearer to the *La Patience*. "And," he said in a more subdued voice, "...prepare to help the lady come aboard."

Soon the longboat was alongside the ship, and the rowers reached out to secure the ladder. A young lady of incredible physical dexterity quickly ascended the ladder and was ushered by the captain's quarters in total silence. The First Mate returned to where his uncle could see him and nodded.

The captain concealed himself in the cabin and closed the door. He turned to Pierre and said, "There's no time to waste. Get the crew back on deck, and let's get underway. I want to get through the inlet while we still have some light."

Soon, the crew was back on board and at their respective workstations. They helped the captain guide the bouncing ship into the choppy sea, but with many unasked questions on their minds.

By the 15th of October, the ship had enjoyed three weeks of uneventful sailing. To date, they had only lost one passenger, an infant girl, lost to pneumonia, but the boat still had a long way to go before they would touch dry land in Annapolis.

On the first day of the fourth week at sea, Anton Smith, the ship's new tailor, approached a group of veteran sailors who sat on the deck eating their evening meal. The sailors took turns dipping their large tin cups into a cast iron pot of beans and salt pork. One of the "old salts" turned to the tailor and asked, "How are you liking being a sailor so far, mate?"

"Not so bad," Anton nervously smiled and replied, "If I were not already a master tailor, I might consider the sea as a life. But I'm afraid I want a more settled life with a wife and a family and a permanent home."

His response to the pointed question brought an immediate roar of laughter from his other crew members.

"Aye, you seem to enjoy sailing, for now," the jester responded, "but you haven't seen the worst of it yet."

"What do you mean?" Anton inquired, but at the same time, fearing he was asking a baited question.

"Well, I guess nobody told you, but we're in the height of typhoon season. Those storms are terrible."

Anthony looked puzzled.

"Aye. You do know what a typhoon is—right?"

"Yes, of course, I do," Anton answered in a tone that betrayed his contempt at the childish jab.

"Well," the sailor continued, "We also have elephants this time of year in the Atlantic. You never know when you might come upon an elephant at sea."

Anton felt like he might be better off not to ask, but he asked anyway. "An elephant? What's an elephant?"

The old salt's eyes widened as he pointed toward a vast dark cloud and said: "Just like that, mate. A big black cloud hangs down its trunk into the sea like a giant elephant sucking up water to quench its enormous thirst. The trouble is, it sucks up everything in its path—ships included. Many a ship has disappeared because of the elephants between May and November. It's a dangerous time to be at sea, don't you know?"

Anton dipped his cup into the beans and pondered the sailor's words, all the while looking up at the dark cloud and trying not to reveal his

uneasiness. He could see the smirks on a few of the conversation's partici-
pants' faces in his peripheral vision. On the faces of others, Anton saw
genuine concern. It was difficult to know whether this was one of the
torments he must endure as a new sailor or whether the crew member was
sincere. Either way, the man's comments about typhoons and elephants
affected them.

CHAPTER SIXTEEN
SAILOR TRAINING

First Mate, Pierre, was proud of the recruits he had selected for his uncle, Captain Beloux. The three new sailors soon proved to be perfect matches for their respective assignments: Bojko as sail rigger; Raiko as ship's purser; Anton as ship's tailor. By the end of the second week at sea, it was difficult for the casual observer to distinguish between the new sailors and the old salts. The actual tests of their character, however, were yet to come.

Anton

After two weeks at sea, Anton climbed out of the lower deck and stood in the fresh air on the morning of October 18th. He looked to the east and gazed in wonder at the beautiful but haunting, red glow that had spread its magnificent hues across the vast horizon. The sun seemed to be struggling in vain to illuminate the new dawn from behind the thick dark clouds.

The captain's nephew, Pierre, called to him from behind the ship's wheel. "Aye, beautiful it is, mate, but I'm afraid that it's a bad omen manifesting itself in the morning sky."

"But the sky is beautiful this morning," Anton said, pointing toward the sunrise. "We must be in for a gorgeous day."

"Don't you know anything at all about sailing, you landlubber," Pierre replied, shaking his head. "Haven't you ever heard: *'Red sky in the morning; sailor take warning?'*"

"Yeah," Anton recalled, "somewhere in the Bible."

"Look at the sky and then look at the sails. No wind is moving at all. I'm afraid this is what we call 'the still before the storm.' We could be in for one fright of a storm."

"Do you mean like a typhoon?" Anton asked.

"You had better pray it's no typhoon," Pierre replied, "If it is, may God help us all. Go to my uncle's—I mean the captain's—cabin and tell him I need him here straight away."

Anton, frightened by the probability of an oncoming storm, hurried immediately to Captain Belioux's cabin. As Anton raised his right fist to wrap on the captain's door, he heard something that caused him to hesitate. Anton thought he discerned a woman's voice speaking in French from within the cabin. *It must be my imagination,* he paused, but the pressing matter of the oncoming storm caused Anton to dismiss the thought immediately from his thoughts. Anton rapped hard on the door.

"Who is it?" he heard the captain ask from behind the cabin door.

"It's me, Captain… Anton Smith. The first mate sent me here to get you. It may be an emergency, sir." He replied. "He thinks we may be heading into a bad storm."

The curtains Captain Belioux had ordered installed in his cabin to conceal the presence of his female passenger worked well in concealing his cabin "guest." Still, adversely, they prevented the captain from seeing the morning sky. All he was aware of was the ship's gentle movement on the sea. The cabin door opened a little, and the captain stuck his head out of the door just far enough to look. Anton could see shadows and hear the movement of chairs across the cabin floor from behind the door. The fragrance of lilac perfume permeated from within the room.

"Confound it!" the captain shouted. "I don't need this to happen when we're so far from a safe port. Go tell the first mate I'll be there straight away."

Captain Belioux withdrew his head into the cabin and shut the door with a slam.

Anton reported the captain's message to the first mate and waited at the wheel with Pierre for the captain's arrival. They didn't have to wait long.

"I need to know how fast we're moving, and I need to know now!" the captain ordered. "I'll take the wheel, and you have Smith help you cast a log." Looking up at the sails, he added, "There is practically no air movement at all. Go! Get the job done."

"Come with me, Anton," Pierre ordered as he headed toward the back of the ship. "This'll be good training for you."

"What did the captain mean by 'cast a log'?" Anton inquired.

"Don't you know anything, tailor? He means we are to take a reading on the ship's speed. In other words, he wants to know at how many knots we are moving."

"What's a knot?" Anton asked with a puzzled look on his face.

"Listen up," Pierre said, obviously frustrated by Anton's lack of sailing experience, "and I'll show you."

The first mate stood beside a large spool to which a long rope containing equally spaced knots wound about a wooden spool. He tied a triangular-shaped board with a lead weight on one end to the end of the spooled rope.

"We will throw this weighted panel into the water. The lead weight will cause the panel to be stationary as the ship moves away from it."

Then he reached inside a cabinet and withdrew a small sand-filled timer that resembled an hourglass.

"This," Pierre said, "is a thirty-second timer. You will turn the timer over when I give you the signal, and we will count how many knots turn off the spool within thirty-second-time limits. If we move away from the panel five knots every thirty seconds, we move at a speed of five knots. Do you understand?"

"I don't understand all of the details, but I understand enough for now."

"Good," Pierre replied, "I'll explain it in more detail after we get the reading, but for now, try to work with me so I can get my uncle off my back. Take the timer and the panel attached to this rope to the back of the ship. Drop the board straight down into the water when I give you a signal. As soon as the board resurfaces, signal me, and immediately turn the timer over. When all the sand has passed through the glass, signal me again. It will take us a couple of readings, but if we work together, it won't take long to determine our speed."

Anton moved to the rear of the ship and looked over the railing. The ship's movement in the ocean's light swells made him feel dizzy initially, but he soon adjusted.

"Look at me!" the first mate yelled, "You need to pay attention and wait for my signal."

Anton turned to look back at Pierre, who stood with his right hand on the reel, and his left hand elevated above his head.

'Now," Pierre shouted as he dropped his left hand down to his side.

Anton released the weighted panel directly into the sea and waited to surface again. "It's up," he said as he turned the timer upside down and watched the sand begin to flow into the bottom compartment of the glass.

As soon as Anton turned over the timer, the first mate released the reel, and the rope with the knots spaced approximately 14.4m[8] apart. The knotted line began to feed out slowly. When the top glass of the timer was empty, Anton signaled Pierre to stop.

Pierre shook his head as if he did not believe what he counted. He turned back toward the wheel and shouted, "Two and a half knots, Captain. I'll measure it again."

"Just leave the chip log in the water and signal me when you are ready to start the timer," Pierre instructed his helper.

Anton raised his left hand into the air, turned the timer upside down, and then dropped his hand. The rope began to feed out once again. This time the line seemed to move out even slower than the last. He raised his head and looked up at the sails. There was minimal movement in the canvass. Anton did not need to read the knots to understand the ship was nearly dead in the water.

---

8 47.3 inches

"Two knots, Captain," the first mate called his uncle. "There's just no wind."

Pierre rewound the knotted rope onto the reel and safely stored the chipboard and timer in its cabinet. He then returned to the wheel with Anton to relieve the captain.

"I'm afraid we may have a serious storm headed our way," the captain said as he returned the steering responsibilities to his nephew. He pointed out into the distance and continued, "The lack of wind and the calmness of the sea concerns me. It seems like the swells are rising higher without the help of the wind. That tells me there are strong winds somewhere out there that just haven't reached us yet. After breakfast, I want you to start securing the ship." Turning to Anton, the captain commanded, "And don't go spreading panic among the passengers either." Then, almost as an afterthought, he said, "And one more thing while I'm thinking about it…keep your mouth shut about anything you see and hear in my cabin. Do you understand?"

Anton knew the captain was referring to the source of the lilac fragrance he had smelled coming from the captain's cabin. There was no doubt now, in Anton's mind, that the captain had been hiding a woman in his cabin. Anton answered without acknowledging he had heard or seen anything, "Aye, Captain. Your business is your own."

"Good then. See to it that there is no scuttlebutt among the crew." The captain then turned and walked to his cabin.

Bojko

Bojko was a natural. Everyone, including the captain and the first mate, was astounded at Bojko's agility on the riggings. He exhibited no fear of height, and his balance adjusted quickly to the ship's rolling pitch on the sea. His ability on the riggings earned him the nickname "Monkey Man," eventually shortened to simply, Monkey. However, the acknowledgment of Bojko's ability among the captain and crew came an equal measure of jealousy from Henri, his trainer, and his boss. Within two short weeks, Bojko had demonstrated the ability to outperform his trainer. That did not sit well with Henri.

"I think I resent my new nickname," Bojko confided in Raiko. "That name is demeaning and makes me feel like a dumb animal. Why can't they call me by my proper name?"

Raiko, the eternal optimist, smiled and put his hand on his brother's shoulder. "Don't worry about it, brother," he said. "They mean it as a term of endearment. It's their crude way of saying they admire your ability on the ropes. The name is a compliment."

"Yep, just like when they call the captain 'Old Blubber Sides?' Or, maybe when they call his nephew 'Weasel' because he listens to our conversations and then slithers into his uncle's cabin to tell him everything he hears? Bojko looked away from his brother and down at the deck in a boyish display of embarrassment. "You may be right, but I don't like it. The crew can keep their compliments to themselves. It makes me angry to be called a monkey."

By the second full week of sailing, both Captain Beloux and the first mate had full confidence they could rely upon Bojko to perform his job better than any of the more experienced crew members. "I'll hate to see that little monkey leave us when we arrive in Annapolis," Henri overheard the captain tell his nephew. Bojko should be the one in charge of rigging instead of that old man we have in charge now."

"Do you mean Henri, Captain?" Pierre responded.

"Of course, I mean Henri. He's done a fair job for me for many years, but don't you think he's getting a little too old for that kind of work? There comes a time in a man's life when the best thing to do is to step down and let a younger man do the job."

"Dream on, Uncle," Pierre said. "Bojko and his brother are dead set on going ashore and staying on dry land. They'll never consider becoming sailors."

"Well," the captain said, rubbing his gray beard, "maybe I can entice him with money as an incentive. Maybe I should give him a position of real authority."

"Hey, wait a minute. You already have a first mate. Besides, whatever happened to blood being thicker than water?"

Captain Beloux smiled and turned away to return to his cabin. He and his nephew knew he could never fire his only sister's son. The boy's mother depended upon him for her support. Pierre was right; blood is thicker than water. Nevertheless, he wished there was some way to keep both Bojko and Raiko aboard ship as permanent members of his crew. For now, that could only be a dream. Little did he know the two Gypsy boys had enough money to buy and sell his entire ship and crew.

Raiko

Raiko's experience as Bernardo's circus manager had prepared him well for his job as the ship's purser. In a short time, he put the captain's accounts in better order than they had ever been. He managed the ship's inventory down to the last bag of grain and keg of rum. He distributed the foodstuffs to the ship's cook, and he set the Captain Beloux's finances in a form the captain understood better than ever before. Just as Bernardo had trusted Raiko, the captain also did.

Still, on the matter of trust, there was one issue Raiko had a difficult time dealing with: Why did the captain never allow him to enter his cabin? No matter how often they met to discuss the accounting, the captain would never meet with him in his cabin. Regardless of the weather, they either met on the deck or didn't meet at all. *What is the captain hiding in his cabin?*

On the evening of October 21st, with the air heavy and still and the sky only partly cloudy, Bojko and Raiko sat talking as they watched the sun setting on the western horizon. Several passengers, including Maisha, the African woman, and her husband, were topside stretching their legs.

"I'd love to know what's going on in the captain's cabin," Raiko said to his brother. "The captain keeps his door and windows closed all the time and never invited me inside. Doesn't that seem just a little strange to you, Bojko?"

"Yes, actually, it does seem rather strange to me too," he replied. "Every time he opens the door to his cabin, I could swear I smell perfume. He doesn't wear any fragrance on his person. Sometimes, I wish he did—or at least take a bath. The fragrance only comes from inside the cabin. The scuttlebutt might be right. He might have a woman inside there with him."

"I don't know," Raiko replied. "But I do know that something strange is going on inside his cabin."

"There's something else," Bojko added.

"What?"

"Remember that night in Alcatel when I had an altercation with Father Thomas? Well, there was a woman in the coach with him that was wearing a fragrance with that same lilac smell."

"Oh, come on, Bojko," Raiko laughed. "The woman in the carriage can't be the only woman in the world who wears lilac perfume. Are you trying to tell me Father Thomas and that woman from Erlach are in the captain's cabin?"

"I know it sounds crazy," Bojko added, "but one time, I thought I heard their voices coming from within the cabin. Surely, Father Thomas and that woman haven't followed us here?"

"Listen to me, dear brother, if Father Thomas were here on this ship, we would be dead already. I think you're just paranoid because of all that's happened. You're overly cautious when it comes to that wicked priest, and I understand why. I am too. But, come on, we're on our way to a new world to begin a new life, and our problems with Father Thomas are far behind us."

Behind the post in front of which the Gypsies sat talking, a black woman stood silently listening. Maisha thought: *A young French woman fond of lilac perfume and in the company of a priest? Could it possibly be? Surely not. It would be too much of a coincidence.*

Emilie De Fontaine

Captain Beloux awoke as the mantel clock in his cabin struck 04:30. He arose from his bunk, walked to the cabin window, and pulled back the curtain. He hoped for a clear sky to enable him to take a sighting with his sexton. Gazing up at the night sky, he could see nothing but heavy clouds. In the distance, he could see an occasional glow of lightning, and in his sails, a slight fluttering of a breeze. Perhaps now something would happen to give him a little wind to fill his sails and get the ship moving along again. Privately, he hoped the weather he saw forming was only a tropical storm, but he feared the worst. He turned to walk back to his bunk.

As the captain crossed the floor of his cabin, he could hear the faint breathing of Emilie and smell the fragrance of her perfume. He lit a candle and sat at his table to study his nautical charts. Instead of looking at his charts, he glanced across the cabin and cast his eyes upon the sleeping beauty. The captain shared his cabin in close quarters with Emilie for three weeks. A wiser man would have forced himself to look away, but he did not.

He watched longingly at the slow rising and falling of her breasts beneath the soft fabric of her nightgown. It had been a warm and breezeless night, and Emilie was sleeping with her blankets pulled back, revealing much more of her body than the captain was typically privileged to see. He liked what he saw.

The captain was not a young man, but he was a man, with his longing for a woman alive and well. He had endured watching her day after day, brushing her hair, bathing behind a curtain, and hanging her garments to dry in his cabin. He dined with her, he chatted with her for hours on end, and he slept near her. *Does she have the same attraction for me that I feel for her?* He didn't know, but he was the captain, and he was able to find out.

The captain got up from his chair and crept across the cabin, stopping to pause beside her bed. He trembled in anticipation as he dropped his nightgown to the floor and reached down to pull her blanket the rest of the way off her body. He slipped into her bed beside her.

Then, the unexpected happened. In one swift movement, Emilie withdrew her arm from beneath her pillow, and with a knife in hand, she held the sharp point of the blade against the captain's left unshaven cheek.

"What do you think you're doing, you smelly fat old man?" she whispered intensely through her gritted teeth. "I'll cut your throat from ear to ear and feed your miserable carcass to the sharks."

"Don't you dare talk to me that way, woman! I'm the captain on this ship, and I can do what I please."

"Not with me, you won't. I'll have you remember I'm a special emissary of King Louis XIV of France. If you even breathe hard in my direction, I'll have your fat carcass hung from the mast of your ship until the buzzards eat all the flesh from your miserable skeleton."

With those words, she drew the point of her razor-sharp dagger three inches across his cheek. The blade opened a shallow but nasty cut.

"Damn you!" the captain shouted as he grabbed for his face. Blood ran freely through his fingers, and he rolled his weight away from Emilie and toward the edge of the narrow bed. The captain quickly rose from the mattress, placing his bare feet on his cabin's plank floor. He rushed toward a washbasin that was sitting on the nightstand. He quickly dipped his hands into the water bowl and splashed water on his wound.

"That, my dear captain," Emilie said, "is the first time since we began this miserable journey that I ever saw you wash your face. It would be best if you did it more often.

"And never forget that I am a special emissary of His Majesty, King Louis IV. If you ever so much as touch me, I'll have you hung."

Captain Beloux burned with anger, but there was no time for rebuttal or confrontation. A brilliant flash of light illuminated the cabin, followed by a loud thunderclap. A strong wind appeared without warning, and the ship began rising and falling on huge swells. A storm was upon them.

CHAPTER SEVENTEEN
THE STORM

On the captain's paneled wall, the clock completed its seventh baritone gong as he fought to open the door to his cabin against the force of the increasing wind. Captain Beloux gripped the cabin door with both hands and then turned to close it as gently as possible.

The captain struggled to keep his heavy-set frame on his feet and struggled across the pitching deck of the bouncing ship to get to his nephew's side. Pierre gave little notice to his uncle's efforts and struggled desperately to steady the ship's wheel. Just as the captain reached Pierre, a brilliant flash of lightning streaked across the heavens and revealed a three-inch gash on the captain's right cheek.

"What in heaven's name happened to your face, Uncle?" Pierre shouted across the noise of the storm.

"It's nothing. I just cut myself shaving," Bijoux snapped back. "But it's none of your business," the captain replied in an unmistakable tone of embarrassment and irritation.

"But Uncle, I've never known you to shave—ever. What in the world ever possessed you to shave in the middle of this storm?"

"Maybe this gash on my face will help you to understand why I never shave," he said as he attempted to cover up his recent indiscretion with Emilie. "Now, tell me about this storm. How long has it been with us?"

Pierre thought for a second, trying to recollect the details of the past hours. "The swells came on us gradually, beginning—I don't know—

about three hours ago. I could see lightning flashes over the southern horizon, but I wasn't sure. At first, I thought it could be the sunrise, but then I realized it was simply too early for that. Do you know how sometimes your eyes can play tricks on you when you have been on duty all night? About two hours later, when the ship's tailor came on deck, I could see the sun's earliest signs were beginning to come up. Smith mentioned how bright red the sky looked behind the black clouds. It was eerie." Pierre looked toward Anton, who was nodding in agreement with his story.

"The swells began to get more severe, and they began to lift ship higher. They were much higher than I've ever seen them, except in a tropical storm. That's when I realized this would not be a simple thunderstorm. I figured we were in for one beauty of a storm."

Even as Pierre spoke, a strong wind from the south pushed hard against the flapping sails, and the dark clouds moved menacingly in the sky above the ship. Brilliant flashes of lightning illuminated the heavens, and foamy white caps surrounded them for as far as they could see into the distance.

"Get the entire crew on deck immediately," Captain Bijoux ordered. "We'll need to be prepared for one devil of a storm. Typhoon season ends in November, but I hoped we'd get lucky and sail typhoon-free. So much for luck!"

The seriousness of his uncle's voice filled the first mate with fear. He left the captain immediately and started below to gather the crew. By the time Pierre reached the crew's quarters, he had found every man up and dressed. Some had already begun to ascend the ladder to the top deck.

Pierre found the ship's new purser dressed, but confused about what an accountant should do in this emergency. Raiko had a look of questioning fear in his eyes as he watched the rest of the crew hurry to the top deck. The Gypsy turned to the first mate and asked: "Is this one of those typhoons that Henri told us about?"

"At this point," Pierre answered, "I don't know what to call it. Let's hope to God that it's not a typhoon. Yesterday I prayed for a wind, but this is ridiculous."

"Maybe you need to be careful what you pray for, " Raiko joked. "Do you think it's going to be bad?"

"Bad? It's already bad. The storm's coming on us like a tropical gale with winds of over thirty-five knots and building. Technically it's still typhoon season. It's just that it's awful late in the year for a typhoon or tropical storm. The typhoon season normally runs from June through the end of November, but I've never known one earlier than July or later than September. What worries me about this storm is its wind direction. Like most tropical storms, this storm is coming at us from the Southwest. This storm is bad is a bad one, no matter what we call it."

"What do you want me to do?" Raiko asked. "I don't know what my job is supposed to be during a storm?"

Pierre thought for a moment, and then answered, "You can do the most good by going below to help with the bilge pumps. The more the storm blows water across the deck, the more water we're likely to take on. It's a back-breaking job, but without operating the pumps, we'll sink for sure."

"I'll do what I can to help," Raiko said as he turned away to go below.

Raiko began his descent down into the dark hull of the ship. It felt unlike anything he had ever experienced. Raiko needed to calculate every step with the ship's rising and falling with the increased pitch. He felt like he was descending into the belly of a great fish. The deeper he went, the darker the hallways. In the third-class section of the ship, the air was rank and stagnant with human odors. The lack of proper lighting made it difficult to see. He could hear vomiting and crying all around him. The smell of overturned toilet pots permeated the air with the sickening smell of ammonia.

I think I am beginning to feel a little bit like Jonah did when the whale swallowed him, he thought. *The only difference is I'm going into his belly voluntarily, while Jonah had no choice. Come to think of it, I may not have any option either. Oh please, Lord, don't make me stay down for three days.*

As he passed through the passenger decks on his way to the bilge pumps, what Raiko saw made him sick to his stomach. The passengers began to feel the intense rising and falling of the ship's movements as it moved across the swells. Everywhere he looked, he could see and hear passengers spilling the contents of their stomachs. He passed an African woman in the third-class deck hallway, trying to help a man ease to the deck so he could lean against the wall. She held a towel to his face to catch the regurgitation that flowed forcibly from his mouth. Maisha turned and looked up at Raiko as he passed by.

"How bad is out there?" she asked.

At first, he wanted to hide his concern, but instead, he gave her an honest appraisal. "The sky is getting very dark and cloudy. I'm sure you've heard the violent thunder. This trip is my first time at sea, and I don't know much about storms. All I know is I don't like the look of things. The captain ordered me to go down and help with the bilge pumps. Sorry. I can't talk any longer, mademoiselle. You must hurry!"

Raiko's desire to hurry past the scenes he witnessed in the corridor was more of self-preservation than an urgent desire to reach his destination. The sights, sounds, and smells he was experiencing threatened to make him an involuntary participant. Suddenly his stomach felt very queasy. It seemed to Raiko that the lower he descended into the ship, the more difficult it was to get his bearings and more unstable he felt about the ship's pitching and swaying. He longed to be topside, where he could feel a cool breeze and fix his eyes on the horizon. Here, he had no reference point to anything.

When Raiko finally reached the lower deck, he found the trap door to the hull open. He could hear voices below and see the shadows of four men pumping slowly but steadily on long wooden handles fixed to two broad sets of bellows. There didn't appear to be the sense of urgency he had expected to find. He turned and went down the ladder feet first.

"Well," one of the men said when he saw Raiko, "it looks like the first mate sent us some reinforcements. We expected some help would come, but really—a clerk?"

Without saying another word, Raiko removed his shirt to prepare for the task ahead. His muscular torso and well-developed muscles, revealed by removing his shirt, said it all. Raiko was not the kind of man one would want to provoke anger. The other crew members remained silent. They knew Pierre had sent the right man for the job.

Topside, the storm continued to approach with increased intensity. Pierre looked up into the stormy heavens and silently prayed, "Lord, I know you never hear from me unless I need something. Yesterday I prayed for more wind, and it looks like you gave it to me. But would you mind if I asked you to take some of it back? I might have prayed too hard. I didn't need this much wind."

The *La Patience* listed from side to side, and the sea churned angrily about the ship.

The water's white caps began to take on a look of swirling foam, and the swells looked like huge, rounded mountains. The swells rose and fell with increasing fury and bounced the ship around like a cork in the ocean.

Captain Beloux began to bellow orders in rapid succession at the helm, but the experienced crew members already knew what they had to do. There was no need to hear the captain's inaudible commands. Their years of facing every adverse situation and danger on the high seas had ingrained in them the necessary procedures. They seemed to slip into automatic mode.

When Henri and Bojko reached the main deck, the older sailor did wait for any orders.

"Follow me, Monkey Man," Henri called out as he motioned to Bojko. With an uncustomary look of concern, he added, "And be careful. The masts are going to be treacherous, and I don't want to lose you."

Bojko and Henri began to climb the masts with incredible speed and agility. The ferocious winds had increased to seventy miles per hour. By the time they reached the top of the mast, Henri had begun to show signs of tiring under the strain of the storm. Henri was getting older, and his age took its toll on him. By way of contrast, the younger Bojko was living up to his nickname of "Monkey Man."

"The winds will tear these sails to shreds if the mainsails remain in their full upright positions." Bojko looked across at Henri on the opposing mast just as a flash of lightning struck just above Henri's head.

The top of the mast broke off as though it were only a twig and went crashing to the deck below, narrowly missing Captain Beloux as he stood tethered to the ship's wheel. A foot or so would have been certain death for the captain to the left.

The lightning flash temporarily blinded Bojko, but he saw Henri dangling from the mast unconscious and with his foot tangled in the ropes when his sight returned. The Gypsy could only whisper a plea to Almighty God that his co-worker was still alive. He grabbed a rope and swung from his perch across to where Henri hung dangling as crew members below on the deck watched in amazement.

His movements were as graceful as any performance he ever did on the trapeze. On his first attempt, Bojko swung into Henri's inverted body and grabbed the victim's motionless legs. He lifted his boss's torso to turn it upright, and in a display of incredible strength, he held him with one arm while cutting the rope that had tangled about Henri's legs. The freed weight of Henri's body strained both Bojko's and the rope's strength to the maximum. Bojko was able to swing both he and the rescued to a rope ladder.

Two other crew members had managed to climb the constantly swaying masts' ropes by this time. They reached out to take the still unconscious victim from Bojko's grip. The three rescuers, with much difficulty, finally laid Henri on the deck. The jagged bone protruding through the skin on his left leg revealed a compound fracture, and his body bruised, but his prognosis for recovery appeared good. They took him below for the needed medical attention.

The storm raged on for two hours, and then the winds ceased to blow almost as suddenly as they had begun. The swells continued to bounce the *La Patience* about in the waves like a cork in a raging river. The main-sails were re-hoisted by the halyard as far as the broken mast would allow and assisted by the jib sails, Captain Beloux, once again, had the ship under control. The sea calmed seven hours later, and the exhausted crew retired to their bunks for a well-deserved rest.

CHAPTER EIGHTEEN
SAILING UP THE DELAWARE RIVER

Anton tossed and turned restlessly in his berth, annoyed by the unceasing snoring of his fellow crew members; their abrasive inhales and exhales timed with the rising and falling of the *La Patience* as it moved steadily through the roll of the Atlantic toward Philadelphia. The ship's nauseating motion rolled left to right and front to rear. It wasn't the severity of the ship's movement that got to Anton; it was the ship's never-ceasing motion.

I'd have thought my body would have adjusted to this motion after seven weeks of sailing, but it never seems to rest. What I'd give to be able to walk to the apple orchard back home and see that double-knotted scarf. If only I could see Anne and hold her in my arms.

Perhaps it was the confinement of the ship with its cramped quarters getting to him, or seasickness, or loneliness, but Anton felt the sudden need to get some fresh air into his lungs and to clear his head.

Timing his movement with the pitch of the ship's rise, he swung his left leg over the side, pushed away from the wall, and dropped to the deck. In the berth beneath him, the sailor disrupted his snore for a moment, then rolled to his side without wakening. Anton stood still and waited until he heard the man's rhythmic breathing resume before he continued.

Anton reached up to his empty berth and felt along its edge, in the darkness, until he found his canvas jacket and knit hat. He quietly dressed and then moved to the end of the berth to retrieve his boots. Anton picked them up and quietly carried his boots to the ladder leading to the top deck.

The moist December air felt colder with each step up the ladder toward the deck. He pushed up and opened the hatch. A cold blast of winter air hit his face. He swung the hatch cover aside and set his boots on the deck, and looked up at the sky. He stared in wonder at the breathtaking sight of a brilliant full moon set in a crystal-clear sky. The tranquil scene was soon interrupted by the sound of Captain Beloux's deep voice.

"Sailmaker," the captain called out, as he stood at the wheel, beside his nephew, "is that you?"

"Aye, Captain. It's me. Anton Smith."

"Well, then. Don't just stand there like a sea turtle with its head *stickin'* out of its shell. Get over here."

Anton pulled himself up and sat on the end of the ladder while he put on his boots. Then he climbed the rest of the way out of the opening, closed the hatch behind him, and approached Captain Beloux.

"I'm glad you showed up when *ya* did," the captain smiled.

Pointing toward the jib, he said, "I need *you* to *get* up there with that monkey and adjust the sails. When we leave the bay and sail up Delaware, we're *gonna* be *sailin' agin* a powerful current."

Anton nodded, and without a verbal response, he turned and looked up at Bojko, already on the mast. As Anton moved across the deck toward the rope ladder, tied to the mast, the *La Patience* hit the Delaware River's oncoming current with a sudden and profound dip. The current's rushing force threw Anton hard against the ship's railing and nearly knocked Bojko from his perch high above.

The young tailor turned sailmaker, grabbed the railing, and hung on for dear life. He turned his head and looked back through fearful eyes at a grinning captain and his nephew.

"I thought we were *gonna* lose *ya* both there for a minute," Pierre said with a wide grin. "I *should a* warned *ya*, but I wanted to see the expressions on your faces when we hit."

A strong southwesterly wind blew at Anton's back and caused him to hold onto his knit cap. Anton didn't share the captain's morbid sense of humor in endangering lives. The wrong move would have jolted overboard, but he remained silent and continued toward the ropes. He ascended the ladder toward Bojko, grateful the journey would soon end.

Pierre looked up from the helm at Bojko, wide-eyed with terror and trying to figure out what had just happened. Bojko had lost his footing on the crossbeams.

"Give 'er full sail, Monkey Man," he commanded. "We've got a favorable wind from the southeast, but we'll be *goin' agin* the current. Gotta make good time while we kin."

The young Gypsy adjusted the mainsail and jib to catch the maximum breeze with as much ease as any old salt.

"Just look at that boy," Pierre said as he pointed in awe toward Bojko and shook his head. "You would have thought he's been sailing for all of his life." Then, as an afterthought, he added, "Sure hope we can persuade him to sign on permanent like."

I don't think that's going to happen, Anton mulled. *Raiko and his brother are determined to get a new start in Penn's Woods. That's all they ever discussed.*

The captain seemed to be on the same wave-length as Anton as he turned to Pierre and replied, "Good luck with that one. I think he and Raiko are determined to have one of those 'Circuses' they talk so much about."

"That could be, but ya can't blame me for wanting. As I always say, Captain, if you're gonna want, want big."

With the southeast wind behind them, the La Patience continued edging against the current toward the northwest port of Philadelphia.

CHAPTER NINETEEN
A MYSTERIOUS DEPARTURE

The *La Patience* moved steadily along the Delaware River toward Philadelphia, driven by a consistent cold wind, out of the northeast, beneath an overcast sky. By 3:00 pm, the day's light began to fade into early darkness, and snow flurries turned to heavy, wet snow.

"Looks like this could be a true '*Nor' easter*,' if I ever saw one," Captain Beloux shouted to his nephew over the sound of the wind. "Go tell our guest to make sure she's ready and packed. Then get back here, straight away, and help me try to spot League Island. I want to anchor there for the night to make our rendezvous. If we miss the island in this storm, there's no turnin' back until we get to Philadelphia—a place our passenger needs to avoid."

Pierre gave a half-hearted salute and turned toward the Captain's cabin with a devilish grin. There was nothing he liked more than to see their beautiful passenger.

Pierre stood before the cabin door and contemplated his next move. *Should I knock or walk in and hope to catch her in a compromising position?* He opted for the latter. Quietly his finger pulled the latch, and he slowly began to push the door open. The door had only opened a few inches when it was slammed back against him with deliberate force, striking his face and bloodying his nose.

"What the …" Pierre shouted as he pulled his hands up to his aching face. After regaining his composure and suppressing his anger, he wiped the blood from his nose, took a deep breath, and said in a stern voice, "The Captain wants you ready at a moment's notice. Make sure you're ready when it is time to go."

No reply. Not surprising. Pierre turned away and returned to the wheel, leaving the captain.

"What in the world happened to you?" the captain said, laughing.

"I fell against the cabin door when I went to tell that witch to be ready to go."

Captain Beloux laughed, not believing a word his nephew said. "It looks to me like she's more of a tigress than a witch. I told you before, don't mess with her—she's as deadly as a viper and politically connected, I might add.

"Now, get your butt forward and look for a signal fire onshore. I can barely see through this snow, and I doubt if the spotters can see our lanterns. Not only that, but I'm also afraid of running aground. When you see the signal, we'll anchor nearby and wait for nightfall to transfer your tigress, or should I say, witch, ashore?"

Pierre moved to the ship's bow without an appreciation for his uncle's cruel humor. He didn't have long to wait. Thirty minutes into his watch, he smelled the smoke of a fire and saw the flickering glow of the signal through the heavy snowfall.

"Uncle," Pierre shouted as he pointed toward shore, "that must be it! I see the signal fire dead ahead. Should I get, the crew topside to set the anchor. We'll be on top of them before you know it."

"No, you idiot, this is a covert operation. That's why you barred the hatch door, so they can't come up. You'll have to do it yourself"

Pierre gritted his teeth and suppressed his desire to talk back. He knew better. At the command of his uncle, he moved into position and dropped the anchor to the river floor.

When the agents on shore saw the *La Patience* positioning to set anchor, they immediately extinguished their signal fire. They withdrew into a wooded area, back from the shoreline, where they had built a lean-to. Darkness had already begun to overtake the day, and the continuing snowfall helped to form a white curtain of concealment. All that remained was for the crew to go below and settle in for the night. The wind and the cold, wet snow provided the perfect incentive for going below for warmth. Out of the cold weather, the captain's order went below received an enthusiastic response from his shivering crew.

The snow flurries continued to fall all evening. Just before 11:00 p.m., Captain Beloux's cabin door opened, pushing the accumulated snow back, and Pierre emerged from within, carrying two lanterns. He went directly to the hatch and set them down long enough to place a bar across the hatch to prevent the crew from coming out.

He waited there until the cabin door opened once again. A lady emerged with a sword strapped to her side. She carried a small suitcase and a sea bag. Beneath her hooded cloak, she concealed two small pistols.

Beloux was close behind her, dragging a massive trunk across the slippery wooden deck. "Get over here, you idiot, and help me with this trunk," he demanded.

Pierre left the lanterns beside the hatch and hurried to his uncle to help. "Sorry, Uncle, I mean, Captain," he replied and took the lower end of the trunk by its leather handle. They struggled with the massive chest until they arrived at the north side of the ship, facing League Island. Pierre dropped his end with a loud thump beside the railing and went back to the hatch for the lanterns. When he returned to where his uncle stood shaking his head in disgust, he handed one of the lanterns to the captain. They began waving the two lanterns back and forth as the ready signal.

Anton, Raiko, and Bojko heard the footsteps and the baggage trunk dragging across the deck above them from below the deck.

Bojko looked up at the ceiling and asked: "What in the world is going on up there?"

Anton puzzled himself, shrugged his shoulders, and questioningly shook his head. "I don't know, but a few minutes ago, I climbed up the ladder and tried to open the hatch, but it wouldn't budge. Let's get over to the cargo hold and try to look up through the grating."

The trio worked through the ship's hull to the cargo hold. Then, Bojko used his gymnastic skills to help Anton climb up to the cargo boxes' top. Together, they peered through the grating and could see the captain and Pierre waving their lanterns in the night. Beside them stood a shorter, more delicate figure, leaning against the railing and staring into the night in expectation.

"Can you hear them? Bojko asked. What are they saying?"

"I don't know. The men onshore are too far away, and the wind is howling."

Suddenly, the captain raised his lantern above his head and pointed at something in the distance. Soon afterward, Pierre threw a rope ladder over the side with a loud thud against the ship's side.

"That can only be one thing," Raiko called up to his brother and Anton, "a longboat has come alongside the ship."

Sure enough, a scarf-covered head came over the side of the *La Patience*. The newcomer tied a rope to the end of the chest, dragged across the deck, and lowered it down to the still unseen longboat with Pierre's help.

"That has to be a female, Anton," Bojko said. "Look at the way she moves."

Suddenly, all the peculiar events in the captain's cabin during the voyage made total sense. Emilie's movements confirmed Anton's suspicions. But who was she?

The scarfed man handed Captain Beloux what appeared to be a heavy leather bag. Beloux loosened the rawhide strap that held the top closed and poured what looked like gold coins into the palm of his hand. He counted the cash and then nodded in approval.

The stranger reached out and tried to take the handbag away from the woman, but she refused to release it. She threw her right leg up over the railing and proceeded down the ladder in haste with the bag in one hand.

The captain waved her away with his hand as if to say, "Good riddance."

CHAPTER TWENTY
ARRIVAL IN PHILADELPHIA

The La Patience spent the night at its anchorage opposite League Island for safety reasons: the wind was strong, the early snowfall was blinding, and the darkness of the cloud-covered night unyielding. To continue would have been a recipe for disaster.

When the Gypsy twins, Raiko and Bojko, awoke the following day, they hurried over to their friend's berth and shook their friend awake. "Anton," Raiko urged, "get up. It's daylight."

Anton pulled his woolen covers down from his face and squinted his eyes to focus on the dimly lit quarters. A single candle illuminated the room. He rolled over and pulled the brown burlap curtain from across the porthole, and light flooded into his eyes.

"What time is it? I can't believe the captain has allowed us to sleep this late?"

He waited for an answer that never came as he looked out the porthole at a snow-covered League Island. The snowfall had ceased, but its effect was over ten inches of cold, fluffy whiteness covering the ground and the ship's deck.

Anton had slept fully clothed after attempting to go topside the previous night. He sprung from his berth and lighted onto the floor as nimbly as a cat leaping from a tree branch. Anton, and the Gypsy twins, moved to the ladder where Bojko led the way up to the hatch. He pressed against it with his hand, half-expecting it to be barred, but to his relief, the heavy, snow-covered lid opened. Bojko lifted the hatch door, which caused snow to fall through the opening and down on Raiko and Anton.

"Come on up, mates," Pierre, who had stood watch all night, called out. "And bring all your mates with you if you please. We need to get this snow off the deck before moving on. The weight has settled us down a good three to four inches in the water.

"And, Mr. Smith," he ordered Anton, "You'll be standin' watch while I get me some shut-eye. Knock on the cabin door when this snow is gone to move on. Clear the masts first, then the decks and the railings. We'll be in Philadelphia afore noon, and the decks will be crowded with departin' passengers and customs officials. I won't be havin' any trouble with injuries, now, will I?" Pierre had Anton stand by the wheel and then retired to his cabin.

Three hours later, the ship was underway again. It sailed around a sharp bend in the river on the east end of League Island and the winding Delaware River. Shortly after noon, the City of Philadelphia came into sight amid a flurry of activity as the passengers, cooped up from weeks at sea, began bringing their precious belongings on deck to disembark.

Captain Beloux guided the *La Patience* as close to the docks as permitted and awaited the longboats to steer his ship the final distance with ropes. When the crew safely secured the boat, Captain Beloux had Pierre ring the captain's bell to quiet everyone down for an announcement.

"Now, I'm sure everyone is anxious to gather up their belongings and get off this ship. However, there are a few formalities that must first observe. All passengers who wish to reside here in Penn's Woods must accompany the customs officials to the State House, where they will be required to swear an oath of allegiance to King George II of England. They will be required to disclaim all allegiances to their former King and Country. There are no exceptions."

The deckhands connected a gangplank to the dock. The passengers were lined up for their trip to the State House by the passage class. A beautiful black woman named Maisha was at the head of the third-class line, accompanied by her French/German husband, Robert DeWitt. She leaned closer and reminded him of something vital: "Be sure to use your best German language skills. Remember, we're not French. Our papers say you are a German citizen of French descent. They'll be very suspicious of us if they know we are French citizens, and we don't want them to search our persons too closely and find our letters of credit."

DeWitt nodded in agreement at what his wife had said. Soon they were walking down the gangplank on their way to take their oath of allegiance. Maisha felt happy to be in the New World and to have the opportunity to start a new life with her husband.

When the last passenger had left for the State House, Pierre and the captain gathered Anton, Raiko, and Bojko together. The captain seemed emotional for the first time since their departure from Rotterdam. "Boys, I know we've been through this a hundred times, but I must ask once more: Is there anything I can do to convince you to sign on as crew members? My inclination is to shanghai you, and keep you against your will, but that wouldn't be right. You have performed admirably on this voyage. Will you reconsider my offer?"

Captain Beloux had no takers. "All right then, mates, grab your bags and catch up with the folks who are on their way to the State House. May God go with you until we meet again."

The trio lost no time in wasted farewells. They grabbed their bags amid a noisy flood of good wishes from the crew, saluted the captain and Pierre, and ran down the gangplank toward their destinies.

CHAPTER TWENTY-ONE
ANNE'S DECISION

Erlach, Switzerland
Early December 1753

The snow had fallen steadily for several days now, and Anne looked from her bedroom window, across the white fields, past the leafless apple orchards to the distant farmhouse where her fiancé had once lived. Memories flooded her mind, and tears filled her eyes as she longed for just one more caress, one more stolen kiss, or even the hint of a smile. But today, she would not let loneliness dominate her thoughts. Anne intended to make today a happy day, filled with joy and laughter. Today her brother and sister would come home for the holidays, and the family would be a unit once again, if only for a few short weeks. She would not let anything ruin that.

Suddenly she saw movement down the lane that led to her family's farm. *Yes. It's them. They're here.* Anne could see the much-anticipated sleigh carrying its two occupants—a young priest accompanied by his biological sister—a nun—dressed in black and smiling from ear to ear. They were happy to be home again after an absence of nearly four years.

"Mama!" Anne Welti shouted. "They're here...they're here. We must make this the best Christmas ever." Without considering a coat, Anne ran to the kitchen door and pulled on the door handle. She pulled hard against the door. It resisted at first until the frozen snow that held it in place gave way. Then she ran to the sleigh now parked at the rear of the farmhouse. Her sister, Maria, had already climbed down from her seat and stood in the snow with her arms outstretched. Anne ran into the embrace of her twin sister. It was like a part of her body had finally been returned to her. It was like an arm, once severed, now reattached.

The girls hugged and cried and danced around in circles of joy until they finally fell into the cold snow.

"Hey, what about me?" her brother, Father François, called out.

Anne struggled to release from Maria's embrace and to stand up. She ran to her brother and embraced him.

"Go inside, children." Ross Welti said to this son and daughter, "You must be frozen. I'll unhook the sleigh and take care of your horse."

Mutter Welti took the hands of her son and daughter and led them into the kitchen, where the aroma of freshly baked *brochten*[9] filled the air. "You two sit down at the table and nibble on some fresh bread while *Mutter* and Anne cook you up some ham and eggs."

"No, *Mutter*," Father Francois insisted, "sit here with us. We can eat later. We want to see your smiling face and to talk with you. It's been too long."

"Go ahead and sit with them, *Mutter*," Anne said as she pulled back a chair for her mother and gently nudged her down. "I can handle the cooking while you visit."

Anne set the table and finished cooking when her father returned to the barn house. Ross washed his hands and joined his family at the kitchen table.

The Welti family caught up on each other's lives while the family feasted on farm-raised ham, hand-churned cheese, and fresh-baked *brochten* sandwiches. The conversation remained upbeat and never once touched about the baby being given up for adoption.

"Let me make some more coffee," Mrs. Welti said as she started to get up from her chair.

---

9 German hardroll

Her son reached out, took her hand. "Wait, just a moment longer, *Mutter*," he said. "Maria and I have something we need to discuss with you, and the sooner, the better."

Mutter Welti, concerned by the severe tone she perceived in her son's voice, sat back down and said, "What is it? What's wrong?"

"There's nothing wrong, *Mutter*," he replied. "I wanted to talk about an honor Father Roten bestowed upon Maria and me. Bishop Roten came to see me last month. He told me about an amazing opportunity for me at a new church. He wants me to serve as Pastor there for at least four years."

His parents beamed with pride at the Church's confidence in their son. Their eyes shifted to their daughter Maria as her father asked: "He said it was an opportunity for the both of you? Are you going to work alongside your brother, Maria?"

Maria reached over and took hold of her mother's folded hands. "Yes, *Mutter*. I'm going to be with François. I'll be serving as a nurse in the hospital there."

Mrs. Welti smiled at first, but then her smile waned as she realized neither of them had mentioned the location of this new church. "I'm almost afraid to ask," she said, "but exactly where is this new assignment?" Total silence fell over the room as all eyes fell on Father François, sheepishly looking down at the tabletop.

"Actually," he said, "it's a brand-new church named *La Visitation-de-la-Bienheureuse-Vierge-Marie* in New France—Montreal, to be exact. But it's only for four years. We'll both be back before you know it."

Tears welled up in his mother's eyes. "New France? Four more long years? You've got to be kidding. That's thousands of miles and an ocean away. Nobody ever sees their family again once they go to the New World." Mrs. Welti crossed herself and looked up as though searching for God. "Lord, what have we done to be punished like this? You're taking my children away from us one by one. After all, I've done to be a good Catholic. Would you have me die a childless old woman?" She put her head down on her folded arms and wept.

Ross Welti tried to remain a man of reason. "Will you be back in four years for certain? We have only your younger brother now to help with the farm, and he's been spending all of his time with that Hildegard Shultz girl."

"I know, Papa," Francois said, "but Maria and I are in the service of the Church and wouldn't be here to help you no matter where we served. The bishop has promised it will only be four years. We'll be back in Switzerland before you know it."

Ross Welti asked, "When will you be sailing?"

"Not until early spring. I'll be helping Father Benedict here at our local church, but Maria and I can help you on the farm until a few weeks before we leave in mid-March. That's when we leave for Paris. We'll be there for a couple of weeks, and then from Paris, we will sail to Montreal."

Maria had remained quiet during the entire conversation and kept her thoughts to herself. *Maybe I'll be able to find my son in New France and see him again. Lord, I promise not to interfere in his life. I only want to see him and know someone is caring for him.*

Anne also kept quiet and had her private thoughts: *I wonder how far New France is from Philadelphia? If I could go along with them, perhaps I could slip away to see Anton in Philadelphia. Please, Lord, let me go along with my brother and sister to Montreal.*

Holiday cheer filled the next three weeks. The *Tannenbaum* was decked with candles and strewn with popcorn strung on string and wrapped around the tree. However, amid all the decorations and excitement, Anne hurdled a constant barrage of questions at Maria about New France:

"How far is it from Philadelphia? How long would it take to travel to Philadelphia? Would Maria and François have any reason to travel to Philadelphia?"

"Why are you constantly asking about Philadelphia?" Maria asked. "It's quite a long distance away from Montreal. Besides," Maria said, "France and Britain are not exactly on good diplomatic terms. Such a trip would be hazardous, if not altogether impossible, to make."

Anne hesitated to tell her sister why she was so interested in Phila-delphia, but the twins had never kept secrets from one another. Anne pledged her sister to secrecy and then proceeded. "A lot has happened in the four years since you left home. I've fallen in love with one of our neighbors." Anne filled Maria in on all the details, including Anton's departure to Philadelphia. They were two very different women now. Their lives became altered by various circumstances: Maria's life by her rape, the birth of her son, and her decision to become a nun, Anne's life by her love for Anton, the refusal of both families to accommodate their relationship. Anne, subsequently, decided to take whatever action she and Anton needed to be together as husband and wife. When Christmas and the new year arrived, Anne's decision was irreversible.

CHAPTER TWENTY-TWO
PASSENGER SCREENING

Seventy percent of all German arrivals in the New World— between 1727 and 1775— arrived by way of Philadelphia, over seventy thousand in all. Great Britain, fearing war with France and suspicious of the political intentions of the Pope, wanted to limit the immigration of the French and the immigration of all Roman Catholics, in general. There were exceptions for Jews, French Huguenots, who suffered religious persecution from King Louis, and Monrovians who worked among the American Indians. However, all immigrants not of British origin were required to take the Oath of Allegiance, in which they disavowed any allegiance to former kings and the Pope. The new arrivals were then required to immediately receive the sacraments in the Church of England to prove their loyalty.

Anton, Raiko, and Bojko ran down the gangplank and across the crowded pier as fast as could to catch up with the passengers headed to the State House for the Oath of Allegiance to the British Crown. They turned the icy corner on Chestnut Street and saw the tail end of their group filing along in the packed snow on the cobblestones. They caught up with them as the group crossed Second Street and Walnut.

Maisha, the tall black African woman, turned around when she heard the hurried footsteps of the approaching trio and tapped her husband, Monsieur Robert DeWitt, on the shoulder. DeWitt turned to see who his wife was pointing at and, upon recognizing the three familiar crew members, waved to Anton, Raiko, and Bojko and waited for them to catch up.

"Are you going with us to take the oath?" Maisha questioned.

"Yes," Anton replied. "We plan to make our lives here too. Do you think there'll be room for us?"

Mashia grinned. "It looks like this wild land has room enough for many more. Come with us. We'll walk with you."

When the group arrived at the State House, constructed only five years earlier, they found it be impressive. It was not at all what they had expected in this new land. The building, built of brick, featured the main facade over 100 feet long, with wings on either side measuring 50 feet each. It was clear the British were here to stay.

During the sail across the Atlantic, the passengers had long discussions about the mandatory Oath of Allegiance requirements. The oath's content bothered Raiko's conscience. He pulled Bojko aside for a private conversation before they went into the State House.

"I feel strange about disavowing the Pope and the Roman Catholic Church," he whispered to his brother. "Our mentor, Bernardo Sculisi, who brought us to Christianity, was Roman Catholic. We've been to the Vatican, worshiped on more than one occasion in the Sistine Chapel, knew several bishops, and considered ourselves Catholics. What should we do? And what do we tell them when they ask us about our national origin? We're darker than most people. They may accuse us of being Islamic."

Bojko, who had given their situation a great deal of thought, replied the way he thought Bernardo would have answered: "Bernardo taught us to take a broader view of Christianity than some others may take. He taught us that Scripture verse from Galatians 3:28:

"'There is neither Jew nor Greek; there is neither bond nor free, there is neither male nor female: for ye is all one in Christ Jesus.'

"Our loyalty is to our Savior, not to any organization. Therefore, I have no problem with any church so long I stay true to the body of Christ."

"While we live in lands controlled by King George II, and he doesn't ask me to violate my Christian principles, I can remain loyal to Britain. If the king requires me to violate those principles, everything changes, and I'll deal with it when it happens."

Raiko thought for a minute and then nodded in agreement. "I'm with you," he said. "But it still feels weird to disavow the Pope. Disavowing the King is not a problem for me. After all, they all wanted us dead when we were in Europe, regardless of what religion the respective king claimed to practice. Come to think of it, even the Roman Catholic Church had policies against we Gypsies. Let's hope for better acceptance here in the Colonies than we had in Europe."

The passengers of the *La Patience* crowded into a large reception room at the State House, where a powdered-wigged official sat at a large table in front of a blazing brick fireplace. His two male secretaries sat on either side of him, each holding copies of the ship's passenger list.

The wigged official stood up and tapped on the pine table with a bejeweled cane to get everyone's attention.

"Ladies and gentlemen, please, may I have your attention?" he spoke with a strained voice of authority as he surveyed the room as if looking for suspicious characters. His eyes settled on Maisha, Bojko, and Raiko.

"My name is Jonathan Heardly. Shortly, you will please form three lines for processing, one line in front of each of the officials. Those accepted people will be required to sign an Oath of Allegiance for His Majesty, King George II of England; those not found to be acceptable will need further processing.

"You will then please remain in the room until the Most Honorable, Governor Thomas Penn, administers the official oath."

Pointing toward the back of the room, he called out, "You three back there, the negro woman, and those two young dark-skinned men, please come directly to my line, now."

As the lines began to form at the table, Raiko, Bojko, and Maisha accompanied by Monsieur DeWitt and Anton Smith, moved to the head of the line in front of Mr. Heardly, Maisha's husband taking the lead.

Robert DeWitt waited nervously at the head of the line until the official quit fumbling his papers and finally looked up at him.

"So, what's your name? Is this negro woman your slave?" Heardly asked in a voice that denoted disgust.

"My name is Robert DeWitt," he replied in firm response.

The official ran his finger up and down the list until it came to rest on the passenger's name. "There must be some mistake, Mr. DeWitt. You are listed here as having a wife by the name of Maisha, not a slave."

"This is my wife, monsieur. Her name is Maisha, and I assure you she is my lawfully wedded wife."

Heardly wrinkled his eyebrows as if in doubt. "Hmm... Maisha? What a curious name, indeed. What is your country of origin, Maisha?"

"Africa," she immediately replied. I am an African—a free woman more recently of Strasbourg. My name means 'life' in my native Kiswabili tongue."

"So then, more recently, you are French? Are you a Roman Catholic too?"

"No, sir," Robert interrupted. We are Huguenots. As I am sure you know, many Huguenots come from Strasbourg because Strasbourg has always been a 'Free City,' if you will, a 'City of Refuge' since medieval times. The one city in France that tolerated all faiths, and one could escape persecution."

"Really. Do you have Baptismal Certificates, then?"

"No. Of course not; at least we don't have our baptism certificates here. Why would we carry them around with us?"

"I'm sorry, M. DeWitt, but without some certification that would indicate you are something, besides French sympathizers, or Roman Catholics, you will need to get back on the *La Patience* and leave Philadelphia. Your options are to return to Europe, go to the Carolinas, or Nova Scotia. The choice is yours, but you cannot remain here in Philadelphia."

Heardly stood and called to his security agents: "Guards!" Please escort the DeWitts back to their ship."

Two guards came forward and removed Robert and Maisha, under protest, and took them directly back to the boat.

CHAPTER TWENTY-THREE
THE OATH OF ALLEGIANCE

Next in line were Raiko and Bojko, accompanied by Anton.

Heardly, already swollen with righteous indignation in thinking he had done King George II service by rejecting the DeWitts, had unjustly formed the pre-gone conclusion that rejecting the Gypsies would be his next act of patriotism.

"What are your names?"

The twins had pre-determined to use their biological father's surname since their adopted name of "Scalisi," an Italian, would be a sure sign of trouble in England's colonial domain.

"Our names are Raiko and Bojko Celje," Raiko answered with pride.

"So, gentlemen, what's your story? Are you French Papists, too?" he said with a vile smirk.

"No, your honor," Raiko responded as he shook his head. "We are law-abiding Christians—businessmen—if you will."

Heardly used his finger as an index to scroll down the passenger list. "What's your country of origin? Oh, yes, here you are. Romanians, huh? Hmm—Raiko and Bojko Celje? —very peculiar names."

"We will have no problem taking and signing the Oath of Allegiance to the King of England."

"You have about two minutes to convince me of that.

"We are Romanian by birth and Huguenots by choice. Our surname is Celje; C-E-L-J-E," Bojko answered.

"We don't have any use for vagabonds or Gypsies here in Philadelphia." He paused and then looked up into Bojko's dark brown eyes. "How do you intend to support yourselves?"

Bojko was furious at the agent's slur against his ethnic origin but fought to contain his temper. "We, sir, are well-funded and intend to start a business. We are certainly not vagabonds."

The mention of "well-funded" immediately caught Heardly's attention.

Heardly fought back a laugh at the claim by these two dark-skinned men, dressed as seamen, that they had money. He pushed his chair back from the table and motioned the guards to come forward for another extraction.

Bojko, realizing he and his brother were about to be rejected like the Dewitts, pulled open his jacket, tore back the lining, and revealed the letters of credit he had sown inside. "Your honor, I can prove what I am saying if only you will give me a chance!"

Just as the guards grabbed the brothers by their arms, Heardly threw up his hands and shouted, "Wait! Let's allow these men to prove their position." Waving his right hand in a gesture of dismissal to the guards, he said, "Remove yourselves. I'll call you back if I need you." Then, turning to Bojko, he said, "Why don't the two of you come over to the corner with me, and we'll see if we can work something out."

Heardly got up from his desk and motioned the brothers to follow him to a secluded corner behind his desk to talk privately.

He put his arms around them and drew them close to him to talk discreetly. He spoke in a whisper. "Gentlemen, you have no real proof, except your letters of credit, to verify anything you have told me is true. As you can imagine, if I allow you to reside in the colony and the government discovers you to be an enemy of the state, it could put me in serious jeopardy. I should like to think that such a risk, on my part, would be worthy of some modest compensation. Shall we say—oh, I don't know— fifty pounds?"

Bojko looked shocked at Raiko and was about to object when Raiko put his hand on Bojko to calm him and said, "I believe fifty pounds sterling would be a reasonable fee, your honor. But we don't have that kind of cash on us. We'll need to go to a banking house, establish an account, and make a withdrawal."

"No problem," Heardly said through a smile. I'm sure I can have one of the guards accompany you there after the oath."

The clock on the wall above the fireplace gonged four chimes. Heardly immediately glanced up at the clock, and his face became panicked. "I... ah...I'm afraid it is getting late, gentlemen. I'll tell you what: The banking houses are about to close, and we must either process you today or send you back to your ship. Why don't I go ahead and send you a guard to the banking house to get the cash for our little transaction? In the meanwhile, I'll take care of your paperwork. When you get back, everything will be ready for you."

"Fine," nodded Raiko. "And I'm sure you'll have no problem processing our friend from Switzerland, Anton Smith, who is standing behind us in line."

"Again, no problem. It's a pleasure doing business with you two fine Christian business people."

They returned to the table, and Raiko, Bojko, and Anton where they were required to sign the following oath:

I do sincerely promise and swear, That I will be faithful and bear true Allegiance to His Majesty KING GEORGE the second, So Help me God.

That I do from my Heart, abhor, detest and abate as Impious and Heretical, that damnable Doctrine and Position that Princes Excommunicated or deprived by the Pope or any authority of the See of Rome may be deposed or murdered by their subjects, or any other whatsoever: And I do declare that no Foreign Prince, Person, Prelate, State or Potentate, hath or ought to have, any Justification, Power, Superiority, Preeminence, or Authority, Ecclesiastical or Spiritual, within the realm of GREAT BRITAIN. So, Help me, God.

I do Solemnly and Sincerely, in the presence of GOD, Profess, Testify, and Declare, I do believe that in the Sacrament of the LORD'S SUPPER, there is no Transubstantiation of the Elements of Bread & Wine into the Body & Blood of CHRIST, at or after the Consecration, thereof, by any Person whatsoever: And that the Invocation, or Adoration of the Virgin Mary, or any other Saint, and the Sacrifice of the Masses, as they are now used in the Church of Rome are Superstitious and Idolatrous. And I do, in the presence of GOD, Profess, Testify, and Declare, That I do not make this Declaration and every Part thereof, in plain and ordinary Words Real unto me, as they are commonly understood by English Protestants, without any Evasion, Equivocation, or Reservation whatsoever; and without any Dispensation from any Authority or Person whatsoever; or without any hope of any such Dispensation from any Authority or Person whatsoever, or thinking that I am or can be acquitted before GOD, or Man, or absolved of this Declaration, or any part thereof, although the Pope, or any other Person, or Persons, or Powers, whatsoever should dispense with or annul the same, or declare it Null and Void from the beginning.

Raiko looked squarely into Bojko's eyes and whispered, "I don't think I can sign an oath like that. We are new Christians, and I still have mixed feelings about worshiping God. I would be a true hypocrite to sign a document that contains matters I don't fully understand."

"Me too," said Bojko. What do we do now?"

Raiko, noticing the hurried look on Heardly's face, took advantage of the circumstances. "Your honor, we don't have time to read, with due diligence, this important oath. We are running out of time. If you don't mind, we'll go ahead and proceed to the banking house while you handle the paperwork."

"Shew!" the magistrate said with a wave of his fingers as if chasing them away. "Get going. I don't want you to get to the banking house after closing. Just go!"

Bojko turned to Anton and said: "Please wait for us, outside, if necessary, until we get back."

Anton nodded.

Relieved they would not have to perjure themselves; the Gypsies were escorted out of the State House by the appointed guard and hurried down the street to the banking house.

Anton had no difficulty dealing with the oath's content, so the Honorable Mr. Heardly immediately processed his acceptance.

When all acceptable applicants were cleared and had signed the oath, the government officials gave a short, matter-of-fact speech and a brief appearance by the governor. Then the oral Oath of Allegiance is followed immediately by a giving of the Sacraments. Four hours after their arrival at the State House, the immigrants became legal residents of Pennsylvania.

When the twins got the necessary cash from the banking house and returned to the State House, they found Anton waiting patiently outside the locked building under the guard's supervision.

"Where will you go now?" Bojko asked of Anton Smith, saddened by the realization that he and Raiko were saying goodbye to their friend.

"I'm a tailor and fashion designer," replied Anton. "Twenty-thousand people live here in Philadelphia, with more arriving every day. Philadelphia is where the people are, and this is my best opportunity to launch my career. What about you two?"

"Well," Bojko replied while trying to conceal a smile, "we have somewhat of an inheritance that will see us through. Our dream is to start a circus, as we told you about during our way here. First, however, we want to see the frontier and to see these so-called 'Indians.' Secondly..." Bojko stopped there as if embarrassed to continue.

"Secondly, what?" Anton asked.

"Secondly, Raiko answered for his brother, "We want to find suitable wives."

Anton laughed. "I know that concept all too well. As soon as I get settled with a regular income, I will send for my beloved Anne, about whom I've already told you. I miss her desperately."

"Where will you live, and how will you survive until you get started?" Raiko asked.

"I have a little extra money the captain paid me for making his new uniform and some money I could bring from home. It won't last long, but it should get me started."

"Let us help you," Raiko pleaded. "We have more than we need."

"Yeah, sure. That's why you worked for your passage. Right?"

Raiko again looked embarrassed. "You don't understand. We worked because we didn't want anyone to know we were carrying letters of credit. Discrimination has followed us all our lives, and we don't want to be taken advantage of anymore. Please allow us to help you. It's the Christian thing to do. It's something our benefactor, Bernado Scalisi, would have wanted us to do."

Everything within Anton wanted him to accept their help, but he couldn't do it.

The guard looked through a window and saw Heardly waiting impatiently in front of the fireplace, drawing on his long pipe. The guard tapped on the window. Heardly, turned around, and glad they were back, he rushed to the door with papers in hand to let them in.

Raiko put his hand on Anton's shoulder and said, "Please, Anton, this should only take a few minutes, wait for us, and we will find a place, together, to spend the night. At least allow us to treat you to dinner?"

Anton nodded in agreement as the sound of Heardly unlocking the door was heard behind them.

Heardly held out the immigration papers in hand. "No need to delay you, gentlemen, any further than we already have. I took the liberty of signing the oath on your behalf. Hold up your right hands, please.

"Do you promise to be good citizens? "

"Yes," they both replied.

"Good. With the power invested in me blah, blah, blah, and so on, here are your papers. Now get out of here, and by the way, keep our little transaction secret, or you'll not know what hit you. Understood?"

Raiko nodded as he handed Heardly the cash. After Heardly counted the money, he gave the guard a silver coin, locked the door behind himself, finished buttoning his coat, and turned and walked away.

Happy they did not need to sign the oath or take it, Raiko and Bojko departed the State House joyful to have this part of their lives behind them.

Raiko turned to Bojko and hugged him intently. "Do you realize, my dear brother, this is the first time in our lives we have ever lived anywhere legally? Smell that air, Bojko. What do you smell?"

"Smoke from wood burning in fireplaces?" he replied.

"No, you silly man. Freedom. That's what you smell—freedom."

The three friends walked the streets of Philadelphia full of hope for a brighter future, searching for a place of lodging.

CHAPTER TWENTY-FOUR
A CHANGE OF PLANS

The *La Patience* sat higher in the water now with its lighter load. Most of the passengers, some of the crew, and its legal cargo had departed the ship. A pathway through the snow on the deck enabled better footing, but the stubborn ice clung to the masts, and every horizontal surface glimmered in waves of shimmering light in the afternoon sun. The *La Patience* possessed the eerie appearance of a crystal ghost ship: lifeless, without its former vitality, and dead in the water. The melting ice dripped a steady rhythm of water onto the deck, tap, tap, tap, like the persistent tapping of a musician's metronome. The only sign of life was a lone sentry. He stood on the pier at the bottom of the gangplank, shivering beneath a heavy, brown woolen coat, his head covered in a stocking cap, and shifting his weight from leg to leg in an apparent effort to keep the circulation moving in his cold toes. His orders were to allow no movement on or off the ship.

Maisha DeWitt, wrapped in a royal blue cape, given to her three years earlier by her former teenage charge, Emilie De Fontaine, walked cautiously across the snow-packed planks of the pier. She approached the ship's sentry, accompanied by her husband, and a British guard from the statehouse. The sentry held up his hands in front of him to indicate they should stop.

"Permission to come aboard to speak with Captain Beloux," requested the husband.

The sentry, who recognized the DeWitts as passengers who had planned to remain in Philadelphia, nervously looked at the British guard and then back at Robert. The sentry did not want to arouse the suspicion of the British guard. It would not be in Captain Beloux's best interest for the British customs officials to come nosing around their ship. "What is your business with the captain?"

"We need to discuss the passage with him," Robert responded.

The sentry walked to the top of the gangplank and called the captain in a loud voice. Soon, the door to Beloux's cabin opened, and his bearded head peeped outside. "What is it?" the captain inquired.

DeWitt called out from the bottom of the gangplank before the sentry had a chance to answer: "We need to talk with you about booking a new passage."

The captain, no longer dressed in the colorful new uniform Anton made him, stepped outside, and motioned the couple to come to his cabin. The British guard, anxious to return to the warmth of the state-house and satisfied that his charges were safely delivered into responsible hands, turned, gave a mocking half-hearted salute, and started back.

Beloux wore a puzzled look of surprise inside the captain's quarters and seated the couple at his table. He pushed his cup of hot tea aside, without offering refreshment to his guests, and asked: "What are you doing back here? I thought you were intent on staying."

"Believe it or not," Robert DeWitt replied in a tone of disgust, "the government won't allow us into the colony. I can't believe it, but the magistrate ordered us to leave immediately because of our French origins. Where do you sail to from here?"

Beloux hesitated to answer spontaneously because his destination was forbidden to sail under a British flag and registry. He paused while he rubbed his beard in thought. "Let's just say we'll be sailing someplace north of here, where people of *our* national origin are welcome."

"Someplace north?"

Beloux smiled and walked to his porthole and looked outside as if for assurance, and nobody was watching. Then he walked to his armoire, pulled a folded, red, white, and blue bundle from the shelf, and held it close to his body while his back was still to the Dewitt couple. When he turned around to face his guests, he stood rigidly at attention, clicked his heels together, and said, in a verbal salute, *"Pour la Couronne et le pays!"*

CHAPTER TWENTY-FIVE
THE WHITE HORSE INN

Darkness came early to Philadelphia in December, and with the night, closed storefronts, and thinning traffic, as residents hurried home to the warmth of the family hearth and a warm meal. It was slightly after 5:00 pm, and already the sun withheld what meager heat it had miserly dispensed through the gray, cloud-covered skies. A cold wind blew steadily off the water as three deeply chilled newcomers wandered through this unfamiliar city, searching for lodging for the night.

"That looks like a popular spot," said Raiko as he pointed toward a large wooden sign that hung down from a wrought iron frame that hung out prominently from a brick facade. It had a large white horse painted on the sign and read: "The White Horse Inn."

"Let's go there and see if they have any rooms. The tavern looks crowded, and the smell of the food coming from within smells delicious."

"I... I don't know," Anton said. "It looks as though it might be a little too pricey for my budget."

"Come on, Anton," Bojko said, "We already talked about this. We agreed we would buy you dinner in return for all you've done for us. As far as the lodging is concerned, we can share a room. But, if we don't find a room before they fill all the vacancies, we might end up sleeping out in the cold." Bojko reached into his pocket, pulled out some British currency, and then handed it to Anton.

"What's this for?"

"We'd like you to arrange for the lodging while we wait outside."

"Why?"

"We'll tell you about it, later, over some ale," Bojko replied. "But for now, let's just say our dark skin may be a problem with some people."

Racial prejudice was a new concept for Anton. He had heard about the rejection of Gypsies and knew there had been some controversy about Gypsies in his home village of Erlach, but he had never met one. He was also eminently familiar with religious prejudice—that's what drove him to the colonies—but he had a tough time understanding Bojko's concerns.

"I don't understand why you're afraid to make your reservations, but I'd be happy to take care of the lodging for you since you are willing to let me stay with you."

Anton proceeded inside alone while Raiko and Bojko watched him through the inn's front window. They watched him approach a large, kindly-looking bald man behind the tavern bar, who wore a stained white apron.

"May I help you, young man?" the plump man said.

"Yes, please. I need a room for three men. It needn't be especially large or fancy."

"I think I can accommodate you," the proprietor said as he held out his right hand. "I own this establishment. My name is Richard Jennings."

Anton shook the proprietor's hand and replied, "Pleased to meet you, Mr. Jennings. My name is Anton Smith. I'll only need the room for one night, but it could be longer."

Raiko and Bojko peered through the inn's window and watched as Anton conferred with the innkeeper. They watched as he paid for the room, received change, signed a massive ledger, and the innkeeper handed him a brass skeleton key to the room. He turned toward the window where his friends waited and waved for them to come inside. Anton thanked the innkeeper and went to the door to meet his friends.

Anton attempted to hand Raiko the change from the money he had given him for the room.

"Why don't you hang onto that money for now. We can square up with each other after we eat," said Raiko. He pointed across the dimly lit dining room with its magnificent fireplace and low, hand-hewn ceiling beams toward a dark corner. "Let's hurry. I see only one empty table left at the back of the room."

Anton put the money into his pocket, and they tried to push their way past the bar to get to the table before someone else could claim it. They had proceeded only a few feet when an intoxicated patron grabbed Bojko's arm and shouted, "We don't allow Redskins here!"

The room fell silent, and Bojko stood frozen, unsure how to answer. Anton spoke on his behalf: "If you please, sir, release my friend's arm immediately. I assure you, he is not a 'Redskin,' as you called him. He is a Jew. This man received his immigration papers not one hour ago."

"Don't look like no Jew to me," the drunk said, still holding onto Bojko's arm. "Besides, a Jew ain't much better than a Redskin anyhow."

Just then, a young British officer forced himself through the crowded and smoke-filled tavern to defuse what had the potential to become an ugly confrontation. "Good afternoon, gentlemen. My name is Lt. Beck. May I be of some assistance here?"

The young Scott looked barely old enough to be a military officer. Anton guessed him to be about twenty years old. He was five feet, eleven inches tall, weighed about one hundred and seventy pounds, and had bright red hair and a handsome, freckled face.

"This here Redskin is claiming to be Jew, and I was just about to throw him and his Iroquois friend out into the street," the drunk said in a tone of righteous indignation.

Lt. Beck could tell the accuser's alcohol level had him at a point where he was far beyond his capacity to reason. He knew he must act before this situation got totally out of hand. He placed his hand on the man's shoulder in an agreeable manner and said: "I can handle this from here, sir. Thank you for your concern. Please release the man's arm."

The man released his grip on Bojko's arm. Lt. Beck turned to Bojko and said: "Did your friend say something about papers a moment ago?"

"Yes, sir," Bojko replied and withdrew his folded document from within his wool coat. He handed the papers to the officer.

Beck read the documents and then held them high over his head. "These documents," he shouted across the room so everyone could hear, "were issued to this man and signed by the governor so recently, the ink isn't even dry. As you all are aware, the Crown is not in the habit of issuing immigration papers to Iroquois." Then, turning to the Bojko and Raiko, he held out his hand and said, "Gentlemen, welcome to Philadelphia."

Beck turned to the ruffian and, with contempt, ordered him to leave the tavern and then disappeared into the crowd as abruptly as he had appeared.

The patrons soon went back about their business, and Anton, Raiko, and Bojko were seated at the table they had spotted earlier.

"Now, do you see why we wanted you to arrange for the room?" Raiko asked. "In one form or another, we have faced prejudice all our lives. As children, we watched our parents beaten, almost to the death, in Romania, and then watched as their owners sold them to a slaver. One of our reasons to come here to the colonies is in the faint hope we might find them."

Anton shook his head and paused in deep thought for a moment. Then Anton inquired, "Where do you intend to begin your search?"

"We're not sure," Raiko replied. "We have it on good authority they are in New France."

"New France? Then what are you doing here?"

"Well, we thought once we were here, we could..." Raiko lowered his voice to a whisper. "...we could slip into New France."

Anton leaned in closer to Raiko and motioned for Bojko to lean in too. Bojko drew closer.

"I believe you should talk to our friend, Captain Beloux," Anton suggested. "Trust me when I tell you he can get you there."

"How?"

"I overheard him and his nephew, Pierre, talking about it. I believe he has some cargo to be delivered to New France after leaving Philadelphia, but you had better talk to him soon. He leaves on the morning tide, the day after tomorrow. May I suggest you see him down at his ship at first light? Going from here to New France is illegal, but it's also possible."

A large bosomed blonde waitress came to their table wearing what looked like a low-cut German *dirndl* with a floral border. Instinctively, Anton looked up at her and said: "*Guten Abend[10].*"

At first, taken by surprise, the waitress asked: "*Was trinken Sie[11]?*"

Bojko looked up at the waitress and replied, "I'd like an ale, please."

She smiled and then took their orders for food and drink and left them alone at their table.

Anton, realizing that he and the waitress had conversed in Deutsch, turned toward Bojko and asked, "You understood what she said in German?"

"Yes, Raiko and I speak Romanian, Italian, French, and German—with several words and phrases of other dialects thrown in. We traveled extensively across Europe for several years with our adopted father, working in a circus. We had to learn these languages. After our adopted father, an Italian named Bernardo Scalisi, died, we traveled all over Europe to stay ahead of the henchman and stay alive. It is our inheritance from Bernardo that is the funding for our letters of credit, which has financed our stake in the New World."

Anton had wanted to ask them a question for almost the entire trip. Now that they were becoming fast friends, he mustered courageously to ask. "Please forgive me for asking you this extremely personal question, guys, but what's the story on your ears? In Switzerland, the government removes ears from Gypsies, and I couldn't help noticing that you both are missing the right ear. You keep your secret well concealed beneath your long hair, but I've been traveling with you for several weeks."

Both Raiko and Bojko hung their heads in unjustified shame. Raiko spoke first. "Yes, we are Gypsies. I was amazed when you told the lieutenant we were Jews because we told people in Europe to hide our true ethnic identity. But a shoemaker we worked for in Erlach, Switzerland,

---

10 Good evening
11 What do you want to drink

kept our due wages, and with the help of an evil priest, we met in Rome, betrayed us to the authorities. What you saw is the consequence of his betrayal.

That priest, who has absolutely no belief in anything except himself, has pursued us all over western Europe. We lived with French Hugue-nots, slept in the frigid cold, hid in barns, were imprisoned in Germany and hunted like animals, swam the ice-cold Rhine River, lived in the attic of a Catholic church in Erlach, Switzerland..."

"Whoa! Wait a minute!" Anton exclaimed, holding up his hand. "Did you say Erlach?"

"Yes. As fate would have it, we discovered the evil priest who had devoted himself to our demise was the assistant pastor at the same church where Good Father Benedict was protecting us."

Anton's mouth dropped open. "I know about whom you speak. You mean Father Thomas is the priest who persecuted you, don't you?"

"Yes, but how could you possibly know that? He raped a sweet young girl and then almost killed Father Benedict because Father Benedict caught Thomas in the act. To shift blame, he accused us of his dastardly crime, but we escaped."

"Incredible. Not only am I from Erlach, but my betrothed is that young girl's twin sister! Father Benedict recovered from his injuries, and his testimony, rumor has it, resulted in the immediate defrocking of Thomas. He disappeared soon after the incident and has not been heard of since," Anton added.

"We hid out," Bojko concluded, "for almost a year, until our adopted father, Bernardo Scalisi's estate, was settled. After the settlement of the estate, we met up with Bernardo's Jewish friend and confidant, who gave us our inheritance."

Anton, Raiko, and Bojko continued to marvel at the series of events and crossings of paths they shared as they dined the evening away at the White Horse Inn. God, they concluded, had brought them together. They talked the night away comparing notes. Anton and the Celje brothers pledged that no matter how many miles and years separated them, they would remain friends for life.

CHAPTER TWENTY-SIX
RETURN TO THE SHIP

December 10, 1753

Raiko curled in a fetal position as his muscular body shivered and ached beneath his brown woolen blanket at the White Horse Inn. His five-foot-ten-inch length was longer than the inn's blanket could accommodate. His aching muscles reminded him he hadn't been exercising to the standard to which he had become accustomed as a circus strongman.

Still half asleep, he had a feeling something was wrong, but couldn't apply reason to the problem. He pulled his blanket down from his face and sat up immediately in bed in a panic. *Where am I?* Then he remembered as he looked toward the dim morning light that filtered in from the room's single window. *Of course. The White Horse Inn.* Then he realized the cause of his feeling of disorientation. *Tonight, is the first night in weeks I slept without the ship's pitch and rolling on the ocean.* His acclimation to life on dry land would take some getting used to, but maybe his journey was not yet over. He remembered last night's discussion about asking Captain Beloux to take him to New France. Raiko reached over and shook his brother. "Bojko...Bojko. Wake up. We need to go see the captain."

The walk to the ship for the three friends was precarious. The water from the previous day's snowmelt had settled down between the cobblestones and frozen during the drop in the night's temperature. As they walked, puffs of white vapor blew from their nostrils in the cold morning air like smoke from fire-breathing dragons. They rounded the corner at

King and Front Streets intersection and saw the familiar *La Patience* still docked at Carpenter's Wharf. The sailor on watch was the same sentry who had greeted the DeWitts return to the ship the previous day.

The sailor smiled in surprise to see his former shipmates. "What's this? Do you want your old jobs back? It seems as though half the folks who left the ship have returned." The guard's former shipmates knew about the DeWitts' return and needed no explanation of his comment.

"It could be that we do want our old jobs back," Raiko replied. "May we speak with the captain?"

Captain Beloux had been in his cabin sharing breakfast with Maisha and Robert DeWitt and heard voices at the bottom of the gangplank. He went to his porthole, now with its curtains pulled back, and looked out.

"Well, I'll be," he said, delighted to see his three favorite sailors had returned. Before the guard even had a chance to call for him, the captain opened his cabin door and called for them to come up.

They arrived at the captain's cabin door and greeted its occupants.

"What are you doing here?" Beloux asked as Maisha, and Robert looked on in wonder. "You either came back to say good-bye, or you want your jobs back. I'm hoping for the latter."

"We need to speak with you about going with you to your next...destination," Bojko blurted out.

Beloux looked around to make sure nobody else was listening. Then with a nervous quiver not typically heard in his deep, confident voice, he said, "Good, I'm beginning to think too many people know about my 'next stop.' Please, keep your voices down."

The captain paused as he contemplated the consequences. Beloux did not want the British authorities to get wind of his intentions. He felt the need for an immediate departure. "Who all is going? All three of you?"

"Not me," Anton inserted. "I'm where I want to be."

Captain Beloux held out his arm in a farewell handshake and said, "Then this is where we must part company. I'm sure you'll understand my insistence that you keep your mouth shut."

"Of course," Anton said. He shook hands with the captain and embraced his two Gypsy friends. "This is not our final farewell. Our paths will cross again." Tearfully, Anton turned and left the ship with a void in his heart he hadn't experienced since leaving Anne back in Erlach, Switzerland.

Captain Beloux closed the cabin door, ushered the Gypsies to his round oak table, and shouted, "Cookie! Bring that big pot of tea you just made over here to warm our innards." Then he turned his attention back to his guests. "I know why the DeWitt couple want to head north, but what's your story?"

Raiko was about to start talking but hesitated until the cook set fresh cups on the table and poured tea into them. He set the large copper pot in the center of the table and left without saying a word.

Raiko picked up his cup and blew the steam off the top. He realized it was still too hot to drink and set the cup back on the table. Then he looked with a sad face at the captain and began: "Our parents..." and continued until he had told the captain the exact details, he and Bojko had told Anton back at the White Horse Inn.

"So," the captain said, "you think you can find your parents in New France after all these years? That was nearly twenty years ago. They could be dead now, for all you know."

"We'll take that chance, "Bojko interrupted, "but most of all, we want to bring closure to a huge cloud of doubt that had hung over our heads since the time our parents were taken away from us."

Captain Beloux shook his head in wonder that these young men, safe for the first time in their lives, would want to risk everything on this seemingly futile undertaking. "Here's the deal:" the captain said. "I'm not saying I'm going to where you want to go—that's illegal—but if, let's say, I need to pull into a French port for emergency repairs and you happen to jump ship, that's not my fault. Do you understand what I'm saying?"

Raiko jumped to his feet and smiled a broad smile of gratitude. "Thank you, Captain. Thank you."

"Now, you need to get out of my cabin and find my nephew, Pierre, who is somewhere in town drinking himself silly and probably shooting off his mouth about matters that could get us all hung. If you're going to serve under me, there is no time for lollygagging. Find him. I intend to sail tomorrow."

"So soon?" Raiko inquired.

"Yes, for two reasons. First, too many people seem to know my business. Secondly, this is December 10th. I want to be at my destination before the Winter Solstice. You probably don't know what the Solstice is, but..."

"Of course, we do," Bojko interrupted. It's when the planet tilts on its axis and begins the first day of winter. It happens every year between December 20-23. What date is the Solstice this year?"

"Well, I'll be..." the captain replied in amazement. "How do you know about astronomy?"

"Our stepfather, Bernardo Scalisi, saw to it that we received a good education. Please don't assume we're ignorant because we happen to have dark skin."

Captain Beloux looked embarrassed, and Maisha gave a resounding, "Amen to that!"

"It is likely that the St. Lawrence River will be frozen by January 1st. Even if the river is not frozen, there will be a high risk of icebergs sinking my ship. Depending on ice conditions, I may have to drop you off and have you make your way to Quebec City overland.

"The truth of the matter is that I need to get my cargo to Quebec City and unload it before the British government stops me and searches my ship. So, if it is possible to take you to Quebec City, you will need to stay with me long enough to help us quickly unload and get out of the St. Lawrence River before La Patience ends up crushed in the ice. Is that understood?"

The brothers smiled widely and nodded in unison, shook hands with the captain, and left the cabin to go search for the First Mate.

The brothers bypassed the most likely taverns along the pier to search for Pierre and went directly back to the White Horse Inn. They stopped at the tavern's bar and asked for the proprietor, who promptly appeared. After a brief conversation, they handed the innkeeper something, shook hands, and turned to leave when they ran straight into Anton, who had come downstairs and was about to depart the inn.

Anton was surprised to see them again. "Hey, what are you guys doing back here? I was on my way back to the *La Patience* to see how you fared. I was concerned about you."

Raiko smiled. "We wanted you to know, Anton, we've arranged for passage to where we believe we will find our parents. We sail tomorrow. After last night's conversation with you, we realized what we must do—at least try to do. We need to search for our parents and buy them out of slavery if we can.

"Why don't you walk us back to the pier where the captain thinks we'll find Pierre in one of the taverns? He wants him on board for an early departure tomorrow morning."

Anton agreed to go with them.

They eventually found Pierre in a tavern called *The Whaler*, an appropriately named tavern since Pierre was laying like a beached whale, sound asleep, in a booth at the tavern's rear.

It required all three men to carry him back to *La Patience*.

Anton left his friends at the ship's gangplank and returned to the White Horse Inn. He ate a meager breakfast of bread and coffee and then prepared to search for employment.

CHAPTER TWENTY-SEVEN
ABRUPT DEPARTURE

December 11, 1753

Mid-morning activity aboard *La Patience* had crawled to a snail's pace. Most crew members slept snoring in their berths, resulting from swollen adenoids from two nights of heavy drinking in the taverns along the pier. The same was true for Pierre, the first mate, who shared his uncle's cabin. It had been two hours since the brothers had brought him back to the ship, and by this time, Captain Beloux could tolerate his incessant snoring no longer. The captain pushed his chair back, got from the table, and went to Pierre's berth. He shook his nephew with vigor.

"Wake up, you scallywag," he shouted in a firm voice. "You can't fly with eagles if you flock with the turkeys. Wake up! I need to talk to you."

Pierre held his head in his hands and swung his feet, ever so slowly, over the edge of his bunk. He sat there with his elbows resting on his canvas pants with his fingers gently massaging his temples.

"I should have you keel-hauled for staying out all night. If I must depend on the second mate to do your job for you, why do I even need you? If you weren't my sister's boy, I'd throw you overboard."

The first mate looked up at Beloux through clouded eyes and whispered in a raspy voice, "Well, when you hear why I stayed at The Whaler drinking all night, you'll soon change your tune."

"I doubt that very much. But go ahead and give me your best shot. I'm sure this is going to be more of your poppycock."

"I stayed there because I was pumping information from a chap by the name of—Heardly…or Heardsly… or something like that."

"And what kind of information did you extract that would be of any possible value to me?"

"Well, it just so happens this chap is a person of importance at the State House. Once he got to drinking brandy—which cost me a fortune and for which you will want to reimburse me—he came down with a bad case of wagging tongue. He began to tell me he would lead a surprise inspection of the *La Patience* before its scheduled departure tomorrow morning. He didn't know, of course, I'm the first mate on this fine vessel."

"Heardly," the captain said as if talking to himself. "Yes, I've heard that name before. He's the one who refused to give the DeWitts their immigration papers. Well, blow me down. You finally have done something to pay for your existence."

"Cookie," the captain yelled. "Get my nephew some coffee and some dry tack to eat. We have a lot of work to do. We sail on the evening tide."

Night came cold and early as the *La Patience* sat readied for its unauthorized and unscheduled departure from Carpenter's Wharf. Activity had been restricted on deck to the bare minimum to avoid suspicion. A lone sentry stood to watch on the pier at the bottom of the gangway. The lone figure of the captain came out of his cabin to check the ship's readiness. He was a chronic planner and would wait until the ebbing tide's last possible minute to depart. If he could get pulled away, out of gunshot from the pier, the authorities would not have time to rig a gunship and give pursuit in the shallower tide before detection. They'd have to wait until morning, and the *La Patience* would be long gone.

He would wait until all activity at the taverns along the wharf had ceased before lowering his longboats and crew to connect the tug ropes. The cold dampness of the night had already restricted most of the regular activity in Philadelphia. He glanced at the gangway and noticed the ship had already settled down a foot from where it had been at high tide. Another hour was all the captain needed to execute his plan.

At 20:00 hours, he entered his cabin and aroused Pierre. "Get the crew lowering the longboats over the starboard side, and be quiet about it. Hang canvas between the longboats and the ship to absorb noise from rubbing or banging against the ship. And have the men stoop down below the railings to hide their profiles. We have the advantage of a new moon, but Heardly might have spies watching us. You never know, and we won't look pretty with our necks stretched from a British rope."

Pierre rubbed his neck at the thought of what it might be like to hang. The thought wasn't pleasant. He grabbed his coat and knit cap and departed on his mission to get underway.

The crew positioned themselves. The longboats lowered into the water with tow ropes attached, and the crew began to gently row until the tow ropes were tight against their effort. The captain signaled to the sentry, who had moved to the top of the gangway and hoisted the ramp. The crew secured the gangway and retrieved the ropes that held the ship to the dock, and the *La Patience* slipped silently away into the night.

CHAPTER TWENTY-EIGHT
ANTON'S START IN PHILADELPHIA

December 10, 1753

Anton left Raiko and Bojko at the *La Patience* and stopped at a bakery to get something to eat. The bread was cheap. He purchased two loaves of bread and a block of cheese. Everything was different here, and he was unfamiliar with the cheeses offered for sale. *I'll get used to trying new foods. It'll be fun to learn,* he told himself to remain optimistic. He ate one loaf while strolling back to the White Horse Inn. Anton entered the inn with the second loaf hidden under his arm because he was embarrassed about bringing food to his room. His plan to walk past the bar unnoticed failed when he heard the proprietor call out his name.

"Just a minute, Mr. Smith," the innkeeper shouted. "I need to talk to you. Would you step over here, please?"

Anton felt a surge of anxiety. *What could I have done wrong? I know I paid for the lodging when we checked in. Maybe he's upset with me because I'm bringing food to the inn instead of dining in his restaurant?*

The innkeeper disarmed Anton's anxiety with a wide smile. "How are you this morning, Mr. Smith? I noticed you were up and about quite early."

"Yes, sir," Anton replied. "My friends needed to talk with the ship captain of the *La Patience* this morning. I went there with them. Is everything all right?"

"Everything is quite fine," Mr. Jennings replied, still smiling. "I'm surprised you didn't pass your friend Raiko on your way here."

Anton turned quickly, ran to the inn's door, and looked down the crowded street in vain for Raiko. He didn't see him. Frustrated, he returned to the bar.

Mr. Jennings continued to smile. "Anyway, he's a most generous young chap. He insisted on paying for your lodging. He gave me enough money for you to keep your room for two weeks."

Anton was dumbfounded. "Two weeks? I don't know what to say. I never expected that."

The innkeeper looked at his guest with empathy and suggested: "If you don't mind me butting in where I may not belong, I have an idea that might be of some help to you." Without waiting for an acknowledgment from Anton, he continued. "I have a few rooms on the third floor that are small but less expensive than the one you currently occupy. If you are willing to take one of those, you could stretch your lodging out to almost a month. Let's go ahead and round it off to a full month." Handing a key across the bar, Jennings said: "Why don't you go have a look at number 301. I'd go up with you, but I'm needed here at the front."

Anton was immediately excited about the suggestion. "That's not necessary," he said. "I'll take it. Let me go move my things now, and I'll return the other key." Anton gratefully took the key and bounded up the stairs, skipping every other step and thrilled that something had finally gone his way. He gathered his belongings and went directly to the third floor.

The third-floor hallway was much darker and narrower than the second floor, illuminated by a lone window at either end. Most of the rooms Anton passed on the way to room 301 were marked "storage," and an odor of mustiness hung in the air. Anton correctly reasoned that the rooms on this floor seldom saw occupants.

Anton found his room at the north end of the hallway. He desperately tried to remain optimistic. *The door to the room is near the hall window, where I will have enough light to see the keyhole.* Anton pushed his key into the lock and tried to turn it. The lock resisted his effort. With more pressure than his first attempt, he tried again but became concerned the key might snap off in the process. He felt the metal key bend slightly, but then the tumblers in the lock clicked, and the key turned. *I would guess these rooms don't get rented out very often.*

He turned the doorknob and pushed the door inward. It opened in a three-quarter swing and then stopped against an obstruction. He tried again, but the obstruction was unmoving. Anton peeked his head around the door and saw that a single bed, stripped of linen to the bare mattress, blocked the door. He squeezed through the partially open door, placed his suitcase on the bed, and turned to get a better look at his room.

The room was ten feet wide and twenty feet long with a single tall, narrow window covered with a yellowed—once white—lace curtain that moved hauntingly like a ghost when the draft blew through the window that was badly in need of caulking. *At least I'll have a constant supply of fresh air.* Anton navigated his body around an armoire, much too big for this small room. He then went to a small wooden desk and chair situated in front of the window. *Great. I'll have plenty of space to store my clothes, and the armoire will help block the light—and draft—from the window if I decide to take a nap during the daytime.* Such as the room was, it was affordable, and it was home.

All in all, he was happy with his choice of necessity. This room was all he needed, and it enabled him to stretch out his finances for a long time. *Indeed, with my training, I'll find employment in short order.*

Filled with optimism at his newfound good fortune, the young tailor left his room without unpacking and began his search for employment as a tailor with high expectations. The first few rejections hurt his feelings, but following rejection after rejection, his enthusiasm began to wane as the day wore on. He trudged down cobblestone streets covered with ice and down mud streets soaked in dirty wet snow that stuck to the soles of his boots. He went from the tailor shop to tailor shop with always the same answer: "Sorry, but we don't need any help right now. We have all the seamstresses we need."

Dressmakers? Are they ridiculing me? Yes, I think they are. They're suggesting that I want to do women's work. Why can't they understand that I'm a master tailor who is not only worthy of hire but probably better than the best tailor this city has to offer? I've tailored for King Louis IV of France, for crying out loud.

But being employed by the nemesis of King George of Great Britain was a lot closer to a hanging offense here than it was a strength of resume. He would need to keep that part of his career a secret. *If only I had the financing to start my shop, I know I'd succeed—but I don't, and I probably never will.*

Hunger beset him, and his feet became colder. His leather boots grew wetter with each labored step. The bitter weather and grey overcast skies seemed an omen of worse things to come. The streets became dark, and the shops began to close. It was 5:00 p.m. and Anton had presented himself to every tailor shop he could find in this section of the city. Business hours had ended, and he had no recourse left for this day. Anton returned to the inn and went directly to his room. There he prepared a sandwich from bread and cheese he had purchased on his way home, prayed over his meal, and retired to bed early.

Three weeks passed without any prospects of finding a worthy position and the futility of Anton's job search became more apparent with each passing day. By the end of his first month in Philadelphia, he had presented himself to every commercial tailor shop in the city—some twice—without success. His finances were in dire straits. His small, rented room on the third floor of the White Horse Inn was due for payment, and he was out of cash. Just when Anton reached the depth of his despair, and his sanguinity had turned to pessimism—his hope to hopelessness—the proverbial light appeared at the end of the tunnel.

Anton had just finished eating his last morsel of food and was about to admit defeat when he heard loud voices coming from the tavern on the first floor. He was angry at first that the people in the pub were having such a good time when he was so desperate. Anton laid in his bed for a while and listened to the conversation in the room beneath his. He struggled to distinguish the words uttered so loudly in the fervor of discussion beneath. Anton leaned across his bed and pulled open the door for better clarity. He couldn't tell for sure the context of the conversations, but he could tell from the pitch of the voices, and the vast number of patrons, something extraordinary was taking place. His curiosity piqued. Anton sprang out of bed, quickly dressed, and then hurried toward the steps leading down to the inn's tavern.

Anton's arrival at the landing on the stairs confirmed his suspicions of the importance of this gathering. The number of spectators seated on the stairs to listen to the speaker prevented Anton from descending farther. The speaker remained yet unseen by Anton. He pushed his way down the stairs stepping carefully between the men seated there. One of the men sitting on the stairs looked up at Anton when he noticed someone trying to get through the crowd. Anton leaned down to the man and whispered, "What is all the commotion?"

CHAPTER TWENTY-NINE
MONTREAL

December 20, 1753

The skillful navigation of Captain Beloux and good fortune brought the *La Patience* into the Saint Lawrence River without detection by the British Navy. Once inside St. Lawrence, the captain issued the order his French crew had long awaited: "Bring down the Union Jack and raise our true colors! For once, the weather is in our favor, and we will enter Quebec City."

A quick cheer went up from the crew. Had it not been for the intervention of Beloux, the French crew would have burned the British flag once it reached the deck.

"Don't be foolish," he ordered. "We may need that flag again. It's saved our hides more 'a once." Following his decree, he and Pierre folded the British flag, almost in reverence, and the captain took it into his cabin and put it in his armoire where he had previously stored the French flag.

"Enough of the celebrating for now," Beloux ordered. I want two long-boats over the side and out about a hundred yards in front of the ship as we navigate Quebec City. We need to be on the lookout for ice packs on the river. The last thing we need is to put a hole in the side of this ship."

The *La Patience* edged its way toward its destination.

The ship stopped for papers inspection at Fort Quebec, where Captain Beloux received permission to proceed to Montreal. Passengers Maisha and Robert DeWitt and shipmates Raiko and Bojko Scalisi-Celje stood in the cold wind at the ship's rails and tried to catch their first glimpse of Montreal, perched high atop the riverbanks.

"I know it's too much to hope for, brother," Raiko said as he turned toward Bojko, "but wouldn't it be wonderful if we found *Mutter* waiting at the dock to greet us?" When Bojko turned toward his brother, tears were streaming down from his brown eyes. "Maybe a wish like that isn't so silly after all. I was thinking the same thought. But even if they are here, they'd have no way of knowing we are coming. I'm afraid it's going to be a long, hard search."

Raiko refused to allow his brother's skepticism to dampen his optimism. "Well, brother, when you consider," Raiko said as he pointed up to the sky, "how He has directed our paths so far, nothing could happen that would surprise me. I have faith that something good is going to happen."

"I'm glad you have such confidence, but how do you know what will happen will be good?"

"The reason for my optimism is Romans 9:28: 'All things work together for good...'"

"Yea," replied Bojko, "but how do you know it will be good?"

"The answer is simple, my brother. We must believe that God is still the One in charge even if we don't like our prayers' outcome. The outcome will be for the total good—no matter what—even if we can't see the good at the time."

Bojko didn't answer. Instead, he looked at the outline of Montreal's walled fortress and silently prayed they would find Florica and Jànos, their Gypsy mother and Romanian-Magyar stepfather.

The *La Patience* docked at Montreal, and ever-caring Maisha turned to the twins and asked, "Where will you boys be staying?"

"We don't have any real plans yet. As you know, we intend to ask around for clues on where our parents might be. Captain Beloux has agreed to use his influence to inquire with the immigration officials to see if our parents appear on the immigration records as having arrived here. What about you and Robert?"

Robert intervened. "That's why we asked you about your immediate plans," he said. "Beloux told us about a business opportunity we may be interested in pursuing. As you know, my wife and I have experience running an inn. Beloux will introduce us to an elderly gentleman he believes is ready to go back to France and wants to sell his inn. We're considering it an option if it's a good fit and a good price for us. We were hoping you could come with us to check it out. Two extra sets of eyes would be a big help. The captain can't get away from the ship for a couple of days to make the introduction, so we thought we'd check into the inn unannounced and check the place out while incognito. By the time the captain gets there, we'll already have a pretty good idea of the inn's character. Will you come with us?"

"We'd love to come with you," Raiko answered.

"And be sure to keep your immigration papers from Philadelphia well hidden. They can only get you into trouble here."

"Not to worry," Raiko said as he patted his coat, "I've already sewn them into my lining."

Immigration in New France wasn't much different than in Philadelphia—only in reverse. Since 1627 when Cardinal Richelieu instituted the "Seigneurial System," only Roman Catholics were allowed to inhabit New France. So, in Quebec, the boys did what they needed to do. They used the name "Scalisi," after all, they were legally adopted by the Italian circus owner, Bernardo Scalisi. Declaring their Roman citizenship, they claimed to be Roman Catholics and swore allegiance to the Louis XV of France. A minor monetary consideration to the immigration official was necessary to speed up the paperwork. Maisha was questioned about her status as a free woman and had to produce the essential papers of her citizenship in Strasburg, France. Robert DeWitt had no problem at all. Within an hour, all four arrivals had their immigration documents.

The Celjes and DeWitts went directly from immigration to the La Fleur, the inn Captain Beloux had suggested to Maisha and Robert. It was an older building located on Rue Saint-Paul. Constructed of wood, it was one of the few survivors of the great fire of April 1734. The foursome entered the inn, and Robert approached the front desk under the proprietor's watchful eye.

"Good morning, monsieur," Robert spoke. "We'll be needing two rooms, one for my wife and me and one for our two friends here."

The innkeeper looked everyone over very carefully. "I'm sorry, but we don't take your kind here."

Robert's first instinct was to reach over and pull the older man across his desk, but better judgment prevailed. "Our kind?" he replied. "Exactly what do you mean by 'our kind?' Are you referring to the fact my wife is black, and my two friends are people of color?"

"Hey, look, monsieur," the old man said, "I don't want any trouble. But ever since Montreal was burned back in '34 by that black woman, *Marie-Josèphe dite Angelique*, and her white lover, Claude Thibault, folks around here are suspicious of your kind—you know—mixed couples, that is."

"Are you serious? That was twenty years ago. What happened?"

"You never heard about it? Most of the buildings along rue Saint-Paul burned to the ground, including Hôtel-Dieu Hospital, run by the Hospitaller Sisters. Since then, the governor passed a new ordinance requiring all new structures to be brick or stone. The sisters rebuilt the hospital out of brick, of course. As for me, I had considerable damage, but I was lucky not to lose my entire inn. As you will notice, the inn is one of the few remaining wooden structures."

"So, what became of the couple who started the fire?" Robert inquired.

The innkeeper smiled. "The woman was found guilty, then tortured and executed, of course. Thibault disappeared soon after the arrest of his black lover and was never heard of again. I guess that he's living somewhere out in the wilderness and married to a redskin squaw. But the one thing I do know is he had better never show his face around here again. The citizenry of Quebec will shoot Thibault on site.

"As for you folks, I'd suggest you either get back on your ship and leave here or consider moving thirty miles downriver to Quebec. Yes, now that I think of it, Quebec City would be a good place for you. It's a bit more of an outpost, less civilized, where folks are less sophisticated if you know what I mean."

Maisha could tell her husband was about to let his temper get the better of him. She took his hand and squeezed it gently. "Merci, Monsieur," Maisha said. "I think you have told us all we need to know. We'll try to find lodging elsewhere." She pulled on Robert's hand and led him away from becoming a significant confrontation. They departed the inn and walked through the muddy streets of Montreal in search of lodging.

"So many of the buildings look new," Bojko said. "Look over there. That church looks brand new. Let's go inside. I feel the need to pray for help in finding our parents."

They removed their muddy boots and went inside the beautiful, but simple church completed only the year before. They knelt side-by-side before the alter, crossed themselves, and stood beside the prayer candle rack. They each lit a red candle and placed it on the stand. Robert dropped a coin in the contribution box near the candles. Bojko glanced over to a dark corner of the church and saw a tall priest standing with his back to them. He was gesturing with his hands and engaged in an intense conversation with a woman who wore a headscarf and seemed very upset. The new arrivals went to a nearby pew and knelt in prayer while the priest and woman continued in a heated but controlled conversation, both careful not to let their voices rise to an audible level.

The voices—which got louder by the minute—were the only other sounds in the quiet sanctuary. After a few minutes, Bojko reached over and grabbed his brother's arm. "Raiko! Listen to that voice. I'd know that voice anywhere. Don't you recognize it?"

Raiko cupped his hands and held them to his ears to listen, but it was all in vain. "I can't hear it. You know I've got a hearing problem. I'm sorry I can't understand a word of what they're saying. But how could you possibly recognize the voice of a priest in Montreal? We just got here."

Bojko began to tremble. "Raiko, I'm telling you that priest is none other than evil Father Thomas from Erlach, Switzerland!"

CHAPTER THIRTY
A GLIMMER OF HOPE

December 22, 1753

Captain Beloux filed the necessary paperwork with the customs officials and returned to the *La Patience* to supervise his unloading military cargo. "Pierre," he shouted, "tell those idiots to quit smoking immediately." He ran over to the nearest crew member, pulled his pipe from his mouth, slapped him so hard the sailor fell to the deck, and threw his clay pipe overboard into the water. The captain looked furious as he surveyed his crew, who was now giving him their full attention. "I'll have the next one of ya hung from the mast who's stupid enough to smoke while we have a cargo of black power on board. Now throw those pipes into the water; every one of ya." Seven disgruntled seamen gave a series of begrudging "Aye, aye, Sirs" and hurdled their pipes into the Saint Lawrence River.

He turned to his nephew and said, "Now, if I can trust you think like a seaman, instead of a baboon, I'm going to leave you in charge while I go into town and take care of some pressing business."

"Aye. Where will you be in case, you're needed back here at the ship?"

"I'll be at your uncle's inn, the La Fleur. But if you send somebody to disturb me, it had better be for something of vital importance."

"Aye."

When he arrived at the La Fleur, he found his wife's brother, Louis Trudeau, behind the bar. It was mid-afternoon, and the inn was virtually empty. They hadn't seen each other for several months. They embraced.

"Well," Beloux said, "Don't keep me in suspense. What did they think?"

"What did who think?" Louis replied with a puzzled look on his face.

"The couple I sent to you about buying this flea trap—that's who, you idiot."

"I'm confused as to what you're talking about," Louis replied. "Trust me. I'd remember if anyone came to me about buying this inn."

The captain looked around the empty room to make sure there were no listeners and then leaned in close to his brother-in-law's face to whisper in his ear. "Did you not see an attractive negro woman and her French husband who came here to register for a room? Maybe they didn't tell you the reason they're here. Perhaps they were waiting for me to come and make the introductions. I hope you gave them a nice room?"

Louis' face became white as a sheet. "I...I... sent them away. How could I have known?"

"You what? You sent them away where?"

"I don't know where they went. I suggested the couple search for a room in Quebec City."

Beloux became livid. He grabbed his brother-in-law by his lapel and pulled him so close their noses touched. "You stupid little fool. I sent you two suckers, and you sent them away. I own ten percent of this dump, and I need my money out of it before the hostilities begin. Once the fighting starts, God only knows whether the British will burn this place to the ground. Trust me. I've seen what the Brits have invested in their colonies and the size of their population. We have what—fifty or sixty thousand French against a couple of million British settlers? If the king thinks he can win this one with those odds, he's dreaming."

Beloux relaxed his grip on Louis Trudeau, and his brother-in-law pulled away to straighten his wrinkled shirt. "Well," Beloux said in a calmer tone of voice, "Montreal isn't that big. I'll have to go out and walk the streets and hope to find them." He shook his head and turned toward the door. As he passed through the doorway, he said, "You idiot!"

Raiko came out of the Church of the Visitation, beneath its single bell tower that rose above the doorway. He pulled his woolen coat collar up around his neck just as he heard a distant clock strike three gongs. He turned to his brother and said, "It's 7:00 p.m. We need to find lodging very soon, and if we're going to Quebec City tomorrow, we should stop by the livery stable and arrange for transportation."

Bojko wasn't about to leave Montreal without looking for his mother. "You can go to Quebec City with Maisha and Robert if you want to, but as for me, I'm not leaving here just because some nasty old man suggested we move on. We have business here to finish, and I'm staying."

Maisha intervened. "I think Robert would agree with me that we aren't ready to leave here either. Perhaps we will, but it will be because we have decided ourselves. We won't be run off by prejudice. Besides, how many forty year-old Gypsy women could there possibly be in Montreal? If we get a fresh start tomorrow and split up four ways, we should cover the entire city in a couple of days. Then, if we wish to move on to Quebec, we will at least know they're not here."

Robert also offered a suggestion. "Look. It's getting late, and it'll be dark soon. Why don't we go back to the ship for the night and start fresh in the morning, as Maisha suggested? Besides, I have a hunch we should inquire about your parents at the livery. We passed it a short distance from the pier."

"The livery?" Bojko asked.

"Everyone and anyone who needs a horse or owns one will eventually do business with the livery. Besides, didn't you tell us your stepfather—Jànos, isn't it? —was a horse trainer. Who would need a horse trainer more than a livery owner?"

Daylight was already failing when they arrived at the livery stable. The wooden sign that hung above the entrance to the office read, "Arquette's Livery." Bojko's heart was racing with anticipation when they entered the livery office. The cold weather did little to suppress the intense odor of horse urine in the stable office. A filthy man with a grizzly-looking beard sat behind a cluttered desk in an armed oak swivel chair. He spun about when he heard them enter his office and looked suspiciously at the variety of ethnic mixes. "What do you want?" he growled. "I don't allow slaves to use the front door." He turned his attention to Robert. "Your servants will have to wait outside. Get them out of here."

Robert took the lead. "I can assure you, monsieur, that there are no slaves here. We are all free persons."

"Even the Gypsies?"

Robert glared at the dirty little man at the desk. "How'd you know they're Gypsies?"

"You've got to be kidding. I own a couple of Gypsies, myself. Gypsies are good workers. You say they're not slaves, huh? Are you sure these two aren't for sale? I'll give you a good price for them. Gypsies are the best horse trainers in the world. I think they can speak horse language." His teeth showed yellow through his bearded grin. It was the first sign of humor he had demonstrated.

"What are your Gypsies' names?" Raiko blurted out.

Arquette, who had foregone the courtesy of introduction, jumped up from his chair so forcefully the chair slammed against his desk. "I wasn't talking to you, boy. Shut your mouth, or I'll shut it for you. Freeman or not."

Robert grabbed Raiko's muscular and trembling arm. He could feel the anger and strength the young man possessed. He acted immediately in his precarious new status as a negotiator and forced a smile before rephrasing Raiko's question. "We're searching for a Gypsy woman who might have come here with her Romanian husband about eighteen or twenty years ago. Name's Florica; husband's name Jànos. We'd be willing to pay for information concerning her whereabouts. Do you know of them?"

No answer was needed. The livery man's mouth dropped open, and he was at a loss for words for the first time since he began talking.

"You can't take them away from me."

"Ah, I see. That's better," Robert said while suppressing his excitement over Arquette's apparent admission of knowledge. "Then you are familiar with the couple we're trying to find?"

"Hey, look. I was a mere teenager when my father bought them from a Dutch slave trader who came here regularly with his cargo of slaves to sell. It's all legal. I have the proper papers at my house."

The twins pushed forward, but Robert again gently held them back, fearing their comments would impede his progress in the negotiations by putting Arquette back on the defensive. "Are the Romanians here now?" DeWitt asked.

"No. They're not. The army is preparing for some military exercise along the Allegheny and Monongahela Rivers to the south. Jànos is working with them to get enough horses trained in time for the new troops scheduled to arrive here in the spring. I expect him back here the day after tomorrow."

"What about his wife? Is she with him?"

Arquette didn't answer at first. He looked down at the mud-clump-covered floor in shame, and without looking up, he said, almost in a whisper, "Florica isn't well."

Bojko couldn't remain quiet any longer. He lunged forward and shouted, "What have you done to my mother?"

Arquette jumped back and raised his weapon again to shield himself from an impending attack by the Gypsy. "I didn't do anything to her. She became pregnant with Jànos. She's in her early forties—too old to be having babies. She's due any day now, and my wife's caring for her at our house, but I'm afraid she's not doing too well. Her pregnancy has taken its toll on her."

"Please, for the love of God and everything decent, take us to her. We couldn't bear to lose her again. You must! You must!" Bojko pleaded.

Arquette was a man of little compassion, but not totally without reason. He could hear the anguish in Bojko's plea and see the tears in Raiko's eyes. "Alright," he agreed, "I'll take the two Gypsies, but not you two," he said, pointing toward Robert and Maisha. "I can handle two of you—and be forewarned I'll be armed—but I don't want to have to deal with the whole lot of you. I'm about to close for the day anyway. Come back in an hour, and I'll take you there. Mind you, though, no funny business or I'll shoot your mother at the first sign of a problem. She's my property, and I can do with her as I wish."

Maisha and the Romani became angered at the horrible threat, but Robert remained calm and said, "Monsieur Arquette, we believe every word you've said. Count on us to comply with your conditions. The boys will return in an hour." Robert nudged his three companions toward the door. "Merci," he said over his shoulder as he closed the door to the livery behind him.

Once outside, Maisha asked, "What now, Robert? It's getting dark, and we still don't have a place to stay."

DeWitt knew he and Maisha had done all they could do for Raiko and Bojko. From here, they would have to manage on their own. "Arquette," he said, "has made it quite clear we are not welcome to go along to his house, and the guys still have an hour to kill. I suggest we all go together to *La Patience* and seek permission to spend the night aboard the ship. These bags are becoming a nuisance to carry everywhere, and I'm wet and cold. Once we settle in, Raiko and Bojko can go back to the livery and meet up with Arquette."

"Do you think he'd do it?" Maisha asked.

"Do what?"

"Do you think Arquette will shoot Florica if the boys give him any trouble?"

"Don't be ridiculous. Arquette is a real money-grubber. While he may be devoid of compassion, he and his wife are not caring for Florica because they're humanitarians; they're caring for her because she is worth a lot of money. If Arquette were to shoot Florica, it would be the wasteful destruction of a valuable slave. Additionally, he'd lose her baby, which will also become his property. And after he shot her, he'd be standing there with an empty pistol and these two young bucks wanting to kill him. That's just not going to happen. But he might shoot one of the boys and have the law on his side because they were trying to steal his property. These young men know how to take care of themselves. I watched them work on the ship, and you can believe me when I tell you Arquette would not want to get them angry. They'll be fine."

The snow began falling again, and the rapidly approaching night became colder. Raiko and his brother remained silent as they walked down the street and felt the damp wind blowing off Saint Lawrence. This day is the day they had hoped and prayed for at the Church of the Visitation. The day was what they always believed would happen, but they didn't know how to handle their circumstances.

Captain Beloux, still upset with his brother-in-law and still walking the streets of Montreal in search of the Dewitts, was not at the ship when they arrived at the pier. Pierre, however, was and agreed to accept compensation to provide a night's lodging aboard the ship. The brothers threw their bags on the bunks they had used as crew members and headed back to the livery. Maisha and Robert entered their cabin, and Maisha locked the cabin door.

Robert had his back to her and struck a match to light the brass lantern secured to the wall. He removed the glass chimney from the lamp and held the lit match to the wick when Maisha came up behind him and blew out the match. "What are you doing, Maisha?" he said. "That was my last match."

Robert felt Maisha put her arms around him and pull him close. "I was proud of you today," she whispered into his ear. "You've come a long way from the cowering man who hid in the tree outside of Monsieur De Fontaine's office in Strasburg and witnessed his murder. That Robert DeWitt no longer exists. You've become a leader; you took charge of today's situation at both the inn and livery. Seeing you assert yourself and acting as a negotiator makes me love you and respect you, and yes, want you even more."

Robert felt Maisha's warm breath on his ear and turned to embrace her. "That was quite a story about the couple who allegedly set fire to Montreal back in '34, wasn't it? Do you think they did it?"

"I don't know. How can we ever know? Things being what they are, they might have been scapegoats for somebody else's carelessness. But I do know one thing for sure: I'm about to become guilty of starting a fire of my own—and we won't need any matches."

"The weather is growing colder, and the wind blowing stronger," Captain Beloux lamented to his nephew. "The river is showing increasing signs of freezing. We must embark immediately or face entrapment in the ice."

"Wake the men and get the guide boats into the water immediately."

Pierre looked back at his uncle with raised eyebrows. "But Uncle, it is Christmas morning. Most of the crew celebrated last night with generous portions of rum. They won't be much good this early in the morning."

The captain took another glance at the river and reiterated his command. "If we don't leave now, they are going to have a bigger problem than a hangover. Do as I ordered!"

An hour later, *La Patience* was towed from her moorings and set sail for the warmer waters of the Gulf Stream.

CHAPTER THIRTY-ONE
THE PRICE OF FREEDOM

The muddy rue had begun to freeze, and the three inches of freshly fallen snow would have given it a fresh new look were it not for the influx of horse owners who wished to board their horses at the livery. "Bad weather is good for business," Arquette told the brothers who arrived promptly at 5:00 p.m. "but as I explained to your earlier, I'm short-handed with Jànos out of town. You'll either have to help me stable the horses or sit and wait until I've taken care of them myself."

"Always looking for slave labor," Raiko whispered to his brother. They had little choice except to help Arquette.

An hour later, the Celje twins were free to find their mother. They walked several blocks to Arquette's house and approached what amounted to a small shack in the house's back. From inside the hut, they could hear a woman's anguished screams. The three men ran to the house and flung open the door. There, they found Mademoiselle Arquette wiping their mother's forehead delirious with pain.

"Get out of here, you fool. And shut the door. Can't you see this woman is about to give birth?" The men quickly retreated from the one-room shack.

"She looked terrible," Raiko wept. "I'm not even sure that's our mother. I've waited all these years to see her, and now that I have, I'm almost sorry I did. She looks like she's on the verge of dying."

Arquette brushed the snow from his coat, removed his snow-covered hat, and banged it against his leg. "You were both only seven years old. Would you have recognized her even under the best of circumstances?"

Bojko thought about the question for a minute and then answered. "I would like to think I'd recognize her. Sometimes she would come to me in a dream and warn us of impending dangers. She saved our lives more than once. I have only the face I saw in my dreams to recognize her. Her images in my mind from when we were children have faded and become unclear and unrecognizable. Sometimes I lay in bed at night and try to remember her face, but I can't, not really."

Arquette, more out of self-need than benevolence, said, "I need a glass of wine, and I'm not going to stand out here in the cold until that woman decides to have her brat. Let's go to my house. My wife will come for us if anything changes." When they arrived at the back door of his big house, Arquette said, "You boys wait here in the mudroom. You're not going to track mud into my house. I'll bring the wine to you." He removed his muddy boots, left Raiko and Bojko waiting for him in the cold mudroom, and entered his house. Ten minutes later, he returned with three glasses of sherry. They all took a sip from their respective glasses without a proposed toast.

"We'd like to make you an offer, Monsieur," Raiko said. "We propose to buy the freedom of our parents."

Arquette quickly lowered his glass and cocked his head to the side. "Buy their freedom? That, I'm afraid it is something you could not afford."

"Don't be so sure," Raiko added. "How much did your father pay for them?"

Arquette took so long to answer that Raiko knew he was about to lie. "I believe my father paid 1,200 pounds British for them. By now, considering how much I have invested in them, not to mention the fact Florica is about to give birth to a child who will make them even more valuable, I'm guessing their worth to be at about double that."

Raiko struggled not to become angry. "Here's the deal as I see it: Jànos is in his mid-forties and getting older by the day. By your admission, Florida is not well and may die in childbirth, perhaps her child too. Anyone can see that even if she lives through this childbirth, she's too old to have more children. They are both of an age where they will soon become a liability to an owner." Raiko felt strange negotiating for his parents but felt now was a good time to do so. "The honorable thing for you to do," he added, "would be to emancipate both right now for their years of faithful service. Are you brave enough to do the honorable thing?"

"Set them free? Do you think I'm a fool? I need their services."

"You paid 1,200 pounds for them. A free unskilled laborer would earn one hundred pounds per year, a skilled worker—which they are—twice that or about 2,400 pounds per year. I'd say you've done well with your investment. Here's our offer: I'm giving you 1,000 pounds for both right now. If the baby is born after the transaction, it comes as part of the deal."

There came a sudden scream from the shack behind the house. Arquette's wife yelled, "Help. Come quickly! I need help!"

Arquette rushed to where he had left his boots and began to pull them on.

"Is it a deal? Answer now, or the price will go down if Florica or the baby doesn't make it."

"But I need Jànos for a few more months to train the horses. I must fulfill my contract with the military."

"Here's our final offer: We will remain with Jànos and help him train the horses until the end of April. But he and his wife and child will remain as free persons. Is that a deal?"

"I don't suppose you happen to have your 1,000 pounds with you?"

"We do, indeed." Another unintelligible scream of anguished came from the shack. "Is it a deal or not?"

"It's a deal," Arquette said with a tone of frustration. He held out his hand for a shake and sealed the deal on the spot. Raiko reached into his coat and counted out 1,000 pounds. Arquette didn't take the time to count the money. He shoved it into his pocket.

"Not so fast, Arquette. I want a receipt, and I want it now." Arquette ran into his kitchen, muddy boots, and all, and hurriedly improvised a receipt. He returned to the mudroom and thrust it into Raiko's hand. Now, if you don't mind, it's your mother, after all." They were out the back door in a flash and ran to the shack to help deliver Florica's new baby girl.

CHAPTER THIRTY-TWO
A JOYOUS FIDDLE

The door to Florica's five-hundred-square-foot shack opened, and Arquette stuck his head out. "Come see your new sister." he said, "My wife's bathing her now."

Raiko and Bojko removed their hats and entered the building. The twins saw their mother in the dim light of the lantern and the amber glow of the fireplace. They walked over to where she lay and covered her with a blanket. Florica's eyes remained closed, and her face was pale. Concerned, Bojko asked, "Is she dead?"

Mademoiselle Arquette turned from where she was working with the screaming baby and smiled. "I certainly hope not. We need her to nurse this hungry brat. I think she just passed out from her ordeal." She dried the baby with a coarse white towel and brought the naked child over to her brothers' lantern. "She looks just like her mother: dark skin, deep brown eyes, and black hair," she said as she offered her up for Bojko to hold.

"Oh no, my hands are too cold to touch her, but she is a beautiful baby. Please cover her so she doesn't freeze." Bojko moved over to the fireplace and placed another log on the dying fire. "It's cold in here. Do you want them to die of pneumonia?" he asked.

Arquette's wife answered in a tone of disdain. "Firewood costs money, you know. It's not free." Mrs. Arquette carried the baby she was holding over to the mother and pulled down the blanket. She laid the crying baby at the mother's swollen breast. The little girl needed no instruction in feeding. Florica stirred and then, seemingly instinctively, folded her arm around the baby to hold it secure. Then her midwife pulled the blanket up to Florica's shoulders to keep them warm.

Florica never opened her eyes, but she seemed to be smiling through her slumber. "I think *Mutter's* smiling," Raiko said. "*Mutter*, can you hear me? It's Raiko and Bojko. We've come to find you, *Mutter*. You're a free woman." Florica made no further signs of stirring. She was too exhausted.

Arquette's wife glared at him. He was at a loss for words. He knew the news of Florica's freedom would be a shock to her—news he had hoped he could deliver to her under more favorable conditions. Without a word, he reached into his coat pocket, pulled out the money Raiko had given to him and handed it to her. Arquette's wife grabbed the money from him and moved closer to the lantern, where she immediately counted the money. Not realizing the money was for Florica and Jànos, she smiled at what she thought was a good deal. She shoved the money down the front of her dress, and she and her husband went back to the main house. The twins pulled the two kitchen chairs over close to their mother's bed and made themselves as comfortable as possible while maintaining their night vigil.

Raiko was the first to be awakened by the crying of the baby. He smelled a profuse odor that permeated through the air. Bojko's bad hearing spared him from being the first to pull back the blankets and to discover the mess the infant made over her mother's body and bed coverings.

Raiko turned to his brother, sitting in his chair asleep, and shook him. "Bojko! Bojko! Wake up. We have a problem," he half-shouted.

Bojko rubbed his eyes and tried to wake up. "Whew! What's that awful odor? Is that you, Raiko?"

Raiko shook his head. "No, but the odor is the source of our problem." Pulling the blanket down from the baby, he showed Bojko the odor's source. "What do we do now?" Raiko asked as he looked toward the fireplace where an iron kettle of water hung on an iron hook. He went over to the kettle and tucked his hand into the sleeve of his coat he still wore. He swung the kettle away from the fire using his cuff as a glove. Then he went to the nightstand beside the bed, retrieved the washbasin full of cold water, and poured it into the hot water to cool it down. He used the cloth he had seen Arquette's wife use to blot Florica's head and dipped it into the warm water. "Bojko," he said, "bring that towel from on the nightstand over here and spread it on the kitchen table. We're going to get our first self-education lesson in bathing our little sister."

Bojko reluctantly complied, and between head-turning, nose-holding, half-gagging, and near-vomiting, the two men managed to get the job done. "Get a dry towel, Raiko, and let's wrap her bottom in so this doesn't happen again."

Raiko handed his brother a dry towel and then opened the cabin door and threw the dirty water outside. Then he refilled the basin with fresh water and gave it to his brother. Bojko just stared at the basin of warm water and asked, "What are you going to do with the basin? To wash my hands?"

"No. You'll need to wash *Mutter*. She's filthy."

"Oh no, not me. I'd feel weird washing my mother. When Arquette's wife laid the baby at Mutter's bare breast, I about passed out. I can't do that. You do it."

A prolonged argument was averted when a knock came at the door. "Raiko, Bojko, are you in there?" It was Maisha's voice. *Thank God. There's a woman here to help,* they thought. Maisha agreed to help Florica while the men went to a nearby inn for breakfast.

Raiko noticed his brother kept looking out of the dining room window as they ate breakfast. "Why do you keep looking out of the window?" he asked him. "Is there something of particular interest out there?"

"I don't know," Bojko said. "Maybe I can't get used to being a free man who doesn't have to keep looking over his shoulder anymore, but I can't shake the feeling that someone is watching us. Ever since I saw that priest at the church who reminded me of Father Thomas, the old feelings of persecution have come back to haunt me."

"You need to get over it, brother. We're not in Europe anymore. Here we are, free men."

Bojko tried to believe his brother was right because he wanted him to be. But walking to Florica's place, he kept turning to look over his shoulder.

When they returned, Robert's wife met them at the cabin door. She quietly closed the door behind her and stepped out onto the small stoop.

"Your mother woke up while I was bathing her. She's awful weak, but I explained who I was and told her about her sons. I'm afraid she tired herself out in the excitement of it all, but I managed to calm her down. She's sleeping now. Let me go in and wake her and tell her you're here. When she's ready, I'll come to get you." The boys could hear their mother's excited cries from within the shack. They could wait no longer and opened the door and rushed inside while Robert waited outside. Maisha had propped her up on her pillows, and Maisha was now holding the infant for her. The pure excitement of seeing her sons for the first time in more than eighteen years brought joy to her heart and color to her face. She tried to speak, but no words found their way past her lips. Florica managed to hold her arms outstretched to receive her sons into her longing embrace. They ran to her and dropped on their knees beside her bed. Both brothers cried tears of joy they had been waiting all these years to release.

"*Mutter*," Raiko said, "you're a free woman now. We bought your freedom."

"What about Jànos and the baby?"

Florica always puts everyone else first. Her sons filled her in on the details, including the fact they had agreed to help Jànos train the horses until the end of April. By then, the baby and her mother should be healthy enough to travel, and they would plan to leave New France as a family unit again.

"Where will we go?" Florica asked.

"We'll go back to Philadelphia. We have papers that declare us as citizens there. In Pennsylvania, we can live as free people and never hide our identities as Gypsies again. You'll be welcomed there as our parents and enjoy the same freedoms we have. Here, you will always have the stigma of being a slave."

Florica smiled freely for the first time in days at the news. "Jànos is a free man now?"

"Yes," Bojko said, "But he doesn't know it. He doesn't even know he's a new father."

"Then please send for him. I know the weather's bad, but he'll come right away."

"Can we tell him the good news?"

"Of course. Jànos needs to know about his freedom and know about his new baby. Go get him."

Bojko saw a fleeting shadow across the wall in front of him. He turned quickly and looked toward the window. Nothing was there. He got up from beside his mother's bed and went to the door, opened it, and looked outside. Nothing!

"Still edgy, brother?" Raiko asked. "Maybe so," said Bojko. "I apologize for being so on edge."

Maisha stayed with Florica throughout the remainder of the day, taking care of the infant and allowing its mother to rest. Robert, Raiko, and Bojko searched for new temporary housing for the parents. Remaining in such deplorable living conditions was not an option.

Jànos got to the shack where his wife, baby girl, and stepsons waited for him just before nightfall. It was an incredible reunion that night, with seven people crammed into its tight confines.

"What shall we name our beautiful little daughter?" Jànos asked of Florica. "Her birth has brought us such good fortune and joy."

"Joy? Why not? Joy would be a great and fitting name for her. Yes. Let's name her Joy." And, so it was.

Jànos took down his violin from above the stone fireplace, and soon joyous Gypsy music filled the air late into the night. This celebration would be the best Christmas season in this Gypsy family's lifetime.

CHAPTER THIRTY-THREE
FULFILLING THE CONTRACT

December 20, 1753

A wagon borrowed from Arquette's Livery and pulled by two oxen lumbered through the early morning snow past the Church of the Visitation. The eyes of all six of the wagon's nervous passengers fixed upon the rectory windows.

"I think I saw the curtains moving at one of the upstairs windows," Raiko said.

"I saw them move too," Bojko added. "The priest seems always to know what our next move is. He must have spies everywhere. I'm glad we'll be miles away from him in Quebec City and out of view from his ever-seeing eyes."

"Don't be so sure, "Raiko said, " He seems to have eyes everywhere. As we've already learned, he's relentless and evil."

Behind the curtains of a second-floor bedroom window, a dark-eyed priest watched the passing wagon with interest. *Go to Quebec City if you wish, but there's no place for you to hide. I'll not rest until I see you all stretched from taunt rope with your feet kicking as you fight for your last breath.*

"Come back to bed, sweetie," a woman's voice called from across the room, "it's too cold to be standing by that drafty window. Get under the blankets with me, and let me warm you up."

The wagon departed Montreal by its east gate and trudged ever-so-slowly along the half-frozen, half-muddy road toward Quebec City. From the plateau along which the road edged, they could look down and see the Saint Lawrence River, broad and majestically flowing toward the ocean with large chunks of ice, barely above the water's surface. "It looks as though the ice floats will get to Quebec long before we do," Raiko commented. "True," Maisha said, "but we'll get there just the same, and we'll be safer there together. We need to be more like the oxen pulling this wagon—steady and true to our purpose."

The extended family—the Celje brothers, their mother and stepfather, and the DeWitts—arrived in Quebec City, a town of fewer than 6,000 people, late in the afternoon of December 20. They immediately sought lodging at a local inn run by Andre Lamour.

Lamour asked, "So, you say you are looking for a house big enough to accommodate all of you? For how long?"

"Well," Maisha answered, "we'd take it on a yearly lease, of course, but if that's not convenient for you, we'll take it for whatever period you can allow. We would at least like to have it until we can find something else. Why do you ask?"

Monsieur Lamour immediately began to see an opportunity to earn some quick cash. "I do have a furnished house I rent out, but it's been promised to the French military to quarter their officers beginning some-time in mid-April. That's when their new regiment will arrive. I'd be willing to lease it to you on a six-month basis, but you must be willing to move out the moment their ship arrives—with no refund for unused lease time. Who knows? Bad weather could delay the ship's arrival, but the arrival could also be earlier."

"We'll take it immediately," Maisha answered without hesitation. "Consider it done."

The extended family immediately moved into the house, sight unseen, and agreed to split the lease's cost. It was a large frame house near the Quebec City branch of Arquette's Livery. "What good fortune," Maisha said as soon as they were alone without their new landlord, "to find this magnificent house for just the time we needed it. When the military comes, we leave, and everyone is happy; us, the military, and Monsieur Lamour."

To make the house a home, Maisha utilized her excellent taste, acquired during her nearly twenty years of living in the De Fontaine household in Strasbourg. Florica set about reacquainting herself with mothering skills and getting to know her sons and her new daughter, Joy. Monsieur DeWitt spent his daytime hours talking with local traders about the intricacies of running a trading business with trappers who traded furs among the river systems of New France. Once established in Pennsylvania, he spent his evening hours making lists of supplies he and Maisha would need to run their trading post. Raiko and Bojko worked diligently with Jànos to fulfill their agreement to help him with the arduous and dangerous task of training one-hundred-twenty horses for the French military. They all worked hard, and the winter seemed to pass quickly as they awaited Captain Beloux and their passage out on the *La Patience*.

CHAPTER THIRTY-FOUR
TO NEW FRANCE

March 1, 1754

Father François and Sister Maria arrived in Paris amid the country's prepara-tions for war. The streets of Paris were alive with men in uniform who talked of French patriotism, the enthusiasm for which was dependent upon social class-more intense at the top of the social ladder and less enthusiastic on the lower rungs. French troops were having their last hurrah before being shipped to New France. King Louis XV had ordered the construction of twenty-six new forts along the Allegheny and Monongahela Rivers to keep the British on the Alleghenies' eastern slopes and eventually connect French claims territory from Nova Scotia to New Orleans.

March 15, the nervous soldiers, along with the brother and sister ministry team, boarded riverboats and began their trip down the La Seine River to Rouen, about seventy-five miles from the sea, where the deeper waters allowed for ocean-going ships to dock. Some of the soldiers boarded a ship named *La Patience*, originally a ship of British registry that had recently returned from the colonies. *La Patience* was now flying a French flag as it continued downriver for their last stop at Le Havre on the English Channel before sailing to New France.

The trip from Le Havre to Quebec usually took between sixty and ninety days, depending on favorable winds and the number of passen-gers to provide ballast—the better the ballast, the smoother the trip. The ship's captain, Beloux, was pleased to have the soldiers aboard, not so much due to his patriotism, but rather for the Crown's fees and for the ballast weight the soldiers would provide for his ship. The return trip would also be helpful due to cargo shipped from New France to the European Continent.

After dinner, Captain Beloux and his nephew, Pierre, sat in the captain's quarters and reviewed navigational charts. A loud knock came at the door. "Find out what they want," the captain said to his nephew, "and don't keep the door open while you talk. I'm freezing already."

Pierre went to the door and opened it. He was surprised to see the sentry he had left at the gangplank standing there with an attractive young woman. "What do you want, Mademoiselle?" he inquired.

"I want to book passage on your ship to Montreal," she said, somewhat sheepishly. "I've been told you will sail on the morning tide. Is that correct?"

Captain Beloux couldn't help overhearing the conversation and called to his nephew, "Tell her we're booked to capacity and close that door!"

The young woman desperately wanted an audience with the captain and would not be easily turned away. She squeezed her way past the first mate and into the cabin, where Beloux still sat with his back to the door, half-heartedly glancing at the charts. He heard his nephew call to the young woman as Pierre tried to stop her from entering the cabin. The captain immediately pushed his chair away from the table, and rose to his feet. The captain's action was too late to prevent the woman's entry. He found himself face-to-face with a desperate woman who was not about to back off.

"I'll pay double passage," she said before he had a chance to say anything. "I need to sail with you and can't wait for another passage."

"But I already told you we're full. I have over one hundred soldiers onboard and the raunchiest crew you'd ever want to see. I can't be baby-sitting you for two months while we sail to Montreal."

"You already have one woman on board, do you not?"

"A woman? Well, yes, if you can call a nun a woman. But men don't look at a nun as a woman the same way they'd look at you."

"I'll pay double passage."

"We don't have quarters for you."

"I'll stay with the nun."

"She might object to that," the captain replied.

"Don't tell her I'm on board until we are well underway. I'll get a room for tonight at an inn and come back before sunrise. I'll remain in your cabin until you have guided the ship out to sea. By the time you need your cabin back, we'll be too far away from port for her to turn me away. Besides, she's a nun and will be delighted to help me."

Captain Beloux, a man familiar with taking on clandestine passengers and never a man to allow reason to take priority over profit, agreed.

The young woman shivered in the shadows of the pier until the last possible minute to board the ship. When she saw Pierre come to the gangplank and pull out his pocket watch, she knew she must board now or never. She ran to the gangplank, holding her small carpet bag in her right hand and using her left hand to hold the hood of her cape from blowing off her head in the wind. Pierre saw her coming and motioned for her to hurry.

"You made it with not a second to spare. I was about to bring up the gangplank and sail off without you. The tide is moving, and so must we," Pierre said in a scolding tone of voice. "The captain is at the wheel. He told me to get you inside the cabin and then for me to help him get us underway." Pierre led her to the cabin, opened the door, and said, "There are hot tea and baguettes on the table—help yourself. But don't touch anything else. Once we are sufficiently underway, I'm supposed to take you and introduce you to Sister. It'll probably be about an hour from now." Pierre shook his head in disbelief that a young woman would pay double passage on a ship full of young men and then take a chance the nun would allow her to share her cabin. *What incredible audacity!*

It was closer to two hours before Pierre returned to the cabin with Father François and Sister Maria. Without knocking, they entered the captain's quarters and found the new passenger with her head down on her folded arms, sleeping at the table. The sound of the opening door awakened Anne, and she jumped to her feet and looked directly into the nun's dark brown eyes. They stood facing each other without a word and then rushed, weeping into each other's arms. She released the nun and embraced the priest in the same manner.

"What's this? You know each other?" Captain Beloux asked.

"Yes," Sister Maria answered. "Can't you see we are identical twins?"

The captain leaned down and looked first at the nun and then at Anne. "Well, I'll be!" he exclaimed. "I never guessed it."

"Of course," Pierre interjected, "no one ever looks at a nun's face. And with the habit and all, even the hair is covered. What now?"

Anne's brother, Father François, had many questions. "Does *Mutter* and Papa know where you are? Did they agree to allow you to sail to New France?"

Anne felt awful to tell them the truth, but there was no escaping what she had done. "No. I love Anton Smith, and our parents won't allow us to marry because he's a Protestant. Anton has already sailed to Philadelphia and plans to send for me, but I haven't heard from him. I'm afraid something awful has happened to him, and I must find him."

Captain Beloux shook his head in disbelief. "Did you say your fiancé is named Anton Smith—the tailor?"

Anne was shocked, but hope sprung in her heart when the captain knew his occupation. "Yes. Do you know him?"

"I sure do. Anton served on my crew on the passage to Philadelphia and two Gypsy brothers, with whom he was awful friendly. He stayed there, but his two dark-skinned friends had a change of heart and rejoined my crew and sailed with us to Montreal."

The priest looked suddenly angered. "Did you say Gypsy brothers? Were they about the same age?"

"Why... yes," the captain said. "They claimed to be twins, but they didn't look anything alike."

Maria looked faint and reached out to steady herself on the back of a chair. Her heart began to palpitate, and she felt a shortness of breath. The nun felt an unexplainable feeling of panic as the room started to spin around her.

"Here," Anne said. "Sit here and put your head between your knees. I'll pour you a cup of tea."

"What's wrong," the captain asked. "Is your sister ill?"

"Anne," Father François suggested, "Why don't you help Maria back to our cabin while I speak with the captain?"

Anne gave Maria a few minutes to recover from her anxiety attack, take a few sips of tea, and then be escorted out of the captain's quarters and back to her cabin. The priest, the captain, and the first mate were seated when the sisters left.

The priest leaned forward on his elbows and rubbed his forehead. "Where do I begin? About four years ago, my sister—the nun—was raped in the church's courtyard in Erlach. The perpetrator also severely beat our parish priest and left him for dead.

"Two Gypsy brothers were accused of the crime and condemned to death, but they escaped on execution day.

"Father Benedict, our parish priest, was not expected to recover from his injuries, but he regained consciousness and revealed the rapist was his assistant priest, Father Thomas.

"Maria has no memory of the incident but knew of the accusations against the two Gypsies. Now, whenever she sees a Gypsy or hears anyone talking about Gypsies, she has anxiety attacks."

Pierre's curiosity got the better of him. "So, whatever happened to the priest? Did they hang a man of the cloth?"

"No," François said. "Much to my chagrin, the bishop wanted to avoid scandal. He defrocked Father Thomas and sent him on his way along with his French Jezebel, named Emilie. Both the priest and the French-woman have dropped from sight. I've never met this Father Thomas, and it's a good thing that I haven't. I was not in Erlach at the time. The bishop would have had to defrock two priests because I would have killed Father Thomas with my own bare hands." The priest crossed himself. "May the Lord forgive me for my thoughts?"

CHAPTER THIRTY-FIVE
SISTER MARIA

April 1754

The *La Patience* navigated the St. Lawrence River, first stopping in Quebec City to present its papers, then sailed to Montreal.

Father François arranged for a carriage, and soon excitement filled the air as he and his two sisters arrived at the rectory of the Church of the Visitation.

Maria stepped down from the carriage, pulled her black coat tightly around her, and looked at the church. She turned to her brother and embraced him tenderly as she began to weep with joy. "François, this is a dream come true—to serve the Church I love, with my brother, whom I adore and respect. However, I never expected Anne to be serving alongside us. The Lord has poured out so many blessings upon me that I sometimes feel like I can't handle more."

Anne moved close to her brother and sister and embraced them both while tears of compassion streamed down her cheeks. *Only my sister, Maria, the victim of a rape and beating, could see the good in this world. If any woman deserves sainthood, it is she.*

François carried two pieces of luggage and led his sisters up the flagstone sidewalk to the rectory's front door. He sat the bags down on the doorstep and reached for the brass door knocker. Three loud knocks resonated through the house.

The knock at the rectory's front door sent a paralyzing shock through the male occupant of the rectory.

They are here! Damian shouted in Father Thomas' head.

"Who is here? I don't understand," Thomas said.

Emilie pulled the blankets up around her as a chill of fear embraced her. "Thomas, you are talking to yourself again."

Needing to know who Damian was talking about, Thomas rushed to the bedroom window and carefully pulled back the curtains without hesitation.

François stepped back from the front door and looked up to the bedroom window in time to see the drapes move slightly to the left.

"There's someone at home, girls. I just saw the curtains move above us. I'll knock again."

Anne didn't wait. She shrugged her shoulders, raised her eyebrows, and reached out and beat the door with her hand. "It's cold out here on the stoop. Let's get someone to the door."

The Welti sisters heard footsteps coming down from the second floor and approaching the door inside the rectory. They listened to the dead-bolt slide from its notch and saw the door latch lift on its lever. The heavy oak door swung inward and revealed a tall, heavily bearded priest, thirty pounds overweight, wearing a bathrobe and standing barefoot before them. He squinted at them through one eye and leaned forward to examine the priest and nun. His heart jumped in his chest at the recognition of the women.

Anne stared back at him, suddenly overcome with an eerie feeling of familiarity.

"Who are you, and what do you want?" the bearded man asked in a raspy voice. His voice betrayed the fact that their knock awakened him. The priest was as nervous as a child caught with his hand in the cookie jar.

His eyes shifted from the priest standing in front of him to the two women accompanying him. A sudden panic set in.

Oh, no! I recognize these women. They're the Welti sisters from Erlach. Indeed, they'll remember me, and I'll be exposed. What should I do?

Just relax, Damian said. *They would have said something by now if they suspected anything.*

François spoke: "My name is Father François, Sister Maria, and our blood-sister Anne Welti. I have been sent here as the new parish priest."

There was a long pause while the evil priest further pondered his situation. *But their brother—I've never seen him. Wait a minute. I remember now. That old Father Benedict told me he served as a priest in Zurich. That's why I never met him. He wasn't in Erlach when I was there.*

"Who, may I ask, are you?" Father François inquired. "Rome indicated to us that the pulpit is empty, and this was to be my new charge."

"I don't know how to answer that. My apologies for the confusion. My name is Father Peter, and I've been here for nearly a year now. Communication is so slow now, especially with all the problems with the British on the frontier. There must be an explanation for the mix-up. Please, step inside and warm up while I have my housekeeper make you some tea."

The Welti family stepped inside, and while the door was open, Father Peter looked out to the carriage driver who was waiting for instructions as to what to do and yelled: "Driver, bring the rest of their luggage and set it inside the door." He closed the door without locking it and ushered the new arrivals into his living room and seated them near the warm fire burning in the fireplace. The priest added a new log to the fire and poked the hot coals with an iron stoker. Soon the new dry log was ablaze, and all were seated comfortably.

"Please, make yourselves comfortable. My housekeeper must not have heard me call her. I'll go to see what is causing the delay."

Father Peter walked over to the stairwell and called up the stairs. "Emilie! We have three guests. Will you please make us some tea and serve it in the living room?"

There was no answer, just the sounds of someone rustling sheets and feet shuffling across a hard-wooden floor. Then, footsteps down the creaking stairs. All heads turned toward the stairs as a beautiful blonde appeared. The blonde wore apparel that seemed much too fancy for the functions of a housemaid. The fragrance of lilac perfume filled the air.

"Emilie," Father Peter said without introductions, "Please bring us tea."

Emilie's mouth dropped open, and she stared wide-eyed at the priest in scorn. She regained her composure and took a deep breath. "Will there be anything else, Father?" she replied through a fake smile.

"Yes there is. Bring us some warmed baguettes and jam if you please."

Emilie turned sharply without saying a word and went into the kitchen.

"Well, now," Father Peter said, while he stared at Emilie as he entered the kitchen, "explain to me, if you will, exactly why you are here."

Father François, puzzled at being asked such a question, leaned forward from his chair, raised his eyebrows, and leaned his head to his right and began to explain:

"I was serving in Zurich with my sister, Sister Maria when I received orders directly from the Vatican to come here. We understood that this diocese had an elderly priest in ill health who needed to retire.

"You can understand our dismay, after uprooting and traveling for the past two months across two continents and a very unfriendly ocean, only to learn we are not needed here."

"Oh, yes. You speak of poor Father Anthony. Unfortunately, as you say, he was in ill health, and the diocese couldn't wait for your arrival. As fate would have it, I was on a ship bound for New Orleans that stopped here in route when the good Father took a turn for the worse. What else could I do? I remained behind to care for our brother-in-Christ, and the ship went on to New Orleans.

"May God rest his soul. Father Anthony went on to his reward a week after my arrival. He insisted—contrary to my advice, of course—I take him to Quebec City to visit the members of his parish there one last time. The trip was too much for him, and he passed before we even got halfway to Quebec City. I had no choice. As a servant of the Lord, I could not, in all conscience, leave these good people without a shepherd so I decided to remain here. I sent word to the Vatican I would stay here to care for Father Anthony's flock, but you must have already left for Montreal before they could contact you."

Emilie returned to the living room with a tray and set it on a coffee table. Father Peter welcomed the interruption. It gave him time to think about what he might say next.

Father François once again couldn't help noticing Emilie's fragrance as she moved close to serve his tea. When Emilie had silently served Father Peter and his guests, she excused herself and started back toward the kitchen. The Weltis all watched her with interest as she moved away, carrying herself upright and with a more graceful posture than one would expect from a woman of her station as a housekeeper.

"Pardon me for asking Father, but what's the story on your house-keeper?" François asked as he broke the silence.

Father Peter sat upright in his chair and threw his shoulders back with raised eyebrows as if startled and at a loss for words. "I, ah...Emilie, that is, was aboard the ship that brought me here. Yes, we met aboard the ship.

"She's originally from Strasbourg, France, and came to New France to meet up with her fiancé. Unfortunately, her fiancé died from consumption a month before her arrival. She, who was left financially devasted, and me, without a housekeeper, I offered her a position here at the rectory until she can afford passage to return to France.

"Well, enough about my housekeeper and me. You must be exhausted from your trip. It would only be appropriate for you to stay with us—I mean me—here at the rectory until we can sort this all out, and you can return to Europe. I'll have Emilie make up the beds for you in two guest rooms. Sister Maria and Anne can share the larger guest room, and I'll sure you'll find your accommodations quite satisfactory, Father François."

An eerie feeling of De Ja Vue came over Maria as she stared at Thomas. *That man makes the hair on the back of my neck stand up and I don't know why. I must be exhausted from our journey. I'm sure he is a good man. After all, he is a priest.*

Between the four of them, they carried the luggage up the stairs. Father Peter assigned Father François and his sisters their respective rooms. Father Peter excused himself and went downstairs to join Emilie in the kitchen.

When Father Peter—aka Father Thomas—entered the kitchen, Emilie stood, expressionless at the sink. Her arms crossed confrontationally, and her shoulders settled into place as she exhaled.

"Housekeeper?" Emilie half-shouted through her teeth at the priest. "Housekeeper? 'Emilie,' you said, 'make us some tea; bring us some and make up the beds.'

"Is there anything else you'd like me to do? Your Highness!" With her arms still crossed, she abruptly turned her back on the priest. She took a deep breath and then exhaled completely to demonstrate her outrage at her indignant lover.

Father Peter moved closer to Emilie. "Now, now, Emilie. Don't be like that. What else could I do? What else could I say to explain your presence in the rectory?" He moved closer to her and tried to put his hands on her shoulders. She wriggled from his touch and turned sharply. Emilie placed both hands on his chest and pushed him away.

"Get away from me. I'm in no mood for your patronization."

Upstairs, Father François and his two sisters congregated in the girls' bedroom and discussed their situation in whispers. Anne quietly closed the bedroom door.

"Brother, I hate to be the one to cast false accusations, but there is something very peculiar about Father Peter and what he's telling us."

Her brother moved closer to his two sisters until he was within two feet of Anne's face and asked, "What exactly do you mean, Anne?"

"Well, for one thing," she replied, "how could he have known we were on our way here? And how could he have received clearance from Rome so quickly, giving him instructions to remain here as the parish priest in such a short time?"

Before her brother or sister could speak, she continued: "And another thing I'm uncomfortable with is his relationship with his housekeeper. She is way too well dressed and well poised to be of the working class. That woman is well-educated and accustomed to the finer things in life. Did you see the look she gave Father Peter when he sent her to bring us tea? The fiery darts her eyes shot at him could have killed a bull.

"And another thing is the coincidence that the former priest, Father Anthony, just happened to pass away when he was in Father Peter's carriage on the way to Quebec City."

Father François stepped back a pace and raised his head at the thought of his sister's indignant remark. "Surely, Anne, you're not accusing this priest of foul play?"

Anne gritted her teeth and leaned forward toward her brother. "All I'm saying is that things do not add up. When one considers the timeline for his arrival, his relationship with his housekeeper and her apparent station in life, the housekeeper's disdain about serving us tea, the former priest's demise, and Father Peter's attitude, in general, it doesn't calculate. It raises too many red flags.

"And another thing bothers me. There's something all-too familiar about that man. I can't put my finger on it, exactly, but take off several pounds, shave off the beard, and I'm sure I've met him somewhere before. When he spoke, the hair on the back of my neck stood up. Did anyone else feel that way too?" She looked at Maria, who seemed to be staring out into the distance. Anne placed her hand on her sister's shoulder. "Maria," Anne asked directly, "did Father Peter look familiar to you?"

Maria came back into focus and looked at Anne. "Well, yes, but since I've been working with Brother in Zurich, I've met so many priests that, quite frankly, he resembles a lot of them.

"But, to answer your question, I share your feeling of uneasiness with him. I, too, share your suspicions about his integrity—may God forgive me." Maria did the sign of the cross.

"I must confess," Maria continued. "From the moment the priest answered the door, I felt incredibly uneasy with him. He seemed to stare at me the entire he spoke to us. To be honest with you, I began to tremble beneath my habit, and I was privately praying no one would notice. There was no obvious reason for my uneasiness, except for the fact he kept staring at me. Do you think he knows about my baby?"

Her brother moved forward and embraced Maria. "Don't be silly, Sister. You had the baby in Zurich and gave it up for adoption immediately. Besides, my sweet sister, you were an innocent victim of a crime. You share no blame, no sin, no guilt. You have dedicated yourself to a life of service to the Church, and that is where your focus should remain.

"We'll remain here at the rectory and work with Father Peter until the bishop comes to visit or receive further instructions from Rome. We won't allow that man to push us away until we resolve this difficult issue. I'm sure the Good Lord has sent us here for a purpose."

CHAPTER THIRTY-SIX
ON A CARRIAGE TO QUEBEC CITY

June 1754

The tension in the rectory continued to grow over the next two weeks. Father Peter (Thomas) began to suspect that the Welti family questioned his credentials. The priest knew François and his two sisters couldn't connect all the dots, and their suspicions became manifest in how they behaved in his presence. Thomas held to his belief that the Weltis suspected something was not right. Still, he also realized that the Weltis had nothing to substantiate their suspicions without hard evidence.

Emilie and Thomas discussed the situation in the privacy of his bedroom:

"We can't continue like this indefinitely," Emilie said. "I'm tired of sneaking around this house to have a moment alone with you, and I'm tired of waiting on everyone as though I am a servant. Something must change!"

"I know we've got to do something, but what do you suggest?" the priest responded in the hope of appeasing Emilie.

"Can't you send them away? You're supposed to be the parish priest. Assert yourself. Be a man about it. Just tell them to leave on the next ship. I can't take this anymore," she said.

"Alright. I'll think of something, but it will just make them more suspicious of me."

"Not possible. The Welti family obliviously knows something is wrong with this scenario. I won't be surprised if they haven't already sent letters of inquiry to Rome. Can't you send them to Quebec City to work for a while—maybe indefinitely? That will give us time to leave here. I'm supposed to go to Philadelphia and prepare a report back to the king. You could come with me." Emilie suggested.

"Yes, in due time, but I'm in no hurry to leave here. Rome doesn't suspect anything. I've been sending reports back to Rome in the name of the dead priest, Father Anthony, who I have conveniently replaced."

Emilie looked into Father Thomas' twitching eyes and saw his propensity for evil. "Thomas, please tell me you had nothing to do with Father Anthony's demise. His death was too convenient for your purpose."

"Don't be ridiculous, Emilie. The man already had one foot in the grave when I arrived. The good news is that the old goat is still alive as far as Rome is concerned. Meanwhile, I've been able to skim the treasury enough to accumulate a tidy little fund for our welfare. We can live here in relative luxury and while nobody suspects anything—except, of course, those nosey newcomers.

You're right, though. I need to send our guests off to Quebec City for a while so we can have some time alone."

Don't be a fool, Damian urged Thomas. *Be rid of them all—permanently!*

Thomas did not reply. He stared straight ahead and smiled.

Two days later, the Weltis were on the parish carriage to Quebec City.

"What was that sudden thump, Brother?" Maria shouted as her body thrust forward, and the carriage stopped abruptly and leaned to its right side.

Without answering, Father François opened his door and sprang from the carriage onto the roadway. He saw the driver lying on the gravel and holding his left arm as he anguished in pain. The young priest ran to the driver and knelt to examine his injuries.

"I think I've broken my arm," the driver said through bleeding lips. "When the wheel broke, I was thrown from my seat. Thank God it was only my arm. I could have broken my neck."

Father François helped the driver back onto his feet. "There now, take a moment to steady yourself while I check for further injuries. I can see you have a bloody mouth. Do you think your teeth are alright?"

Before the driver could answer, two dark men on horses seemed to appear from out of nowhere. Father François turned to see them as they dismounted and rushed to assist the priest.

"My name is Raiko." Then, pointing toward his brother, Raiko said, "This is my brother Bojko. Is everyone alright? What can we do to help?"

"God bless you," the priest responded. "Please check on my sister inside the carriage while I tend to the driver."

Bojko stayed with the priest and the driver while Raiko rushed to the carriage. He looked inside the open door and saw a nun holding her head with elbows propped on her knees. "Are you alright, Sister?" he asked. Raiko stepped onto the running board and placed his hand on her shoulder.

The nun turned her head slowly toward him, without a word, and nodded. Raiko looked into her deep blue eyes and felt an immediate familiarity and connection with her. Raiko had never been so close to a nun before—or any woman for that matter. Something about this woman felt special. It was nonverbal; his spirit recognized her before his eyes did. Maria smiled; Raiko felt warm.

"I know you," the nun said with widened eyes and the first genuine grin she had on her face since she arrived. "Father Benedict cared for you while you were hiding out in the church attic in Erlach." Without another thought, she reached across and embraced him. "I'm so happy to see someone from back home. How did you get here? Where is your brother?"

"He's helping the priest tend to the injured driver. Come. Let me help you out of the carriage. He'll be happy to see you."

"That priest, by the way, is my brother. You never saw him because when you were in Erlach, he was serving in Zurich."

Raiko helped Maria from the coach and then approached Bojko. Bojko and the priest helped situate the driver beside the coach.

"Bojko," Raiko said, "Look who's here?"

Bojko turned around and stood up to look. He raised his eyebrows and cocked his head at an angle, and examined the nun with a grin. "Yes, of course," he said. "You are one of the twins from Erlach." Bojko's mind went back to the pretty teenaged identical twins he had seen come to the church to say their confessions to good Father Benedict. However, with that pleasant memory came the memory of evil Father Thomas and Thomas's adverse effect on their lives.

Father François, Raiko, and Bojko worked together to put the wheel back onto its axle. Bojko back-tracked only a few hundred yards when he found the nut that had worked its way off the axle threads. After the men fixed the carriage, they helped the driver onto the carriage. Raiko volunteered to drive it the rest of the way to Quebec City, all the while smiling at Maria and talking about Erlach, the village they had in common. Raiko was happy to learn she and her sister and brother would be staying in Quebec City indefinitely.

CHAPTER THIRTY-SEVEN
AN UNLIKELY RELATIONSHIP

The following week found Raiko and Bojko working diligently alongside their stepfather, Jànos, saddle-breaking horses for the French army with little time off for relaxation. Whenever there was time for rest, it was Sunday, and Sunday would find Raiko Celje in church without fail. Raiko would always make sure he saw an opportunity to chat with Sister Maria and Anne. Raiko always made sure his conversation inadvertently gravitated toward Sister Maria, but he could never manage to talk to Sister Maria alone. Speaking to Sister Maria alone was the one hope Raiko held in his prayers.

One June Sunday, Bojko waited outside the church for his brother. He wasn't surprised when he saw him in the company of Sister Maria and Anne when they came out the front door and then moved to the opposite side of the doorway to talk while Father François talked with parishioners leaving the church. He waited until Raiko had said his goodbyes to the women. Bojko noticed Maria's smile as she watched Raiko descend the stairs. Bojko approached his brother as he came down from the church and met him at the stairs' bottom.

Raiko was surprised to see him there.

"Raiko, we need to talk," Bojko said.

"Sure, brother. What do you want to talk about?"

"Come over here and sit on the steps. We need to talk about you and Sister Maria."

Raiko could tell from his brother's serious tone of voice that the conversation would be more of a lecture than talk and dreaded what he felt he knew was coming.

When they were seated on the low stone wall, Bojko turned slowly toward his brother, placed both hands on Raiko's shoulders, and looked into his brown eyes.

"Brother, you are getting too close to that nun." His voice fell silent, and he waited for a response from Raiko. Raiko dropped his head looked down at the ground to break eye contact.

Bojko butted his head gently against his brother's head and said, "Raiko. Get a grip on reality. I see the way the two of you look at each other. Brother, she's a nun! She's committed to the Church and Christ. You can never have her. You must find someone else to love. It can't be her."

"Get real, Bojko. It's not like that at all. I like her as a friend. And by the way, please stop talking about her as though she is an institution. She is a human being—yes, a woman—and she has a name. Her name is Maria."

"Yes," Bojko snapped back. "She does have a name, and her name is *Sister* Maria. You need to remember her position in the Church."

Raiko felt a twinge of guilt for how he knew he secretly felt about Maria Welti and began to justify his attachment. "I remember hiding out in the church's attic in Alcatel. Remember how we would peep down through the hole in the floor and watch the townsfolk come in on Saturday mornings to say their confessions? And do you remember how we both thought the Welti twins were so sweet and innocent?

"Well, back then, we were admirers from afar. We couldn't even say hello, smile at them, or even let them know we were alive. Only good old Father Benedict had any direct contact with us. He fed us and prayed for us and protected us.

"Then, that evil Father Thomas attacked Maria and tried to kill Father Benedict. Then he blamed his evil deeds on us and turned our lives upside down, and we became fugitives. We're not fugitives anymore, and we don't have to be afraid. Thanks to Bernardo Scalisi, we've become wealthy and found our mother and stepfather. Soon we'll be able to live as a family again and have some dignity.

"Nobody, including the Welti sisters, know of our wealth, yet the Welti family treats us with respect for who we are. Am I asking too much from life to enjoy a friendship based on nothing more than mutual respect? For the first time in my life, I can walk in the daylight and just be me."

Bojko could see the fire in his brother's eyes and hear the passion in his voice as he spoke.

"Now, more than ever," Bojko said, "I'm convinced your relationship with Maria is blinding you to the futility of an affection that could only lead to heartbreak.

"You, my dear brother, are falling in love with that woman. You are going to get hurt because she can't commit to you. I don't want that pain for you, yet no matter what I say to you, you'll resent my interference."

Reluctantly, Bojko tried to offer his best advice: "Raiko, don't take this the wrong way, but you need to back off for a while. You're getting too close to Maria, and you're both going to get hurt. If you don't back off for yourself, at least do it for her."

Raiko gritted his teeth and fought back his anger. "Bojko, we rarely disagree, and we never argue, but this is something with which you need have no involvement."

"So, what you're saying is for me to mind my own business?"

"Thank you, Bojko. I couldn't have said it better myself."

The brothers walked back to their house in silence, Bojko was fearful of saying more than he already had, and Raiko was angry that his brother had verbalized what he already knew to be accurate, but did not want to face the obvious.

The following weeks were devoid of any further conversation between the brothers regarding Raiko's affection for Maria, although Raiko sought increasing opportunities to spend more time with her. He attended every possible church service and volunteered to help with repairs at the church in Quebec City. During one such voluntary pair event, their affection for one another surfaced: Father François assigned Raiko and Maria to build a new prayer candle stand together. At the same time, he worked to oil the hinges on the large double door at the church entrance.

"Maria," Raiko asked, "would you please hold this board in place while I drive in some nails?"

"Of course," she said as she moved closer to Raiko. Their hands touched as they held the board in place together.

Raiko felt her presence as he had never felt it. He could see her slender white hand so close to his and felt the soft, warm breathing from her lips. As he swung the hammer toward the nail, he looked into her bright blue eyes, her face framed in her bonnet. His eyes remained transfixed on Maria instead of following the hammer as he swung it toward the nail. The hammer missed its mark and slammed hard against his thumb.

"Yow!" he cried out in pain.

Sister Maria instinctively dropped the board she was holding and grabbed his hand. She brought the injured thumb to her lips and kissed it. Raiko saw the tears of compassion in her eyes and was overwhelmed by realizing that she cared deeply for him. He took her hand in his and leaned forward, and kissed Maria on the lips. Maria withdrew, but not immediately. For the first time in her life, she felt like a woman, not a teenaged girl ravaged by an evil man, not a nun in the service of the Church, and not a woman with no prospects of finding romantic love. These emotions were new to Maria. Time stopped. She was in an isolated time capsule with no parameters, beginning, end, and consequences. It was the only time in her life that she wanted to be kissed by a man. It was the first time she felt loved for being a woman.

The board stuck hard against the tile floor, and the sound caught Father François' attention. He looked from where he was working on the double doors toward the candle stand just in time to see Raiko and Sister Maria kiss. He saw his sister push Raiko away, and remembering her forced encounter with Father Thomas back in Switzerland, he dropped his oil can and ran directly to the front of the church.

He fought back his immediate urge to grab hold of Raiko and punch him. All he could think of was how much Maria had already suffered. He thought of the attack she suffered that fateful morning in the prayer garden in Erlach. Rage filled his body. His muscles tightened, and his face grew scarlet as the veins in his forehead rose to the surface and looked as though they would pop at any minute.

"Raiko!" he shouted. "What in the world do you think you're doing? Leave now!"

"Brother, please." Maria pleaded. "Nothing happened. It's alright. It was my fault. Raiko didn't mean anything by it."

"Didn't mean anything by it?" Father François responded. "What kind of a man would attack a nun?"

"François, Raiko did not attack me. I'm fine. Raiko hurt his finger, and I kissed it. That's all."

Father François was speechless. What he saw was not just the innocent kissing of an injured finger. The priest had seen Raiko kiss his sister on the lips. What equally disturbed him was that he saw his sister take too much time resisting the kiss.

I should have done something earlier when I saw them spending too much time together. I had hoped that Raiko's interest was in Maria's inseparable sister, Anne—not Maria. I was a fool not to notice.

Maria's brother hurried to where his sister and Raiko were standing, staring into each other's eyes.

"Raiko," the priest said, "I'm afraid you've stepped over the line of decency. You need to leave now and not come back—except for the worship service."

"Brother, please," Sister Maria begged as François escorted Raiko by his arm to the door. Maria continued her plea for understanding as her brother gently nudged Raiko through the church's doorway and pulled the door shut behind him. He turned to his crying sister and looked at her for a few seconds before talking.

"Maria. What part of this scenario is it you don't understand? You are a servant and bride of the Lord, not some silly schoolgirl on her first date.

There is no room in your life for romance. You need to retire to your room and say your rosary and search your heart with the Blessed Virgin to find the right answers."

Maria didn't answer. Without another word, she turned, weeping, re-opened the church's front door, and departed.

When Sister Maria arrived at her shared room with Anne, she found Anne composing a letter to Anton Smith in care of the White Horse Inn in Philadelphia. Anne looked up from her secretarial desk and immediately noticed her sister was upset.

"Maria. What's wrong with you? I haven't seen you so upset for a long time. Come, sit here on the edge of the bed and talk to me."

Maria did as she asked. Anne moved over to sit beside her, put her arms around her, and embraced her. Anne's empathy opened a floodgate of tears as Maria trembled and openly wept in her arms.

After a few minutes of weeping, Anne asked, "Are you ready to tell me what happened?"

"It's all my fault," Maria exclaimed. "Raiko kissed me, and I allowed it. What's the matter with me? I know better than to lead a man on when I'm committed to the church. The trouble is, I wanted him to kiss me."

"You wanted him to kiss you?"

"Yes. What a horrible sinner I must be to want Raiko's affection. I can't help myself, Anne—I'm drawn to him."

"Drawn to him in what way, Maria."

Sister Maria broke eye contact and looked down at the floor. Then she slowly raised her head and looked directly into Anne's eyes. "Anne," she said. "I think I'm in love with him. No, I don't think it. I know I am!"

"Oh, dear me," Anne responded. "We have a problem, don't we? What about your vows of celibacy?"

"Yes. I have a problem, but I've had the problem for quite some time. I have given my vows a great deal of thought, and I'm convinced I took them for all the wrong reasons."

"Wrong reasons? What do you mean?"

"First of all, I have absolutely no recollection of what happened to me in the prayer garden at the church in Erlach. I knew I was hurt, but I don't remember the incident. Then when I found out I was pregnant, the guilt was overwhelming. It must have been my fault."

Anne listened silently to her sister, shaking her head but not saying a word. She knew Maria needed to get it all out in the open.

"Then, equally as bad, I allowed the convent in Zurich to talk me into giving up my son for adoption. They told me they had found the right home for the baby with a wealthy French woman who could care for the baby and give it a loving home. Every time I see a little boy with a French-speaking mother, I wonder, *could this baby be mine?*

"As if that weren't bad enough, the guilt I carried with me for both the rape and the abandonment of my child was overwhelming. I prayed, and I prayed, but the guilt wouldn't leave me. So, I made another wrong decision—I became a nun.

"I figured, somehow, by doing good works, God would absolve me from my sin. I thought no man would ever want me after having a child out of wedlock. Then I met Raiko, and the weight of the consequences of my bad decisions bore down on me. Help me, Anne. What can I do?"

Anne pulled her close and removed the habit bonnet from Maria's head. She smiled through her tears and reached for the hand mirror on the dresser. Anne held it up in front of Maria.

"Look into this mirror, Maria."

Her sister slowly raised her eyes to the mirror and tried to resist the smile forming on her face.

"What do you see, Maria? Can you face yourself with honesty?"

"I see a pathetic excuse for a woman, red-faced, tears in her eyes, confused, and scared, with hair that hasn't seen sunlight for a very long time," Maria replied.

Anne set the mirror face-down on the bed and smiled at her sister. "Do you know what I see?" She asked. "I see a lovely young woman who is the innocent victim of an evil man—I'm sorry, but I can't bring myself to say 'priest'—who did absolutely nothing wrong. I see a woman who keeps blaming herself for every little mishap in life. Maria, you are not responsible for what Father Thomas did to you and certainly are not responsible for getting pregnant and having a son.

"I want you to think about something, Maria. What happened to you just as easily could have happened to me in the garden that day. I seriously doubt he even knew which one of us twins it was he assaulted. I also seriously doubt if it would have made any difference to what girl he attacked. As far as he was concerned, it was going to happen, regardless of who the victim was or the consequences."

"Anne. Where do I go from here? Is it too late to turn back the clock of time, to undo what is? Am I trapped forever in the consequences of circumstances that are beyond my control? I know I made decisions that seemed right at the time, but I made those decisions because I was confused and frightened."

"Whoa, Maria. You are firing too many questions at me too fast. You're panicking again, and panic drove you to make what you now consider to be bad decisions. Let's slow down for a minute and allow reason to set in, so you don't make the same mistake twice.

"The first thing you need to do, my dear sister, is quit blaming yourself for the sin of the entire world. Forgiveness of our sin is God's job, not yours, but you can begin by forgiving yourself. Then, realize you have done nothing wrong regarding that morning in Erlach. It is Thomas who needs to ask for forgiveness. Your part in the forgiveness process is to forgive the transgressor. Remember the part of the Lord's Prayer, which says, '…forgive us our trespasses, as we forgive those who trespass against us?' That's the most challenging part, isn't it?"

"Yes, it is. But how can I forgive a man for an act of which I have no recollection? Yes, the resulting pregnancy and the birth of my son, yes, I can forgive for that. My prayer would be that the Lord will allow me to remember someday and to be able to confront that evil man."

Anne pulled her teeth across her lower lip to avoid speaking. *Should I tell Maria about my suspicions about Father Peter being the rapist and her child's father? Can she handle my unfounded and unprovable accusations that he is Father Thomas? No, not now. It would be unfair.*

"The time of remembrance and confrontation may very well come someday, my dear sister. For now, however, you have other, more pressing issues.

"Regarding your feelings for Raiko, only you can know how you feel, but I do understand the draw of love. I'm here in New France because of my love for Anton. I've abandoned the only home I ever knew, left our parents, and crossed an ocean to search for the man I love. Not a day goes by without my heart longing to see his face, touch his hand, or hear his voice. Yes, sister, I do know love."

"But what should I do about Raiko? François has forbidden him ever to approach me again. I want to honor François' wishes, and I certainly want to honor God, but what do I do about my feelings for Raiko, and how do I make those feelings for Raiko compatible with my vows?"

"My only suggestion would be to follow your heart. Pray about your vows and ask the Lord to show you the way. If you still feel strongly about your decision to make a life with Raiko, talk the situation over with our brother after you've prayed it through. Yes, François is a priest, but he's still our brother."

CHAPTER THIRTY-EIGHT
PUTTING PREJUDICE INTO PERSPECTIVE

April 16, 1754

It would be spring in only five days, but winter showed few signs of releasing its firm grip on Quebec. The trees still looked like skeletons firmly planted in the frozen snow, and spring tulips slept beneath a blanket of white. Crows, blue jays, and cardinals scavenged for food remnants among the garbage heaps piled outside the city during the daylight hours, and black bears prowled the garbage dump by night.

One-hundred-twenty horses, still in their shaggy winter coats, filled the muddy coral at Quebec City, awaiting the French troops' arrival. The Celje men had finished their job of training the horses, as promised. All that remained was to spend their time exercising the horses until Arquette signed off on the papers to conclude the contract. Toward that end, Bojko, Raiko, and Jànos prepared to take the documents to Arquette in Montreal.

"You look like a true Count now," Raiko jabbed at Jànos, "sitting up there on that magnificent white stallion. If it weren't for your dirty clothes, I'd say you were royalty for sure."

Jànos reached across his saddle and patted the stallion's neck in a display of affection. "I have to admit I've taken a keen liking to this horse. He was the first horse I saddle-broke, and we've been the best of friends ever since. I'll be sad to leave him behind, but he'll undoubtedly be cared for by some high-ranking French officer. And by the way, don't forget I'm a Hungarian Magyar, not of the noble Romanian bloodline of you and Bojko. My father wasn't a nobleman, like your father, Count Celje."

Jànos' words hit Raiko like a slap in the face. Jànos hadn't meant any harm, but he was right. *Here we are,* Raiko thought, *carrying letters of credit from our inheritance that would qualify us as wealthy men, but we are training horses. Our bodies are filthy, and our clothing is covered with mud and ice. We have a mother who served as a slave for nearly two decades because she is a Gypsy. Lord, you make us endure all this hardship while our half-brother plays around Europe at his leisure. Where's the justice in this world?*

Raiko began to feel the bitterness of his hatred eat away at him, and he didn't like it. *I've pledged to put this all behind me, and I will. Oh well, getting even is God's job, not ours. I need to let this pass.*

Raiko's thoughts were interrupted by shouts from atop the wall. A man on the catwalk yelled, "Ships are approaching. I can see them now."

CHAPTER THIRTY-NINE
A DEAL'S A DEAL

April 23, 1754

Raiko and Bojko Celje ran to the fortress wall and climbed up to the catwalk. They leaned forward to look over the wooden fortress wall and could see a fleet of five ships still so far out in the distance they looked like children's toys floating on a pond in Paris. "I see the *La Patience*," Bojko said.

Raiko shaded his strained eyes as he struggled to identify which ship was Captain Beloux's ship. "How, in the name of Heaven, can you tell one ship from the other at this distance?" he asked with skepticism.

"It's the *La Patience* in the lead; I'm sure of it. After spending all those weeks climbing on its masts and being called the "ship's monkey," there can be no doubt. Let's run back and tell Jànos. He'll need to get *Mutter* packing."

Raiko had a look of panic on his face when he considered all they'd need to do to get ready. "How much time do you think we'll have to pack, Bojko? We can't afford to miss the ship's departure."

"Are you kidding me?" Bojko replied. "Considering how little we own; we can still pack our sea bags and be gone in ten minutes. On the other hand, *Mutter* will have to pack a lot of stuff for baby Joy. Let's get moving."

The Celjes returned to the coral to find Jànos mounted bareback on the great white stallion. They shared the good news of Captain Beloux's arrival. "Go tell the others to start packing. We'll run down to the customs building to tell Beloux to save us passage to Baltimore," Raiko suggested.

"How much time will we have to get everything ready?" asked their stepfather.

"*La Patience* will spend at least two days in customs here in Quebec City. After that, it'll take a couple of days to unload their goods in Montreal, then a couple more days to load goods to take back. Then, if for whatever reason, we're still not ready, the *La Patience* will have to stop back here on its way out to sea. All in all, I'd say we have at least a week," Bojko said. "Your main concern, Jànos, should be to get Arquette to sign off on your papers so you will be free to go. We already have *Mutter's* papers signed, sealed, and delivered. But it's you we're worried about, and we're not leaving here without you."

Jànos immediately hopped down off the stallion and ran, muddy boots and all, back to their house to alert his wife and the DeWitt couple. Raiko and Bojko ran down the steep hill to the customs house to await *La Patience's* arrival.

It had taken nearly an hour for the first ship to fight its way upstream from where the Celjes sighted it, but Bojko had made the right call. The *La Patience* was the first ship to the dock, and soon the Celjes were waving to former crew members they knew from their time onboard.

"What's with all the other ships?" Bojko called Pierre as he threw a rope to the dockhand.

"Military," Pierre shouted back. "They're loaded with soldiers and supplies. It looks like it will be quite busy around here for a while. We'll get together for an ale once we clear customs, and I fill you in on the details."

"That'd be great," Bojko replied, "because we need to talk with you about your next stop. Raiko and I must go to Montreal today on urgent business. We'll catch up with you when you get there."

The ride back to Montreal was much faster than the first trip to Quebec City in the oxen-pulled wagon. Jànos took the lead on the white stallion, followed closely behind by Raiko and Bojko on their recently saddle-broke steeds.

The three men arrived in Montreal in the late afternoon. The skies had cleared somewhat, and the afternoon sun shone brightly through gaps in the partially clouded sky, but the optimistic attitudes of the Gypsies, fueled by the weather's pleasant change, were soon dimmed by what they saw. They rounded the corner one block from the Arquette's Livery just in time to see a familiar figure leave Arquette's livery and walk with a slight limp toward a black-covered carriage. The threesome came to an abrupt stop as the carriage passed them in the opposite direction.

"Is that who I think it is?" Bojko asked his brother.

"None other," Raiko answered. "I'd recognize that walk anywhere. He's heavier now and has grown a beard, but that is unmistakably none other than our archenemy. I owe you an apology, brother, for doubting you. And did you notice he was smiling that evil smile of his? He's up to something, I tell you."

"It doesn't matter what he's up to," Jànos interjected, "we'll be out of here in a couple of days. He can rot in the pits of Hell for all I care."

The three men dismounted in front of the livery and walked their horses into the stable. They found Arquette instructing a groom on what to do. "*Bonjour*, Monsieur Arquette," Jànos greeted. Jànos' soon-to-be-former master neither returned the greeting nor smiled.

What are you doing here?" Arquette asked in a nasty tone. "I'm quite busy, and the three of you are supposed to be training those horses. Be brief and then get back to work."

Jànos reached into his coat pocket and withdrew an invoice signed by Arquette's Livery of Quebec City manager. He held it out to Arquette. "You will notice, Monsieur; this signed receipt testifies to the fact that there are exactly one-hundred and twenty horses trained and ready for the French military in Quebec City. In other words, we've fulfilled our obligation to you, and I'm to become a free man—as per our agreement."

Arquette snapped the paper arrogantly from Jànos' hand. He carefully read its contents. "This paper is meaningless until I have had a chance to inspect the horses personally. Right now, I'm too busy to bother with it."

The look of utter despair on the Magyar's face was unmistakable. He was furious. It took every ounce of his strength not to attack this man who stood in front of him, ignoring his obligation to fulfill his agreement. "And when do you think you'll have the opportunity to inspect the horses?"

"Oh, I don't know. Perhaps in a week or so. With the weather being so unpredictable, one never really knows from day to day what might happen. I'm sure I'll get around to it sooner or later."

Bojko looked down at his stepfather's strong hands and saw Jànos clench them into fists. "I don't suppose your reluctance to fulfill your obligation has anything to do with a conversation you might have had with a certain priest we saw leaving here a few minutes ago, would it?" he asked.

Arquette smiled for the first time, sheepishly, nervously, but with considerable guilt. "I'm not saying it does, and I'm not saying it doesn't, but Father Peter has told me a great deal about you boys. He told me about your sentence to hang in Switzerland for raping a young girl and killing a parish priest. Is that right?"

Jànos lost it with those words of accusation. He started to lung forward at Arquette when Bojko grabbed hold of him and made him stop. Arquette jumped back in fright.

"Look," Raiko intervened, "You have our thousand pounds, and we upheld our end of the bargain by helping Jànos with an otherwise impossible deadline of delivering one-hundred-twenty trained horses before the end of April. A deal's a deal. We expect you to uphold your end of that bargain too, so inspect those horses and give us the necessary papers for this man's freedom."

Arquette trembled nervously. Three men, any one of whom could have, and wanted to, beat him to a pulp; Arquette also felt the weight of the authority and influence of the Church and the expectations of the priest who had just left. "Go back to Quebec City," he said, to gain more time and to be rid of the current intimidation. "If the weather holds, I should get there by tomorrow evening for the inspection. That's all I can promise."

CHAPTER FORTY
THE ARRIVAL OF THE
LA PATIENCE IN MONTREAL

The Gypsies and their stepfather were waiting when Pierre and the captain arrived at the dock. Beloux disembarked.

"You two Gypsies are like a bad debt that keeps coming back," the captain said as he held out his hand and laughed in a joyous greeting. "Let's go to my brother-in-law's inn, La Fleur. It's nearby, and we can talk there. I don't know about you, but I'm starved and need something good to drink. Are you familiar with the inn?"

"Only vaguely," Raiko answered. "We've spent most of our time in Quebec City, helping our father here," nodding toward Jànos, "train horses for the army." The captain looked astonished. "I don't believe it! You found your parents?" He held out his hand to greet Jànos.

"What about your mother?" Beloux inquired.

"She's fine, and we got a new baby sister in the bargain." Pierre, the captain, and Jànos exchanged congratulations, and the group continued the few short blocks to the inn.

Capt. Beloux, when seated at the White Horse Inn with his friends, proposed a toast: "To my Gypsy friends; former crew members, former passengers, and always friends, whose paths continually cross mine, and always for the better."

"Here, here!" they said in unison as they rattled the metal containers together in agreement with the captain's toast.

"So, tell me now," the captain said, "Pierre tells me you need to talk with us? Don't tell me you want to sign on again."

The Gypsies told Pierre, and the captain about their plans to leave and the delay Arquette had presented them in securing papers for their father. "I'll tell you what I'd do if he gives you any more grief," the captain said. "We'll be sailing in four days with the evening tide, and here's what I'd do if I were you..."

Raiko wasted no time in his desire to contact his beloved Maria. When his meeting with Captain Beloux and his nephew, Pierre, concluded, he spoke. "If you will excuse me, folks, I have some urgent personal business to take care of before we depart New France. I'll meet you back here as soon as possible."

Bojko became suspicious of his brother's motives. "How long will you be?" Bojko asked.

"I don't know; maybe an hour, maybe two." Raiko stood up to leave and excused himself.

Bojko looked sternly up at him and said, "I'll walk you to the door."

He stood up, sympathetically put his arm around his brother, and led him away from the table and out the front door of the noisy inn into the cold air of the quiet street.

"Am I to assume, Raiko, you are going to meet with Maria?"

"So, what if I am? Surely you can't expect me to leave here a few hours from now, like a thief in the night, without explaining why to Maria? What do you think that would do to her to believe I cared so little for her? Of course, I'm going to try, at the least, leave her a message. Better yet, I'll talk to her face-to-face. I owe her that much."

Bojko felt terrible for the heartache his brother felt, and he felt bad he had not been more empathetic toward both Raiko and Maria. *Why shouldn't he tell her goodbye? Maybe his leaving will be best for them both. It will give them time to sort out their emotions and realize the gravity of any decision about becoming involved with one another. After all, him a Gypsy and her a nun? What are the chances a relationship like that could last?*

"Very well, Brother. Do what you must, but I'm coming along with you to make sure you don't get into a confrontation with Father Peter or with Father François."

"Come, if you feel the need, but I'm telling you right now, stay in the shadows so Maria and I can talk privately. I'll tolerate no interference from you or anyone else."

Bojko agreed to his brother's terms and re-entered the inn to inform his friends he would return later. When he went back into the street, Raiko was gone.

The first floor of the rectory was well lighted when Raiko arrived searching for Maria. He quietly approached the kitchen window and peered inside. He could see Emilie standing in front of the sink, washing dishes with her back to Father Peter, while the priest sat at the kitchen table. The priest was nervously fidgeting with a cup of tea he held cupped in his hands while he stared at Emilie's back.

Emilie turned toward Thomas and leaned her back against the countertop while she dried her hands on a tile. "How much longer are you going to continue this charade of me being your housekeeper? You treat me like a common domestic. You humiliate me with orders of 'do this and do that' in front of the others. I am a woman of substance, an agent of the King, and a free woman."

She held out her reddened hands and moved close to Thomas for him to examine. "Look at my poor hands. They are reddened and wrinkled like an older woman. I've had it with you. I'm leaving on the next ship out of here."

"Now, now, my sweet. Don't be like that. It won't be much longer, I promise." He reached up and put his arms around her waist, and tried to pull her closer.

Emilie grabbed hold of his arms and pushed them away from her. She wriggled away from his embrace and backed up to her original position against the sink. "Don't try to smooth this over with your *faux* affection. I don't want your affection now, and I don't want it ever. I'm through with you." She wiped her hands again with the dishtowel she held and threw it across the room to where Thomas was sitting. The damp towel hit the priest on the head and wrapped around his face. Thomas quickly reached up and pulled it away from his face, knocking his teacup over and spilling its contents.

The second floor was dark, and that Emilie and Thomas were talking without restraint caused Raiko to conclude the Weltis were not in the house. The logical conclusion led him to think they must be in the church. He went to the front entrance, slowly cracked open the right door, and peeked inside. He saw Father François and his two sisters kneeling in front of the altar. Silently, he pushed open the recently oiled door and entered the church. The resultant draft from the opened door caused the candles on the altar to flicker. François immediately ended his prayer and turned as he stood to see who had entered the sanctuary.

"What are you doing here?" he demanded when he recognized the man who he had forbidden to see his sister.

Immediately Maria and Anne stood and turned to see their brother was shouting.

Maria nearly fainted at the sight of Raiko. She recovered and ran down the church's aisle and into Raiko's arms. They embraced.

The response from François was one of anger. He walked with urgency toward them, leaving Anne still standing in shock at the front of the church. Anne never expected such a passionate response from her sister at the sight of Raiko. Maria's reaction removed any doubt from Anne's mind about Maria's decision.

When her brother reached Raiko and Maria, the intensity of what he witnessed in their embrace caused him to realize what he had seen a few days before was not a forced kiss from Raiko. It caused the priest to pause as Maria openly wept in Raiko's arms. Like Anne, he realized Maria was in love with the Gypsy. That realization prevented the priest from hitting the Raiko. He realized they all needed to talk.

"Raiko. Maria. We need to talk." He pointed toward a pew at the back of the church and motioned for Anne to join them. Just then, the church's front door opened, and Bojko entered.

"You might as well join us too Bojko," the priest said. "We had better get this all out into the open and get it over with."

Bojko moved toward the pew and sat beside his already seated brother without uttering another word. Anne, Maria, Bojko, and Raiko remained seated while Father François stood in the aisle at the end of the pew. He directed his question at the young couple:

"What do you intend to do about your situation?" he asked.

Maria looked into Raiko's eyes and then looked toward her brother and spoke: "Brother, I have been in intense prayer about this ever since I realized I was in love with Raiko. I'm at peace with the fact that I will not continue as a nun.

"Please don't get me wrong. I've enjoyed working alongside you as a nun, and I must admit it has been the happiest time of my life serving Christ. But I'm also aware that I would have never done it if it weren't for what happened to me back in Erlach.

"I was disgraced, ashamed, and torn. My service has helped me forgive whoever did this to me and my son's resultant birth. But I told Raiko everything I can remember, and he is comfortable with that knowledge. Together, God willing, we will find my son, and I will try to get him back."

Her brother looked down at the floor and shook his head. "That is not practical, Maria. What chance could you have in finding a son who is two years old now? You gave up a son in Switzerland to people you don't even know. Get realistic, Maria. That is not going to happen."

Raiko spoke. "And what chance do you think I had of finding my parents who were sold into slavery in Central Europe over ten years ago? God has allowed me to find them, and now we are a family again. He might do the same thing for Maria."

"He might," Maria's brother responded, "but it's highly improbable."

"Improbable, perhaps, but at least I'll have Raiko. God willing, we'll have a family of our own someday."

"And, speaking of God's will," François added, "what about God's will for your vows?"

Maria reached over, took hold of Raiko's hand. "I do not doubt that God understands why I took my vows in the first place. In His infinite mercy, He knows my heart and will bless a marriage with Raiko. We will serve in another capacity through Christian lives."

"What about my mission here at the church? I need you to honor your commitment to helping me here until we can at least receive an answer from Rome about this Father Peter mess. I still believe there is something fishy about what he told us. When would you leave if you were going to marry Raiko?"

Maria's jaw dropped, and her eyebrows raised as if she were about to speak but couldn't find the words. She looked questionably at Raiko and then turned, once again, toward her brother. "Well, to be honest about it, Raiko and I haven't discussed marriage. Our feelings for one another have all happened so quickly. We need time together to talk about making some plans." She turned back toward Raiko and said, "I'm not even sure he wants me for his wife."

Raiko was just as shocked as Maria was about the rapid change of events. All he knew was he loved her and never got beyond the first kiss. "Of course, I want to marry you," he said as Raiko held her hands cupped in his, "but you're right. We need some time to discuss this, and I'm leaving in a couple of days."

"You're leaving?" Maria asked with newly sprung tears in her questioning eyes.

"Yes," he said. "I will go to Philadelphia and get settled, and then I'll send for you. I have enough money to purchase a house there, and we can live there in peace. I'll send for you by next fall, I promise." Maria kept looking at him without saying a word as the reality of what he had said sank into her mind.

"Well, that's not all bad," Anne interjected. "Maria and I can stay here and help Brother while you get established. That gives us several months to hear from Rome." She directed her attention to the priest, and said, "What do you think, Brother?"

"I'm still trying to sort all of this out in my head. I do like the thought of having time for all of us to allow reason to prevail.

"But, Raiko, what if my sister changes her mind about leaving the sisterhood? Will you be able to accept it?"

Raiko looked at Maria and nodded. "Yes, of course. How happy could we be if Maria had second thoughts about her decision a year or so down the road? I want her to be happy and free of guilt."

Maria squeezed Raiko's hand and smiled. "Thank you for your willingness to give me latitude. I already know what my decision is now, and I know what it will be next fall." She pulled his hand to her mouth and kissed his fingers.

There would not be another chance for Raiko and Maria to discuss their future before his day of departure.

CHAPTER FORTY-ONE
TYING UP LOOSE ENDS

April 28, 1754

It had been more than a month since the Vernal Equinox had begun to tilt the northern hemisphere toward the warming sun. Yet, darkness still came early during the bleak afternoons, and winter refused to acknowledge spring's existence. Winter refused to loosen the icy grip it held on the land.

Like a theater's heavy curtain, the early evening darkness concealed a cast of experienced players who moved in carefully choreographed precision with the silence of mimes. Captain Beloux, with the skilled movements of a concert conductor, orchestrated the opening cue for his cast to begin the work of quietly nudging the *La Patience* from its moorings. Silently and gracefully, the ship started its dangerous voyage down the icy Saint Lawrence toward its rendezvous with waiting friends in Quebec City.

In the rectory of The Church of the Visitation, the Welti twins prepared dinner for their brother and the resident priest, Father Peter. A loud knock came unexpectedly at the door. Father Peter rushed from his study to intercept the visitor. "I'll get it," he called out as he passed through the kitchen, "I think I might know what this is about." The priest opened the door and found a young boy panting and attempting to deliver his urgent message.

"They didn't wait (gasp), for the morning tide (gasp), they left tonight. I ran here as soon as I realized what the Gypsies were doing," the boy managed to get out between breaths.

Father Peter reached a trembling hand into his pocket, pulled out a coin, and handed it to the youth. "Thank you, son," he said, "Go relate this same information to Monsieur Arquette. Have him meet me with a carriage at the magistrate's office."

The faux priest shut the door abruptly in the boy's face. He turned and leaned back against the door as if in deep thought and blew into his clenched fist and said, talking audibly to the demon within.

"I should have known better than to trust that slimy sea captain!"

Kill them all, starting with the Welti sisters and their brother. They're nothing but trouble.

"No," the priest rebutted. "I can't do that!"

You are spineless.

Thomas looked across the room at the puzzled Welti sisters, who had no idea what he was talking about, and said, "I won't have time for dinner. Wrap me something I can eat on the way to Quebec City. I'll return in a couple of days." He ran to his quarters and put on warm clothes. Then he came back and grabbed what Anne Welti had prepared for him, and without any sign of gratitude, he ran out the kitchen door to the magistrate's office as fast as his legs could carry him.

"What was that all about?" Anne asked of her brother.

"I don't know," Father François said. "He seems to be obsessed with capturing your friend, Raiko, and his brother. He claims they're fugitives from justice."

Anne's mouth opened, and she inhaled a sudden gulp of air. The woman's eyes opened wide, and her heart raced. Anne's panic showed clearly on her reddened face. "Maria," she said. "Brother is right. He *must* be talking about Raiko and Bojko. He's going to try to harm them. We must warn them somehow."

Anne's face became pale as she felt a sudden overwhelming experience with déjà vu. A heavy veil of fog lifted from her memory.

"And now I understand!" she screamed. "There was a haunting familiarity about Father Peter that I couldn't place. But when he got angry at the news from that boy, it all began to come back to me. Take away the beard and mustache and about forty pounds of weight, and beneath it all is none other than Father Thomas. I can't believe I didn't see that earlier. Thomas fooled me."

"Surely you don't mean Father Thomas from Alchatel?" Father François asked. "The one who..." He looked across the table at his sister, Marie, and continued with caution. "... Father Thomas, who Bishop Roten defrocked? If that's him, he's not even a priest any longer. He's a total fraud."

Marie's face had a distant look, a look without external focus. She was staring into a place in her mind that had been dark for a very long time. But now, a small and distant glimmer grew ever brighter. A spark of memory began to ignite the illuminating light of cognizance. The dull shades of suppressed events, locked for five years in the recesses of her mind, were suddenly brought into the light of awareness. Her amnesia began to lift, and the missing dots started to connect. "Oh, dear Lord," she said, "it's starting to come back to me." Tears welled up in her eyes, and her body began to tremble. Anne moved her chair close to her sister and put her arms around her as they both wept.

"It wasn't Gypsies who attacked me at all, was it? It was Father Thomas—or Father Peter—or whatever name that evil man goes by. And, if he's the one who violated me, where's my baby? I have it on good authority; a couple brought my son here to New France. I don't know who that couple was—probably him—with that woman named Emilie De Fontaine, but I couldn't find any records of her ever having come here. Everything about that man is a lie."

Maria's eyes widened, and her jaw dropped. "Oh, no. You don't think Emilie—the housekeeper—is the woman who took my baby, do you? The woman who visited the convent in Switzerland was also named

Emilie—and was said to be a beautiful blonde. That would explain why she doesn't fit the role of a housekeeper.

"What am I to believe? Everything is happening too fast: too much information in too short a time." Marie began to break down. "I want to see my son," she cried hysterically. "Where is he?"

Her brother looked at Marie in amazement. "You knew about your baby being brought to New France all along and never told me? How did you find out about Mademoiselle De Fontaine?"

"Please, brother," she cried, "I'm a nun, not an idiot. People of the cloth have their ways of finding out things. You should know that better than I."

Father François moved over to his sister and embraced her. "I'm sorry, Marie," he said, "If your son is in New France, I'll help you find him."

In Quebec City, the Celje and DeWitt families gathered their belongings and prepared for their exit on the *La Patience*, still sailing between Quebec City and Montreal, some one hundred and sixty miles away.

"This is the day Captain Beloux said he'd stop to pick us up," Maisha said. "My husband and I will take Florica and the baby to Monsieur Lamoure's inn and take a room. That way, we will have a warm place to stay with the baby and still be close to the pier. Lamoure expects us to leave and make his rental house available to the military anyway, so he'll be pleased we've moved out. You, three men, need to go to work as usual. That way, nobody will think anything's out of the ordinary. I'm sure the ship's arrival will cause quite a stir in this small town. Believe me, when I say you'll know when it's here. When the ship arrives, don't wait. Make haste to get to the pier and onto the ship. We'll be nervous wrecks until you get there to join us. Beloux won't wait for us very long because he needs to move on before word reaches the harbormaster that he left Montreal without authorization."

"You can count on us," Jànos said, "We have a plan."

Later that late afternoon, the men in Florica's life were glad they had a plan of action. The timing couldn't have been worse, however. The news of the arrival of *La Patience* brought joy to the hearts of many.

When Jànos saw the ship, he raced back to the livery on his white stallion a few miles outside of town. "The priest, Arquette, and four soldiers are headed our way. They can't be more than twenty minutes behind me riding at a cantor. We need to get aboard the ship as soon as possible. I'll ride ahead and alert the women."

When Jànos arrived at the inn, he was about to dismount when he heard Florica's voice calling him from a block away. He hurried down to meet her. "Maisha and Robert have the baby and are going to board as soon as the gangway lowers. Where are my boys?" she asked.

"Get up here on my horse and let me take you to the ship. Raiko and Bojko are putting our plan into action as we speak." He reached down and took Florica's hand, and pulled her up onto the stallion behind him. "We need to get you on the ship. The boys aren't far behind."

Back at the livery, Raiko and Bojko sat mounted on their horses. Raiko was at the gate to the corral, ready to swing it open while Bojko moved to the back of the nervous herd of one hundred and seventeen horses. He kept slowly driving them forward until the lead horses pressed hard against the gate. As soon as Raiko saw their archenemy come around the corner with his entourage, he released the gate, and Bojko let out a mighty yell. The horses panicked into a full-fledged stampede and thundered out of the coral at full gallop toward Father Thomas and his crew. The stampede's thunder and the frightening sight of the approaching herd caused Father Thomas' carriage horses to rear back and overturn his wagon.

Thomas hit the ground hard with his right leg pinned beneath the wagon.

You fool! Damian shouted. *You are letting them get away again. Get them, and this time kill them!*

Thomas grabbed the sideboard with his hands and managed to pull his legs closer to the wagon, but not before a hoof crushed down with tremendous force upon his shoulder, where only seconds before, his head laid. The pain was unbearable, and the ex-priest lost consciousness.

The *La Patience* sat at the ready, moored with its gangway lowered and only two ropes to keep it from drifting away from the dock. Two long-boats were secured alongside the *La Patience*, ready to tow her into the current. The captain's nephew was at the ready beside the ship's wheel. Capt. Beloux stood at the rails with his men in a position to receive his command for departure.

The distant sound of approaching hooves broke the silence of the night air as they pounded, first against the cobblestones of the street, then their hollow beating across the planks of the dock.

Captain Beloux strained his eyes into the darkness and leaned forward against the ship's rails. "Someone is approaching us with serious intent, but I can't make out who it is," the captain shouted to his men. "Have your muskets at the ready…no, no! I can see who it is. Lower your muskets."

Jànos stopped the stallion at the bottom of the gangway. He jumped down from the horse and helped his wife. Florica held baby Joy against her bosom to protect her against the night air, down from the mount.

Beloux smiled. "Mighty fine-looking stallion you have there. "Let's get him on board."

"It's not mine. It belongs to Arquette—actually, to the French army now."

"Seems to me," the captain replied, "he owes it to you. Has the army paid Arquette for the horses?"

"No, not yet."

"Great," the captain said through a smile. "Then it is still the property of Arquette. Has he paid you for your training of the horses?"

"No, he hasn't."

"Even better," Beloux said. "As captain of this ship, I declare you to be the rightful owner of the stallion. Bring it on board and be quick about it. We have no time to be lollygagging."

Gunshots erupted in the distance. Jànos nudged Florica toward the gangway and turned to look up the hill behind him. He could barely make out two approaching riders, who he assumed to be Raiko and Bojko. They were galloping ahead of hot lead, fired at them from the two soldiers who lost their horses.

Captain Beloux leaned across the ship's railing and called down to Jànos, "It looks to me like Arquette tried to double-cross you and the boys. Get that horse up the gangway, and let's get out of here."

The twins arrived at the ship as Jànos ran up the gangway. They didn't bother to dismount, but instead, they rode their horses up behind him.

"Cast off!" the captain ordered. Four crew members strained against long polls to push the ship from the dock and into the St. Lawrence's current. "I want everyone to get away from the railings and get below. I don't want to lose any of you to a lucky shot from those terrible marksmen. I think we're out of range, but we can't be too sure."

Within minutes, *La Patience* was in the current of the Saint Lawrence with the longboats detached. A frustrated Thomas grimaced in pain and leaned against his overturned wagon as he watched the Gypsies elude him once more. "It's not over yet," he vainly shouted to an audience who could not hear him. "I swear I'll get you even if I have to track you to the ends of the earth."

CHAPTER FORTY-TWO
LOYALTIES

Captain Beloux sat in his cabin while a faint fragrance of lilac perfume permeated from behind the drawn curtain that surrounded the captain's bed. His guests were seated around his table as he paused while the cook poured hot tea. The Celje twins, their mother and stepfather, and Robert and Mashia DeWitt were sitting with him. The *La Patience,* well underway and beyond any danger from Quebec City, proceeded slowly behind two lifeboats that guided the ship through the icy waters of Saint Lawrence River.

Beloux spoke to his guests more as friends than as passengers. "Folks, I'm afraid I've put myself in a real pickle. I upset the English when I snuck out of Philadelphia with the Dewitts and Celjes—not to mention a cargo I was not anxious for the harbormaster to inspect—and then I did the same thing with the French in New France. It appears I have made myself *persona non grata* in the entire New World." He snickered as he lifted his cup of hot tea to his mouth. He appeared to relish his defiance and his new status as a rebel.

"Exactly where do your loyalties rest?" Raiko asked.

Beloux blew on his tea and then set the cup back on the table as though in deep thought. "I would have to say my loyalties are first, to myself and my investors; after that, to my family and my friends. But make no mistake of it, for the most part; my crew is as much a part of my family as my nephew, Pierre."

"What I meant was to what country do you owe your allegiance?"

"What country? I've been at sea since I was fourteen years old. The sea is where I hold my citizenship.

Kings are nothing more than thugs. They became 'noble' only because they stole from the serfs and paid men to become soldiers. Kings have bullied the little guy from time immemorial. Then, when they controlled everything they lived in, they began to turn on each other to take the neighboring king's territory. After they murdered and pillaged a large enough area, they called it a 'sovereign country.' Now, Kings Louis and George want what the other has, so they plan to slaughter thousands more men, women, and children to accomplish their goals. After that, who knows? Why not the entire world? Kings are nothing more than land pirates. The only difference between a criminal and a king is how much money and power they have. No, I owe loyalty to neither thug—Louis nor George."

There was a silence at the table. Nobody knew quite what to say. The guests nervously reached for their teacups and drank more to stall for time than because they were thirsty. Robert broke the silence: "Maisha, and I don't care where your loyalties are. We only know you have been good to us, and we are eternally grateful."

"And us too," added Bojko. "Very few people in our lives, outside of Bernardo Scalisi and the old priest at Erlach, have ever shown us that kind of friendship or loyalty."

"Maybe that's why I love you boys so much," the captain said, "you remind me of myself. You've been bounced around by so many countries and so many harsh laws. You don't have any reason to embrace any king, either. Like me, your loyalty rests with your family." Beloux looked at Florica and János and smiled.

"Now, if you don't mind, I'd like to change the subject. What comes next? We can't sail into Philadelphia in broad daylight as the *La Patience*, regardless of what flag I fly. But because I'm no stranger to dealing with governments, I'm going to use one of my old tricks." He got up and walked to the armoire, where he kept various flags and withdrew a wooden plate engraved *"The Shamrock."* "What do you think of this? If you'd prefer another name, I can have the ship's carpenter make us one with a different name.'

Their laughter could be heard from stem to stern as the nature of Captain Beloux's mischievous ways became blatantly apparent. All agreed that the captain's existing plate in his hands would do fine. All was made ready with the plates added to the ship's sides, and a British flag raised overhead. Captain Beloux retrieved the ship's registry's falsified papers from the cabinet and began preparing for his cunning deception. Within a week, *The Shamrock* was in the Chesapeake Bay and about to enter the Delaware River.

The sun had nearly set when the ship began its fight against the river's current and slowly worked its way toward Philadelphia. At the same time, the illegal immigrants waited patiently in the captain's quarters. Conversations ranged from the Celjes' decision to find employment in the city to DeWitt decision to slip up the Susquehanna River to Fort Standing Stone, where they would establish a trading post. Sleep didn't come easy for anyone, and the hours passed slowly. Finally, the anchor's lowering sound over the ship's side aroused the wayfarers to action.

The morning sky appeared dark and bleak as the rising sun's light attempted to filter through the heavy clouds and drizzling rain that often typifies the spring season in the Delaware Valley. "A perfect morning for a landing," the captain shouted as he pulled open the door and entered his cabin. "As you might expect, I won't be taking you the entire way into town. We will stop at a favorite stop-point of mine called Long Island, where I've dropped off a few passengers in the past. A business partner of mine will see my ship anchored offshore. If everything is clear, he'll light a signal fire. We've been through this exercise numerous times before. The only problem is that his boat will be too small to accommodate all of you, so I'll have to send one of my lifeboats ashore with you. Be ready to go at a moment's notice. We can't lollygag. It will get ugly if the officials catch me discharging passengers outside the immigration jurisdiction."

One hour later

Captain Beloux stared into the distance and pointed his finger toward the horizon.

"Nephew, I see, a signal fire lighting the sky on Long Island. Lower a lifeboat over the side."

While the departing passengers were ready, a small rowboat came alongside. It carried a lone occupant wearing a black slicker and sporting a thick gray beard and mustache.

"Ahoy there," the captain shouted to the man below. "Put two in your boat, and the rest of them will get in my lifeboat."

Beloux leaned across the railing and tossed a bag of gold coins into his co-conspirator's rowboat. The occupant looked up at the captain and shook his head. "It's a good thing you didn't miss because it's too bloody cold to be diving for coins."

"I never miss, mate," Beloux shouted. "And remember that. I could have just as easily have chosen to throw the knife at you." Both men laughed, and the passengers continued to climb down the rope ladder and into the boats. The DeWitts went with the small boat, and the Celje family stayed together in the ship's boat.

"Thank you, Captain," Raiko shouted back at the ship, but Beloux had already set about issuing orders to weigh anchor and turn his ship toward the Chesapeake.

CHAPTER FORTY-THREE
DEALING WITH THOMAS

The unauthorized departure of *La Patience* caused more excitement in Quebec City than the area had seen for many years. The noise of the gunfight with a ship in the harbor echoed throughout the city. The sounds brought most of its citizens to their windows or out into the street in a panic.

In Montreal, the chief magistrate began action against one of its most prominent citizens—Father Thomas.

"Your Honor," Father François said as he stood beside his sisters, "I give testimony that the man calling himself 'Father Peter' is not only using a false name, he is using a false title. He was defrocked in Erlach, Switzerland, by Bishop Roten over three years ago. Not only is he a liar, but he is also a rapist who attacked my sister, the nun who is standing before you. He also tried to murder an old priest named Father Benedict, who caught Thomas attacking my sister. On top of all that, he tried to blame both of his crimes on two Gypsy boys."

The magistrate sat at his desk and shook his head in disbelief. He was appalled by the news he had heard.

"How can a man of the cloth do such things?" he asked.

He looked up at Sister Marie and tried to imagine what this sweet young nun must have endured at the hands of such an evil man. He bit his lip and wiped a tear from the corner of his eye before he proceeded with his questioning.

"Sister, do you concur with what your brother has just told me—and if you do, why did it take you so long to come forward about the rape?"

Sister Marie began to tremble and found it difficult to speak. Anne moved closer to her and embraced Marie for comfort. Marie cleared her throat and took a deep breath before explaining. "It wasn't that it took me a long time to come forward after the attack. When I finally regained consciousness, it was apparent that I had been beaten and violated, but I could remember nothing about the incident.

"Additionally, the resultant pregnancy was self-evident that an attack had happened. I didn't name Father Thomas as the man who did it because the incident details had elapsed from my mind. The shock of my brutal beating at the hands of Father Thomas must have caused it; I don't know.

"I later found out that he brutally attacked Father Benedict and left him for dead. The old priest remained in a coma for several weeks, but he identified Thomas as our attacker when regaining consciousness.

"I have regained my memory," Marie said through tearful eyes. "For better or for worse, I remember all too clearly now."

The magistrate rubbed his chin as if in deep thought and then turned to Father François and asked, "So, then why wasn't he brought to justice in Erlach?"

Father François said, "Father Thomas—Father Peter—should have been brought to justice and hanged. Our Bishop had a different opinion on the matter. He was concerned about the impact the priest's conviction would have on the members of our parish. News such as that travels faster than the wind. As a result, Thomas walked free to continue his reign of terror while hiding behind the garb of a trusted priest."

The magistrate nodded. "I emphasize with your Bishop. I am sitting here thinking of ways to rid myself of this menace without a public scandal myself. After all, we are a Roman Catholic community, and his crime's consequences could be significant. What do you suggest?"

"If I weren't a priest, I'd kill him myself. The problem is that I am a priest and must act accordingly. Could we, perhaps, send him somewhere else to stand trial?"

"We can't send him anywhere in New France without word getting back about what happened here. Besides, we can't send him somewhere else to stand trial without sending all three of you along with him to act as witnesses. It gets complicated."

"Consider this," Father François suggested. "What if we sent a messenger to Quebec City to find Father Thomas? The messenger would tell him that he is exposed, and you are on your way to arrest him on various charges, including rape? My guess is he will flee into the wilderness."

"Flee into the wilderness? Do you mean to hide among the Indians? They'll probably kill him," the magistrate replied. "But let's think about the consequences: If we try him here and hang him, we put the Church's reputation in jeopardy. If he gets killed in the wilderness—let's say by Indians or wild animals—people will consider him a martyr, and the Church's reputation will be enhanced."

The priest smiled. "May God's will be done."

The magistrate rose from his chair. He was about to agree to the plan when another thought came to him. "We have one other slight problem that we need to address."

"What problem is that?"

"His son," the magistrate exclaimed. "Father Thomas arrived here with a toddler son who is in his care. Some people say the child is his nephew. Others say the boy is an orphan he found left at his doorstep. Whatever the case may be, the child is about four years old and is being cared for by the Arquette family, who runs the livery."

Father François turned immediately to his sisters. Anne was holding on to Marie, who was about to pass out from excitement. "We must see the boy immediately," the priest responded. There is a definite possibility that the boy is my sister's boy, born due to Thomas's vicious attack. We know where the Arquette's reside. We'll go there while you arrange for a messenger to carry the news of Thomas' arrest to him. Hopefully, both matters will take care of themselves."

The parish carriage stopped in the front of the Arquette residence in the pouring rain. Anne pulled her sister closer to her and said, "Are you sure you're ready for this, Marie? There's no guarantee this child is yours."

Marie trembled with anticipation. "I know it is. I'll know when I look into his blue eyes and touch his red hair. If I'm that little boy's mother, I'll know it straight away."

Father François stepped down from the carriage and held his hand for Marie, but she jumped, unassisted, onto the cobblestones. "Enough of this, I've waited nearly four years to see my son, and I'm not waiting another second. Let's go."

Marie bolted directly toward the Arquette residence's front door and pounded the brass ring that served as a door knocker boldly on the door. The urgency of the pounding brought Mademoiselle Arquette immediately to its source. She opened immediately and looked with some degree of shock at the priest, the nun, and her identical twin. "What's wrong? Has my husband been injured?" she asked.

Marie brushed past her and entered the house. "The boy; where is the boy?"

"What, boy?" Arquette replied. "Do you mean the boy the priest left with us? He's in the kitchen eating his lunch. What do you want with him?"

Sister Marie didn't answer. She continued toward the back of the house and entered the kitchen, the others close behind. She stopped in the doorway to the kitchen and broke into hysterical sobbing.

"What is it, Marie?" Anne asked as she stopped behind her sister and placed her hand on her shoulder as Anne tried to look around her. "Oh my, he's the spitting image of us," Anne said as she joined her sister in tears of joy. "Don't just stand here; go get him."

Arquette's wife was confused by what she had witnessed. She moved past Anne, who still stood in the doorway, and into the kitchen where

Marie was reaching down to pick up a dirty-faced little boy. The nun lifted the surprised lad from his chair, pulled him close to her. She danced around the kitchen in circles. She wept, laughed, danced, and praised God for enabling her to find her son.

"What's this all about?" Mrs. Arquette demanded. "This boy is the nephew of Father Thomas, who is in Quebec City as we speak, with my husband. The boy can't be yours. Whoever heard of a nun having children?"

"He's mine, and I can prove it," Marie said through her frustration at the woman's doubt. "There's a purple birthmark at the base of his spine—isn't there?" She did not wait for a response. Marie turned the boy around and pulled down his pants just enough to reveal what she had declared. "Look. It's just as I told you. He's mine, and he's coming with us."

"But what about all the money that priest owes me? He hasn't paid me for caring for this brat in months. The child is not leaving here until Father Thomas pays what's owed me." She spoke to the backs of Marie and Anne, who had already started through the dining room. Marie and Anne stopped and turned to listen to Mrs. Arquette when they reached the house's front door.

"Just a minute, Mademoiselle," François said as he grabbed her arm to stop her from chasing the sisters. "How much does Peter—Thomas—owe? I'll pay for it." Mrs. Arquette quoted an inflated figure. The priest agreed to pay it. He counted out the money into the woman's hands and then reached in and pulled back ten percent of the money. "There you go, and of course, I'll take out your tithe to the Church."

The priest turned away from the flabbergasted donor and headed toward the carriage where his two sisters sat, introducing themselves to the boy. "Oh my, we forgot to ask about his name," Marie said. Then she added: "It doesn't matter. I'll name him Benedict after the good father in Erlach, who saved my life at the risk of his own."

François smiled in agreement as he cracked the reins and started the horse toward the rectory.

CHAPTER FORTY-FOUR
THE DEPARTURE OF THOMAS

The magistrate, aware Thomas and Arquette had gone to Quebec City, stationed one of his men to observe Mademoiselle Arquette's house. An hour after being posted to watch, he saw a boy of about thirteen—the same boy who had taken Arquette's message to Thomas on a previous occasion—leave the Arquette residence and tuck a note into his jacket. The policeman waited until the boy was out of sight of the house and then stopped him.

"Where are you going, boy?" the officer asked.

"I'm taking a message to Monsieur Arquette in Quebec City. It is of the most urgent nature. Please, sir, it's getting late, and I'm in a hurry.'

The officer took the boy by the arm and led him directly to the magistrate. The letter was opened and read. The letter's content dealt with Thomas's son's seizure and contained a plea from Mademoiselle Arquette for her husband and Thomas to return home immediately.

The magistrate looked at the dirty boy and said, "I'm sorry to have delayed you, son. Please have a seat in the other room for a moment before I send you on your way." He pointed through an open door at chairs lined against the wall in the waiting room and nudged the boy toward them. When the boy was seated, the magistrate closed the door halfway and allowed an opening large enough for the boy to hear what he was about to say.

He turned toward the police officer and winked. "We can let the boy go now. If Thomas receives the letter ahead of our arrival to arrest him on charges of rape, kidnapping, attempted murder, and presenting himself falsely as a priest, all the better. The closer he travels toward us on his return, the less distance we will have to travel toward Quebec City to get him. It's raining, and I don't look forward to the trip." They could hear a chair shuffle in the next room as the boy jumped up and headed for the door.

"Let him go," the magistrate said with a smile. "I'm sure he took the bait."

The boy arrived in Quebec City early the following day and found Arquette and the injured Thomas staying at Arquette's livery office. Arquette immediately tore open the re-sealed letter and handed it to Thomas.

Thomas read the letter and turned red with rage.

The boy couldn't wait any longer to deliver the other news he bore. "You're in real trouble, Father Peter—or whoever you are. I overheard the magistrate tell a policeman he is coming here to arrest you."

Thomas pulled himself from his rage long enough to ask his burning question: "Arrest me? Arrest me for what? He can't arrest a man of the cloth," the former priest said, although knowing in his heart the charges could be for any one of several infractions.

"He said you're a rapist, a kidnapper, and more. But for sure, he said you are not a priest at all. He said you're a fake."

"What does all of this mean?" Arquette demanded in a voice of contempt. "You're not even a real priest? Does this mean I'm guilty of something too? You idiot, what have you gotten me into?"

Thomas grabbed the messenger by his wet lapels and pulled him forward in a threatening manner. "What else did he say? When are they coming?"

"I don't know," the boy said with tears in his eyes, apparently afraid of Thomas. "It was late when he told me, and he is an old man. I don't think he'd leave before this morning."

"Let the boy go," Arquette intervened. "He's told us all he knows." Arquette reached into his pocket and withdrew some coins. "Here," he said, with his hand held out to the boy. "You can rest in the backroom before you head back to Montreal. Tell him nothing about our little meeting if you pass the magistrate along the road. Do you understand?"

"Yes, sir," the boy replied. He headed immediately for the back room, anxious to get away from the angered Thomas, who was still steaming from hearing the bad news.

You are an idiot! Damian exclaimed to Thomas. *We must leave straight away.*

"But I'm injured. How can I travel?"

Arquette, believing Thomas was talking to him, replied, "That's not my problem. Stay here if you wish, but remember that they are coming for you."

When the boy entered the back room and closed the door, Arquette glared at Thomas. "What are you going to do now?" he asked. There are no ships ready to leave Quebec City, and you certainly can't return to Montreal."

"Can't you find me a place to hide here? You know a lot of people, and surely you can protect me."

Arquette looked at the phony priest with disgust and forced a laugh of disdain. "You've got to be kidding me. Protect a rapist, a murderer, and an imposter? I should probably shoot you and win the heartfelt gratitude of the populace. My best advice to you is to saddle your carriage horse and flee into the countryside."

"The countryside? Are you nuts? I wouldn't last a week in the wilderness. I'd be dead in a matter of days."

"Listen to me. I shouldn't help you, but I know a certain Huron Indian named Bitterroot, who would help you for a price. I'm sure he'd paddle you across the river and find you a place to hide among his people, but as I told you, it would be for a price."

"How much of a price?"

"The price wouldn't be in cash. The price would be in guns and whiskey."

"But I don't have any money with me to buy such things. How do you expect me to finance it?"

A wide grin crept across Arquette's face as he prepared to propose a devious suggestion. "What about that gold crucifix and gold ring you're wearing? Also, your horse is of some value. They must be worth something."

"I do believe you've taken leave of your senses, Arquette. I need them."

"You need the crucifix and ring? For what, to continue your career as a phony priest? My friend, let me tell you: the Huron has a history of drowning priests. And besides, you can't take your horse in a canoe. It's time for you to let go and to move on." Arquette watched as Thomas painfully lifted the gold chain bearing the crucifix over his head. He handed it to the liveryman and struggled to remove the gold ring from his finger.

"And the horse?" Arquette inquired. "You'll need to sign a bill of sale for the horse. Your past conduct has shown you are not a trustworthy individual. Priest indeed! What a laugh." Arquette moved to his desk, where he opened a drawer, removed a form he kept on file, and filled in the blanks. "Here, sign this—and use your given name, not the name you used as a priest."

"Alright, but hurry it up. The magistrate could be here any minute." Thomas signed the forms and then looked up at Arquette. "I'll need to shed these church garments if what you tell me about the Huron and their dislike for the clergy is true. Do you have some clothes you can give me?"

"Give you? I think not. But I have some spare clothes I keep in this branch for when working. Clothes are expensive, and I'm not a rich man. You'll need to pay me for them. I know you have some cash in your pocket."

"How could you possibly know that?"

"Because I've seen you pull out wads of cash when you are drinking at the inns, and you buy every pretty woman in the house a drink. I always suspected you were a hypocrite." Arquette held out his hand in expectation.

Thomas reached into his pocket, pulled out a sizeable wad of cash, and unrolled it. Arquette took the liberty of withdrawing a generous amount from Thomas's hand and shoved it into his pocket.

"Please, Arquette, clothes. I've got to get moving straight away."

Arquette crept into his backroom, where the boy was sleeping on a single bed. The boy never stirred as the liveryman moved to an armoire and removed two shirts, a pair of pants, a sweater, and a heavy coat. He returned to the office and put them in a canvas bag, and handed them to Thomas without speaking.

"Now," Thomas said, "where is the Huron you were talking about?"

"Bitterroot? As luck would have it, I know exactly where he is; he works for me. We can find him in the stable now. Come, and I'll introduce you."

An hour later, Thomas sat in the front of canoe paddled by Bitterroot, a heavy-set Huron with coal-black eyes set close together, a toothless mouth that never smiled, and a tongue that never wagged. Thomas had an uneasy feeling about his guide from the moment he met him, and sitting with his back to a man he didn't trust made the trip most uncomfortable. Midway across the St. Lawrence River, he sat in his new set of civilian clothes, with a pocket full of gold coins and a letter of credit from his banking house, and listened to the rhythmic strokes of Bitterroot's paddle. All seemed reasonable to Thomas until the rhythmic splashes of the paddling abruptly stopped. Thomas leaned on his left hand and began to turn to look back at the Huron when he felt the slam of a wooden paddle against the side of his head. He struggled to maintain consciousness but felt himself fading. Then a second and third whack to the side of his head, and Thomas fell backward into the bottom of the canoe.

Thomas hung on the verge of consciousness. He felt the canoe sway from side to side as Bitterroot crawled forward to where he was lying. Thomas was aware of Bitterroot's presence but couldn't make his body respond to his command to strike back. Then he felt the Indian's hand searching through his pockets and removing the gold coins. Bitterroot unwrapped the letter of credit from an oiled cloth Thomas had wrapped it in, but because the Indian couldn't read, Bitterroot didn't understand its value. He crumpled the letter and shoved it back into Thomas' jacket pocket. Thomas felt the canoe lean hard to its right and nearly tip over as Bitterroot lifted him over the edge of the canoe and into the frigid water.

The cold-water shock brought Thomas back into consciousness, but he allowed his body to sink into the depth, rise slowly to the surface, and float away from the canoe. Thomas continued to float on his back and heard the canoe move away. A swift current took hold of him, and he felt his body pushed toward shore. *My limbs are already numb. How long can I endure this cold? I must make it to the riverbank—I must!*

CHAPTER FORTY-FIVE
LOST AND FOUND

A middle-aged Huron woman named Anika walked from her lone cabin, set high upon the tree-lined St. Lawrence riverbank. The short, thick bodied woman walked down to the river's edge to check her woven fish traps. She stopped suddenly, startled by what lay ahead. She saw a large dark mass that appeared to be a bear stealing her morning catch through the morning fog.

So, Mr. Bear, the woman muttered, *Anika has finally caught you in the act of robbing her. This attempt will be the last time you steal my catch and damage my traps.*

A bear had robbed her traps before, and she was determined to end the bear's thievery. If she could react fast enough, she would have bear meat to eat and another bearskin to keep her warm at night. Anika, filled with jubilation, returned immediately to her cabin, retrieved her musket mounted on pegs above the cabin door, and proceeded toward her unexpected catch.

Anika stopped at the top of the riverbank to double-check the load in her musket. The powder was dry, the flint was clean, and the front site was unobstructed. She pulled her long, graying hair back from her face, raised the musket to her shoulder, and assumed at standing stance—left foot slightly forward; right foot back and at a forty-five-degree angle from her body. She pulled the walnut stock of the musket to her reddened face and pushed her nearly toothless gums into her cheek for stability.

There's something not quite right about that black bear, she thought, as she nervously fingered the trigger. *There's no movement. Maybe Mr. Bear got tangled up in the traps and drowned? If so, there's no need to waste my shot.*

Anika lowered the weapon and cautiously approached the traps, ready at any time to resume her stance at the slightest movement from her target. She moved steadily forward until she was five yards from the fish traps. She squinted her eyes as she looked through the fog that clung to the river's surface.

Well, that ain't no bear at all—it's a man—and unless I miss my guess, it's a white man at that!

Anika, not totally convinced the man was dead, stepped forward and prodded the body with the butt of her musket. There was no movement.

Isn't this a fine mess? Now, I not only have to untangle him from my traps, but I'll also have to bury him. Well, forget that. I'll untangle him, push his body out into the river again, and let him drift farther downstream.

Anika removed her moccasins, withdrew her large knife from its sheath, worn on her leather belt, and stepped into the cold, shallow water at the river's edge. She reached forward and dragged the body, traps, and all, up onto the bank. A giant catfish caught in the trap nearest the man's right foot splashed violently to get free. The movement caught Anika off-guard. She let go of the tangled mass and fell backward onto the muddy incline—an unintelligible curse issued from her mouth.

Anika thought the man did that, not Mr. Fish, she said aloud. *Wait a minute; his hand is trembling. Maybe a white man is still alive?*

The woman reached down into the mud for the knife she had dropped during her fall and gripped it in her hand, blade down, ready to plunge it into the man's torso. But for reasons unknown to Anika, she looked at the pathetic creature and felt compassion for him. Instead of finishing him off, she cut him free of her woven fish traps, made of reeds and string, and dragged him farther up the bank.

Anika left the white man on the incline of the riverbank and returned to her cabin. She put a fresh log on her fire, removed her neatly rolled rope from a wooden peg mounted on the log wall near the doorway, and returned to the unconscious white man she had left lying on the river-bank. The squaw rolled him onto his back and looped the ropes under his armpits. She moved four feet from his head and twisted the ropes over her shoulders and then around her waist. Anika trudged forward, beginning her strenuous trek to the cabin.

The wet grass lubricated the drag on the man's body, but at the same time, caused slippery footing as she labored up the hill. It took an hour for her to reach the cabin. Anika was exhausted and sweated profusely. Her now bare and bruised feet bled as she stopped at the cabin doorway and turned to look at the moaning injured man.

"Now to get you over the threshold and into the warm cabin," she said to the man whom she suspected could neither hear, nor understand her.

Anika lifted the man's head over the threshold and then dragged the rest of his body inside the cabin and rolled him onto a straw mat covered with a bearskin pad near the fireplace. She immediately removed his wet clothing and examined his shivering naked body. Her uninvited guest had turned blue from the cold water and shivered violently. The man's nose, fingers, and toes were nearly black. Although she did not know the term *hypothermia,* her experience as a *shaman* and medicine woman had taught her its manifestations. She immediately set about vigorously rubbing his arms and legs to restore circulation.

Three Days Later

Thomas slept on the straw mat, his body curled in a fetal position to retain his body's warmth—one bearskin beneath him, another covered him like a blanket. The hair from the cover tickled his skin and caused the sensation of a woman's hair dangling across his face. The feeling excited his emotions and forced him to fantasize:

"Emily," Father Thomas groaned with half-mumbled words that failed to form audibly on his lips, "Come closer to me and let me feel your warmth." He reached out for her into the cold morning darkness and rolled off his mat onto the dirt floor of the cabin. His contact with the damp, hard floor brought him back into consciousness for the first time in three days.

Outside, he heard a woman conversing in her native Huron tongue with a man whose voice was vaguely familiar to Father Thomas. He pulled back the bearskin and crept across the floor to the cabin door, pulled aside the deerskin covering which hung across the doorway, and peered outside. The woman stood talking face-to-face with an older Indian male just outside the entrance—Bitterroot!

Thomas couldn't understand what they were saying, but the tones of their voices betrayed a feeling of disgust and anxiety. A few minutes later, Bitterroot descended the hill in front of the cabin that led to the river, got into his canoe, and paddled out onto St. Lawrence River. The Huron woman stood with her back to the doorway and watched Bitterroot disappear into the darkness. Father Thomas quietly returned to his bedding and awaited the woman's return to the cabin. She turned and entered the cabin while Thomas feigned sleep on the bearskin.

Anika dropped to her knees and shook Thomas by his shoulders.

Thomas pretended to awaken from a deep sleep. He struggled to sit up and rubbed his eyes. "What? Who are you, and what am I doing here?"

His evil heart seemed to smile.

Well, Damian said to Thomas, *it looks like we have another opportunity for survival. Go ahead. Work your charm on yet another woman. It's what you do best.*

Damian was right. Thomas had found another woman he could manipulate and use for his malicious purposes. His reign of terror was not over.

The Devil Hound would continue to perpetuate his life of deceit and destruction, negatively impacting the lives of all with whom he would come into contact.

ACKNOWLEDGMENTS

My Publisher, Woodhall Press

David LeGere who has guided me through the publishing process, and his partner Colin Hosten.

Amie McCraken – Layout

Margaret Moore – Editor

Independent Publishers Group – Distribution

When Words Count (A literary development group)

Steven Eisner who put together this wonderful organization to find and develop new writers.

Steve Rohr of Lexicon Public Relations who served as a judge and mentor.

Marilyn Atlas of Marilyn Atlas Management who served as a judge and mentor.

Judith Krummeck whose advise and counseling helped give this novel form.

Family and Friends

Janice W. Lamca whose encouragement and editing helped me to publish my first novel, *The Gypsies* and *The Devil Hound*, and who felt I should keep writing and not stop with one novel.

Linda Sampson-Gillis whose encouragement, suggestions, and editorial help made this dream a reality.

ABOUT THE AUTHOR

Franklin Lamca, an author and puppeteer, is dedicated to promoting human rights from a Christian perspective. A victim of child abuse and social type-casting, he spent three years in Europe performing marionette plays where he witnessed the aftermath of the Holocaust and the modern-day persecution of the Romani (Gypsies). Whether the 1915 Turkish genocide against the Armenians, Hitler's reign of terror against the Jews, the Rwandan genocide with child soldiers in Africa, or today's discrimination against the Romani in Europe and South America, the world must change and not forget. Franklin's mission is to build an awareness that will alter the world's view for future generations on the issues of child abuse, religious persecution, and social discrimination. Franklin lives summers in Bedford, Pennsylvania, and winters near Phoenix, Arizona.